ONLY PRETTY DAMNED

ONLY PRETTY DAMNED

Niall Howell

NeWest Press
Edmonton, AB 2019

Library and Archives Canada Cataloguing in Publication

Howell, Niall, 1985-, author
Only pretty damned / Niall Howell.

(Nunatak first fiction series ; no. 49)
Issued in print and electronic formats.
ISBN 978-1-988732-53-4 (softcover).--ISBN 978-1-988732-54-1 (EPUB).--
ISBN 978-1-988732-55-8 (Kindle)

I. Title. II. Series: Nunatak first fiction ; no. 49

PS8615.O942O55 2019   C813'.6   C2018-904444-6
                                              C2018-904445-4

NeWest Press wishes to acknowledge that the land on which we operate is Treaty 6 territory and a traditional meeting ground and home for many Indigenous Peoples, including Cree, Saulteaux, Niitsitapi (Blackfoot), Métis, and Nakota Sioux.

Board Editor: Jenna Butler
Cover design & typography: Kate Hargreaves
Cover photograph from the collection of the Schenectady County Historical Society
Back cover photograph by Darius Soodmand via Unsplash
Author photograph: Alicja Pawlak

All Rights Reserved

NeWest Press acknowledges the Canada Council for the Arts, the Alberta Foundation for the Arts, and the Edmonton Arts Council for support of our publishing program. This project is funded in part by the Government of Canada.

201, 8540 – 109 Street
Edmonton, AB T6G 1E6
780.432.9427
NeWest Press www.newestpress.com

No bison were harmed in the making of this book.
PRINTED AND BOUND IN CANADA

For Alicja

IT'S BEEN THREE YEARS SINCE WALLY JAKES DIED, AND NOT a day goes by that I don't think of the old bastard.

The other chumps around this place, well, I'm sure they think of Wally often too—at least the ones who were around during the infamous Jake-obean era—but not as often as I do. And certainly not in the same way as I do.

See, Wally had a personality that was an acquired taste in the same way that sucking vinegar from a mangy sponge is an acquired taste. Nobody could stand the guy. Nobody except me. But then, I have a high tolerance for all things acidic.

I respected Wally, though I could sure see why others had a hard time digesting him. He was loud-mouthed, crass, insensitive, and horribly opinionated. He rarely shaved or showered, and dental hygiene mattered to him about as much as arithmetic matters to a snowman. And if all that weren't enough, Wally Jakes was also uglier than a couple of rats fucking on top of a pile of trash, which was partially due to a horse booting him square in the kisser when he was a kid, and partially due to him just being Wally Jakes. He was a natural pariah, born to be detested.

But as I said, I respected the guy. He wasn't a performer, like me, but I think that once you got right down to it, he and I were pretty much the same. Now, I don't mean to say that I'm a walking aerosolized can of human-repellant, like Wally, but on the inside, on the inside where it really mattered, we were the same. If you were to take a blade and carve us both down to our respective cores, once you scraped off all the pulpy muck and rinsed away the blood, you'd be staring at a matching set. Two of a kind. You see, like me, Wally did whatever needed to be done to keep things running around here. One day you'd see him tearing tickets, the next you'd see him cramming a suppository into an elephant's ass. Whatever the task, if it needed to be done, Wally would do it. He knew damn well that the show mattered more than anything. More than anything at all.

SOME OF THE SLACKERS AROUND HERE LAY ON THE COLOUR so heavy that they might as well have 'compensation' written across their foreheads in thick black letters. Don't get me wrong, I know that a certain cartoonish quality is necessary to seize the attention of a child. I don't blame the performers for the garishly bright, loose-fitting clothing, the pointy hats, the bulky collars, and the grotesque patterns—shimmering silver stars and malformed crescent moons—that lie scattered across their costumes with no discernible sense of order or even a hint of symmetry. I don't blame them for any of that. It's the faces that get to me. The faces steam my blood. Blue-lidded eyes with lashes so large you can spot them from the parking lot; gaping crimson mouths that stretch from above the upper lip down to the chin, bordered by blushing cheeks nonsensically outlined in black, as if you'd have trouble noticing them on their own against the colourless base they sat against; thick eyebrows that start by the ear and curve all the way up to the bridge of the nose.

The nose…oh, the fucking nose.

That's another thing altogether. Those fat prosthetic bulbs are without a doubt the most embarrassing detail of them all. You wouldn't catch me fastening one of those things to my face in a million years. Not a chance. For me, subtlety is the name of the game. But then again, I don't need to rely on an outlandish getup to arrest an audience.

I don't realize how close I am to the mirror until I exhale and see a portion of my face vanish behind a cloud of fog. Inching back, I stare at my reflection and drink up every detail. The perfect amount of bone-white applied and blended evenly from my skull, down my face and neck, to just below the line of my top. Not a dot of stubble can be seen on my head. I shave it thirty minutes before every performance. I've been doing it since the day I was thrown into this gig, whether it looks like I need to or not. I tell you, I'm so adamant about shaving my head that the hairs burrowed beneath my scalp probably quiver at the thought of even trying to grow—stay subterranean, where it's safe, you little bastards. My nose has been painted on—a tiny red square, right on the tip. A slender black diamond runs vertically over each of my eyes, and my thin eyebrows are arched into a surprised but subtle curve. I'm quite a minimalist when it comes to my face. The only detail remaining is my lips. Those are always the last to be added. I have a routine, you see. I make sure every detail of my face is perfect, then I allow myself one cigarette before adding my lips. I have to have my smoke before my lips go on because I don't want any smudging. A lot of the hacks around here rib me for that; *Toby, you think anyone notices a little smudge on your lips while you're out there flipping around and bouncing all over the goddamn place? Christ, you're like a woman with yer makeup!*, but I couldn't take them seriously if I tried. Just one look at them—with their patchy, caked-on faces and their yellowing, sweat-tainted bald-caps—is enough for me to blot out their very existence.

I let the smoke tumble from my mouth slowly, because I know it's got nowhere better to be, and peek out through the curtain. Julian is just getting started. He finishes restraining Susan and starts working the crowd, pacing around the ring with his knives held high above his head, making damn sure that everybody gets a good look at them, sees how sharp they are. Acts like Julian's are all about the potential of danger, that's their sole appeal. The audience needs to be scared for Susan. They need to genuinely believe that there's a chance that they'll witness some freak accident. Who knows? Maybe Julian's aim is a little off and one of those unforgiving points finds its way into Susan's bicep, piercing an artery and causing blood to spray from her milky flesh as she screams, bound to that giant target and unable to avoid her own spatter as it gushes across her pretty face. Horrific as it sounds, it's what these people pay for—danger. The funny thing about these audiences is they crave peril, but the second something goes wrong, which, aside from a few minor instances, really never happens, they go absolutely bonkers. They scream and they faint and they puke over one little drop of blood. Be careful what you wish for, I guess.

I watch the first knife sear through the air and halt with an abrupt slam just below Susan's hand, then I step away from the curtain to the sound of a thousand sets of lungs vacating. I pace back and forth, finishing my smoke and looking at my reflection, admiring my work. A few nobodies come and offer some unnecessary words of encouragement as I do my lips.

"Knock 'em dead, Toby!"

"Break a leg, Tobe!"

"Go remind 'em why they emptied their wallets at the door, bud."

"Have a good set!"

Have a good set. Christ. I'd have to have one of Julian's knives sticking in my guts for me to lower my set to the level of just plain old good. Bunch of amateurs.

Julian and Susan come running outside, hand locked in sweaty hand. I'm standing a few feet from the opening of the flap, so they let go of each other, go around me, and reconnect on the other side.

I close my eyes and listen to Rowland build me up to the crowd from inside the tent. When he shouts, "Ladies and gentleman, boys and girls, please join me in welcoming the magnificent Freddy Folly!" I charge through the flap, toward the centre of the ring, the spotlight guiding me from above fragmenting the darkness with sharp, angular cuts, illuminating my path through the void. My music—even the most brazen horn—is quickly drowned out by the explosive applause filling the tent.

I kill.

AS ALWAYS, THE BARBECUE FOLLOWING THE SHOW IS exceptional. As always, almost everyone is there. Sal, our resident hypnotist and chef, spearheads the whole operation. He stands behind the grill with the engrossed eyes of a surgeon, spatula in one hand, perspiring bottle of beer in the other, flipping and salting and saucing away until every scrap of chicken on hand has been readied for the consumption of our travelling family. He delegates menial tasks, such as the preparation of salad, to a group of four ring crew members everybody calls the Sycs, as in syco-phants. These four young men, whose real names I don't know, would dance barefoot into hell if Sal told them to. Everyone always jokes that Sal's hypnotic powers must actu-ally work, because since those four joined up with us about a year ago, they've been following him around like a pack of attention-starved puppies, jumping at his every command. I take a swig of my beer. I'm watching the Sycs, and I realize that if I were ever pressed to, I don't think I could tell the four of them apart. They're all slightly short, stocky young men with the same buzzed brown hair, the same beady eyes, the same stoic face. Sal's little zombies. He's probably got a handful of replacements growing in green pods, hidden away behind a secret panel in his trailer. Christ—listen to me. I've got to stop throwing my money away on *Galaxy Science Fiction*.

Once the meat is ready, everyone forms a line. Gloria is five or six people ahead, but when her big hazel peepers spot me, she steps out and joins me near the back. She shoots me a coy smirk and says, "I can't stand that stuff," gesturing with her head to my beer and folding her arms across her chest, pushing up her breasts in a failed attempt at nonchalance. She's still wearing her costume: a navy blue halter-top and short skirt combination decorated in green, yellow, and silver sequins. A line of peacock feathers marks the v-shaped border between the flesh on her chest and the top of the dress, making it look as though her peaks are frowning at me.

"I didn't realize you were old enough to try it," I say, then take another sip.

She feigns offense and gives my arm a smack. "You know I am."

"Yeah, in New York and Kansas."

"*And* Louisiana."

"Well, we're in Baton Rouge soon, so you can buy me a beer there."

"As long as it's not that garbage you're drinking now, you've got a deal," she says, playfully. "What kind of name is that, anyway? *Blatz*. It even sounds icky."

"I think it's Bavarian."

She turns her nose up and whips her head to the side dismissively. "Wherever it's from, it's vile."

I give her the laugh that she's come to expect from me whenever she pulls the cutesy shtick and reach my arm around her. The second my palm makes contact with her bare shoulder, she turns to face me, looking up with mischievous eyes and a grin to match.

"You had a great set tonight."

"You saw it? You really think so?" she beams.

"I did and I do."

"Thank you, Toby! Thank you! I really think I'm getting better. Harriet—er—Miss Lane, she says I'm definitely top-notch. She says with a little more practice, I could be dancing dead centre, leading the whole troupe."

I say, "I believe it," and I think I really do.

The two of us shuffle in form with the rest of the group, slowly inching our way toward Sal and his mountain of poultry. I half-listen to Gloria go on about the new routine they're working out, but the bulk of my attention is focused on the remaining audience members trickling out from the tent toward the parking lot. Their giddy squeals and shouts drift through the night sky over to our barbecue area. I think of the show I put on and, sap that I am, I can't help but smile at the glee of these strangers. Yeah, Genevieve and Andrew were the last act they saw, the headliners, if you want to call them that. But I look at the smiles people are wearing at the end of the night as the result of an accumulated thrill. They're not just smiling because they saw a couple of big names pull off a series of mediocre flying manoeuvres. No sir, not at all. They're smiling because they were dazzled beyond belief by the *whole experience*, an experience I just happen to be a damn big part of. It's like chopping down a tree. Nobody cuts down a big hunk of timber in one swing. It takes a lot of swings. A whole helluva lot of swings from, in our case, a bunch of different axes. And as far as this show goes, I'm the biggest, sharpest axe in the woods. When you think about it, whoever delivers the final blow really has the easiest job of all. The tree's already been hacked to shit when the last person (or, in Genevieve and Andrew's case, *persons*) take their swing. Hell, you can practically tip the tree over with your foot by the time that last lumberjack gets to it.

"Hey, Toby, you fill up on the smell or you actually gonna eat some of this?" Sal says, yanking me back to the moment. He's holding his tongs in front of me, a prime steaming piece of white meat clasped between them.

"Sorry, Sal, you know my mind wanders."

"Well, tether it to a fuckin' pole for a few minutes and focus on the delicious meat that's just been lovingly prepared for ya."

After piling some chicken on our plates and getting some salad from the Sycs' table, Gloria turns to walk toward a group of dancers she knows. She halts when she notices my hesitation to follow her lead.

"You want to eat in your trailer tonight, Toby?" I answer with a nod. "That's fine," she says, "we can eat in the trailer. I like the quiet, actually." A hurt expression begins to spread across her face when I don't respond right away. "It's…you don't mind if I join you in your trailer, do you?"

"Of course not. You know I never mind your company." I force a reassuring smile and wrap my free arm around her, ushering us toward my trailer. "Besides, the only beer they have out here is that Blatz shit you adore so much."

We hustle over to my living quarters before anyone has a chance to accuse us of being antisocial. Before we go in, I crawl under the trailer and grab the bottles of Falstaff I stashed there earlier to keep cool.

Over dinner, Gloria asks where my mind had wandered to earlier when we were in line and she was telling me about her dance number, and I assure her I was just a little light-headed from a mix of a vigorous performance and an empty stomach, and she eats it up like it's a second course. The next hour or so is spent inside my trailer, spread out on the chesterfield, going through bottles like their liquid will be turning into piss at midnight. As usual, Gloria is loaded with questions. She grills me about the supposedly checkered history of Rowland's World Class Circus, and as usual, I let her skate around on the surface while the real stuff swims in the depths below the ice. I can tell she wants to pry deeper, but she's about five beers shy of mustering up the necessary courage, and I'm about two bathtubs of beer shy of being willing to loosen my lips any on certain topics. Once I notice that she's drained her fourth beer, I tell her that we ought to step outside and get some fresh air, knowing how she gets.

"But I like it in here," she protests, a hint of flirtation in her voice.

"So do I, but didn't Joe McCarthy say that antisocial behaviour is a warning sign of communism?" I kid her.

"Who's being antisocial? There are two of us in here. That's not social enough? Besides, if Low-Blow Joe had eyes around here, you'd think they'd all be on Arkady." She begins to laugh, but is abruptly cut off by an ambush of hiccups.

"Arkady, you mean *Andrew*?" I say, unable to mask my disdain, not that Gloria wasn't hip to my loathing of the hack.

Gloria throws back her head and laughs, then takes another gulp of her beer. "I heard he only goes by Arkady. I remember when I first joined, it was just his stage name, but as far as I know he's Arkady to everyone now."

"Everyone, hey? No shit."

"Well, I don't know about Genevieve, of course, but about a month ago, I even heard Mister Rowland call him Arkady," she says, her eyes widening with interest as she shifts so that she's sitting on her knees. It's the kind of position you see young girls in the movies sitting in when they're gossiping with their girlfriends in the privacy of a bedroom.

"That's about the stupidest thing I've ever heard. Tells his own boss to call him by his—Christ! What a pompous son of a bitch! I guess I ought to tell people to only refer to me as Mister Freddy Folly, hey?"

"I guess so." Gloria laughs, then takes a swig so big that she gasps like she's coming up from a diving tank after she pulls the bottle from her mouth. "Stupid hiccups...gotta drown 'em."

"I hear the best way to get rid of hiccups is to scare them out."

She winks. "Too bad our headliners have already performed."

We both have a good laugh, and by the time I remember my earlier suggestion to get some fresh air, I've already cracked open two more beers for us. I assure her that these are our last tonight, having no desire to go through the motions of dealing with a drunken, frisky Gloria. She can be pretty damn determined when she wants to be, and as attractive as she is, I just wouldn't feel right about it; I'll always think of her as a kid, even if she isn't one any more.

I finish my beer in a hurry, and the instant her last drop goes, I tell her that I've become suddenly tired.

"I'm tired too, Toby." She yawns for authenticity and then stretches her arms behind her back, making her frowning feathered breasts bulge out at me. "I could fall asleep right now. Maybe I could just say here. My trailer feels like it's a million miles away."

"Nope. Sorry, kid." I get up and help her to her feet. "My snoring's loud enough to ruin friendships. Off ya go."

I help Gloria down the steps and point her in the direction of her shared trailer. It's dark outside now, must be well after eleven o' clock. An ambitious bonfire is raging in the spot where the barbecue was held earlier, and clusters of performers and crew huddle in circles, swigging booze, yakking away.

I notice the royal couple standing away from everyone else, on the periphery of the fire; the sole members of their own little elite club. Andrew is standing closer to the fire's glow and is completely visible. He's still wearing his costume—a red leotard with bright yellow stripes down the side—but the creeping cold has forced him to throw a wool sweater on. He's talking at Genevieve, and, judging by his slack posture and his graceless gesturing, he's well on his way to drunk. Genevieve's form, on the other hand, is steeped in darkness. The light touching her is so scant, so scant that unless you were looking for her, you wouldn't know she was there at all. Unless you were looking for her, it would appear that Andrew were a delusional drunk standing by himself, yakking his own ear off.

But I know she's there. The burning glow may only illuminate a slight line here, a gentle curve there, but I know what those add up to. I know how to fill in those blanks and see a form so familiar that I wouldn't hesitate to say I've got it memorized.

THE SOUND OF RIGOROUS RAIN TAPPING ACROSS THE ROOF

of my trailer wakes me. The gin I downed after Gloria left has made my mouth so dry that my tongue feels completely alien, and a pounding ache seems to have parked itself directly behind my eyeballs. I can hardly see a thing. I rub my hands over my eyes at least five times before I realize the darkness can be credited to the fact that it's still night and has nothing to do with my disoriented state. With one hand, I grope at the floor beside my bed until I find the small jug of water I always keep there. I bring it to my lips and pour. Much of it leaks out from the corners of my mouth because I'm still lying on my back, but I get enough down the hatch to reintroduce my tongue and dampen the throb of my headache. There are two people fucking loudly in a nearby trailer, though I can't tell exactly which trailer because of the tap-tapping rain. I don't recognize the grunts, but one of them sounds distinctly male and the other sounds distinctly neutral. I think of the other trailers close to mine, but once I realize that the nearest one is inhabited by the Sycs, I pull my pillow over my head, deciding that I have no interest in listening to them bump uglies with anything. The pillow cuts out most of the rain, but I can still hear a faint exchange of thuds and grunts through the cloth and feathers—maybe it wasn't the rain that woke me after all. A few minutes pass and then the noises stop. I realize that it couldn't have been any of the Sycs because I only heard two grunts and those four do *everything* together.

Plagued by the laziness that tends to accompany a bastard of a hangover, I choose not to get out of bed and dig out my pocket watch and instead decide that it is somewhere between four and five a.m. I spend the next two or so hours trying to fall back to sleep, with no luck. Shortly after the rain lets up, I hear someone's door open and decide that I might as well get up and get some fresh air.

"Mornin'," Julian says to me as I lumber out from my trailer, still fidgeting with my pants as I hop down the steps.

"Morning, pal."

"That was some storm last night, hey?" He plucks a pack of Chesterfields from his back pocket and offers me one. I decline with a wave of my hand.

"Thanks, but I'm a Camel man now."

"Huh. No shit."

"Yup. Apparently they're a lot better on the throat," I tell him as I pull out my cigarette case—a nifty silver number with a golden fleur de lis on top that I picked up when I was in Quebec years ago—and take a smoke for myself.

Julian's been with the show almost as long as I have, so you could say we've gotten to know each other rather well over the years, despite our best efforts. I've always thought he was a decent performer (as far as knife-throwers go), and his wife, Susan, is the best kind of riot, but he and I never really hit it off until a couple years ago, our history with the show proving to be a bottomless well for discussion.

He and I puff away as we chat about topics that start off on small-talk turf and slowly migrate into juicier territory. Once you get him going, Julian's like a dam with a hole in its wall. Just as soon as you think you've got him corked, another hole will show up out of nowhere, and, well, you eventually realize you've only got so many plugging-fingers available before you resign yourself to the fact that you're going to get drenched. He tells me about a feud between Susan and Carolyn, one of our dancers, that grew out of Carolyn implying that Susan's ass seemed to be expanding; he tells me that he has it on good authority that Mister Rowland has been nicking the newest bunch of razorbacks on their paychecks and pocketing the extra bread for himself; he tells me that the Sycs are all fugitives.

Sometimes, being the top-tiers that we are, Julian and I will critique the other performers' acts, but lately he's avoided the subject during our chats. I think I maybe put him off when I got a little too worked up a few weeks back during a discussion on aerial technique, but honestly, sometimes I can't help myself. I mean, Christ, this place is crawling with phonies and hacks masquerading as top-bill material, and I can't help but let it get to me sometimes. Maybe I'm a dam, too, I just don't leak as easy. I do all I can to keep it in because I know the water behind my wall is filthy, probably has arsenic or some shit in it.

We've killed four cigarettes between the two of us when Susan emerges from her and Julian's trailer. She's resting one hand on her robe-clad stomach and is sporting a smile that could light up a small town.

"Good morning, Toby, good morning, Julian," she sings. "My Lord," she takes a deep breath in, "I love the way it smells after a big storm."

"Hey, sweetheart," Julian says. He puts his cigarette out on his boot, walks over to his wife and plants a kiss on her cheek.

Susan lingers for a minute, then tells us that she's going to go wash up and that she'll see us at breakfast. I open my mouth to ask Julian what his wife is so chipper about as soon as she's out of earshot, but he beats me to the punch, naturally.

"Hey, Toby," he says, gripping my arm, beaming, "just between us," he checks over his shoulder for spies, "Susan and me, we got a little one on the way! Now, don't you mention it to nobody, because she's only a month or so in, but we went to a doctor the other day when we were back in Little Rock, and he confirmed it!"

"Hey, that's excellent, Jules, congrats, buddy. A nuclear family in nuclear times, hey?" I give his hand a good shake. "And don't you worry, I won't tell a soul," I assure him, knowing that if anybody spills, it'll be Julian himself. "Say, what's that gonna mean for your act, though? You gonna need someone new to whip your knives at?" I'm half kidding, but the other half of me is thinking that Gloria would be perfect to cover for Susan. Don't get me wrong, being a spec girl is great, but Gloria deserves a bigger spotlight, one that she doesn't have to share with so many others.

"No," Julian says, dragging out the 'no' as if I just asked him if he would ever consider a career as a swimsuit model, "Susan'll be fine until she really starts showing in the last few months. I just won't be able to throw the knives anywhere near her belly. Gotta be extra careful, y'know."

And if I didn't know him better, I'd think he was kidding.

WE HAVE ANOTHER SHOW TONIGHT, AND WE'LL TEAR

down right after and hit the road again first thing tomorrow morning. It's around eight o'clock, and most people are still in their trailers sawing wood. I'm making my way to the big top when a couple of our guys pull into the lot. They're coming back from the city, having gone in last night to promote this evening's show and to tear down any of our competition's flyers. We don't end up sharing a city with another show often, but it happens every now and then, and whenever it does, you've got to send a couple guys into the city to do whatever they can to make sure we keep our numbers up. It's all very dog-eat-dog—or sometimes dog-eat-rat—and I've even heard of instances where a group of guys from our show will run into a group of guys from a rival show, and they'll have it out. One time, a few years back, one of our guys came back to the lot beaten so bad we didn't even recognize him as one of our own. It was around this time of year. I remember sitting around the bonfire that crisp summer night, everybody drinking and yakking away at each other, when someone, I want to say it was Susan, spotted this shape hobbling toward the fire. Once the light hit the guy (who, you could tell right away, had been hit by much crueler things that night), all the chatter dissolved, and for a few seconds everyone just stared. The guy was such a mess; one eye swollen completely shut, his mouth hanging open, looking a few teeth short of a full set. He couldn't even talk, he just took another couple steps toward us and then collapsed. A few people rushed to him right away. It was Rowland who eventually noticed the snake tattoo on his hand and realized he wasn't just some bum drifter, but one of our own guys. It was hard to get the full story out of him because he kept fading in and out of consciousness for a couple days, and he had a fractured jaw, among other injuries. But once he was relatively coherent, he was able to write down what had happened. Apparently, he was tearing down a bunch of Ringling flyers and he got spotted by some of their guys. They followed him to a pub, and when he left, they dragged him into an alley and beat the shit out of him. Since then, Rowland has always made sure that at *least* two night riders (that's what we call them) go out to advertise and balance the scales of competition. The two I'm looking at right now don't appear to have run into any trouble in the city. Or if they did, the dark circles under their eyes and the matching looks of weary contentment suggest that it was the good kind of trouble.

We exchange nods and they pass me, heading toward the sea of trailers, and I slip into the big top. I tie the flap open to get some light in the place and walk to the centre of the ring. Moments like this, the place somehow looks even more beautiful empty than it does stuffed to capacity. The emptiness feels so...inviting...inviting, and right. That's it, just plain right. Like home. As if those red and blue flaps I just tied back are gates into a paradise that was crafted specifically for me, and only me. At moments like this, I forget everything else and let this place wrap itself around me.

My eyes always start on the ground, in the dirt, right at the bottom of the ladder. They start at the bottom and then they move onto the first rung and start climbing. Thirty-six steps, one at a time, the rope ladder wavering ever so slightly with each step. My eyes move to the platform. They move to the bar, whose cables descend from above, an intricate web of pulleys and lines that looks messy but is actually the most carefully crafted network you could ever imagine. I see myself swing out into the air, into infinity and...

Christ, moments like these.

Moments like these are just moments. Moments, and nothing more. You breathe them in, and, well, you can only hold your breath for so long, so you breathe them out, and they're gone, and you're back on the ground, you're back in the dirt.

"DO YOU MISS IT?"

"Miss what?" I ask—a desperate grab for a couple seconds to recover from the curveball. Gloria is rarely so blunt. Normally, the cores of her questions were like holes in the ground, sectioned off by flashy orange barricades: obstacles begging to be danced around. I blame her staggering right into one on the gin, and make a note to be leery about offering endless refills.

She chides, "Waddaya mean *what*? Flying! Sheesh, Toby, welcome to the conversation."

I laugh an uncomfortable laugh and rub my hand over my forehead—one of those nervous gestures that you're aware of but can never seem to do a damn thing about.

"Do I miss it? Hell, I don't know. No."

She takes an ambitious sip and then starts laughing with the glass still to her lips, sputtering much of her mouthful back to be enjoyed again later. Likely not much later. "Come on! You must at least miss it a bit. I mean, don't get me wrong, your act now is great. Hell, it's the best part of the whole show, if you ask me, but you must miss flying."

I don't speak. I try to drown in my own drink, hoping that if I don't respond, she'll just move onto something else—*anything* else—sooner or later.

"I can just imagine," she says, "you flying through the air like Super—"

"I wasn't a *flyer*. Genevieve was the flyer and I was the *catcher*." Goddamn it. Leave it to me to be lured in by a technical correction.

"Oh…right. I'm sorry. I. Well, whatever you want to call it, I'm sure it was amazing. I once heard one of the girls say that you soared through the air as if you had your own vault full of Get Out of Jail Free cards for Officer Gravity." She starts to chuckle a bit. "Get Out of Jail Free, you know, like that Monopoly game?"

"Of course I know the game," I say, the words rushing out of me quicker, and maybe more jagged, than I intend them.

We're both silent for a moment. I turn and look out the window, watching the ribbon of highway unravel behind us. It'll be at least another few hours before we hit Fort Worth. I look back to Gloria. Her face and body are framed and fractured by the pale glow of the moon, projecting itself through the trailer's paned window, making it look as though she were compartmentalized into four sections. I can't help but think of that magic trick, the one where they stick a pretty girl in a wooden box, shove a few swords in the side, and then rearrange the enthralled volunteer to the amusement of herself and the audience. A mere push here and a pull there and you've managed to reconfigure an entire human being, just like that.

Because I can't think of anything else, I tell her, "We ought to play it sometime," and Gloria looks at me blankly. "Monopoly, that is. Welcome to the conversation."

"Sure." She sounds disinterested, and I know it's because of me. The way that I get, the way that my tone alters, the way I tense up when certain…things are brought up. It's not something I'm unaware of. But I've told her a hundred times: there are topics I don't care to discuss. Usually she doesn't pry too much, but tonight she managed to jam the tip of the crowbar right into the tiny void around the door of the vault, a void that, it just so happens, a certain nerve likes to call home. And, boy, do I know how she gets when she's met with any degree of coldness. How she begins to withdraw, how she waits for you to coddle her back into comfort, to pet her with your words and assure her that she's wanted. It irks me, but for some reason, whenever I see that baited hook floating in front of me in the water, I always bite. No matter how many times it pierces me, I just don't learn my lesson. It's always a mouthful of worms and a poke through the lip for me.

"You strike me as being one of those cutthroat types when it comes to Monopoly," I tell her. "Like one of those types that puts a big red hotel on every property and bleeds their opponent dry. Hell, I bet that's what you paint the hotels with, isn't it? The blood of your enemies—a warning to any who would dare to cross Gloria, the mighty real-estate mogul."

She turns her eyes up to me and gives me just enough of a smirk to indicate that I'm doing good.

"You betcha, Toby. You're looking at the Queen of Boardwalk and Park Place. We can play sometime, but don't expect me to go easy on ya."

"Oh, I wouldn't dream of it!"

She laughs and wiggles herself up from the slouch that she'd dipped into, then takes a sip of her drink. We spend the next hour or so chatting away, the steady whirr of weathered wheels conspiring with a bottle of gin and the soothing breath of the Indian summer sky to lure us both to the brink of consciousness.

Once Gloria is certain that there's not a drop left in the bottle, she curls up on the bed, closes her eyes, and mumbles goodnight to me. I'm sprawled out on the couch, my eyes getting ready to punch the clock, but willing to put in a few minutes overtime for the noble cause of finishing my drink.

A few minutes roll by. I sip away at my drink. Gloria is snoring faintly. "Sometimes I do..." I start, but stop myself, because I know that she already knew the answer before she asked me the question. She knew, but she wanted to hear it from me, hear me say it out loud. Say it to her. Unfortunately, I don't feel up to offering that kind of satisfaction tonight, whether the set of ears I'm talking to is attached to a sleeping head or not. I just plain old don't feel like it.

WHEN LOUSY PEOPLE CROAK, THEY GET ESCORTED TO A southbound elevator that zips them straight down to Lucifer's inferno. But let me tell you, pal, when *extra* lousy, downright rotten, no-good sons of bitches croak, they get a different kind of southbound trip. They get handed a one-way ticket to Fort Worth, Texas. Keeee-rist! What a town. Unbearably hot, ash-dry, populated by the sorriest bunch of animated corpses you ever saw, and, unlike hell, it doesn't even have the decency to burst into flames.

It's not that we're churning out awful performances. That's not it at all. I mean, naturally *my* act goes off as flawless as always, but everyone else performs just as good or as shitty as they would anywhere else. There's just something about Fort Worth. And I don't know if it's the heat or the dryness or what, but I've never had a good time here, and it seems to me that everyone that lives here isn't exactly having a ball either.

It's the way they watch you that gets to me. Now, when I'm doing my set, I'm usually too preoccupied to notice individuals in the crowd. And, hell, even if I wanted to see the forest for the ugly trees, when you're performing, it's always too dark to see beyond the first row or two. When you're performing, everyone blends together, becomes part of the same shadowy blob. But when I'm not on, I stare out from the curtain at that blob, and sooner or later, my eyes adjust and I see them. I watch the way they watch, the way they clap, the way they cheer, and here in Fort Worth, it's as if they were dragged to the show at gunpoint and told, "Have a good time or I'll blow yer head off, see?"

There's this brat in the front row. This little fucking brat in a striped shirt, a ratty ball cap sitting precariously on the back of his head, licking away at a record-sized lollipop. Christ, the face he's making after each lick, you'd think the damn thing was piss-flavoured—not enough sugar for you, your fucking majesty? You know, I'm one sturdy camel, but tonight that brat is the straw that will make a cripple out of me.

My head's poking out from the curtain—beads of sweat canaling down my face, eroding what's left of my makeup—and I'm watching the crowd who are watching Genevieve and Arkad—Christ! Andrew. Genevieve and *Andrew*. Genevieve and Andrew are doing their act, and the crowd, who, mind you, I warmed up, look like they're actually enjoying the performance, despite what I'm sure are their collective best efforts.

That's not the part I mind. They're having a good time? Well, who the hell can blame them? They've had the privilege of seeing a good show up until now.

But that kid. That kid and his lollipop, with its bawdy, hypnotic swirls, its obnoxious circumference...

Tonight, while I jumped, and juggled, and flipped up a goddamn storm, the hush of the captive crowd that I'm only entirely accustomed to accompanying my set was interrupted by one thing: that slap-slapping of that brat's tongue giving his lollipop a fresh coat of bastard spit. But you know what? Now, with Genevieve and Andrew hamming up the tent, as my eyes adjust to the crowd's darkness and that depthless mass slowly turns into a cluster of faces, I notice that not only has that kid's tongue gone mute, but also that he's ditched the lollipop altogether—he's dropped the damn thing on the ground!

Genevieve and her man have somehow converted this little disinterested shit into a believer.

For a moment, I ponder how. How the hell do they arrest the attention of all these miserable zombies? I ponder this for a second, and when the realization hits me, it hurts—I mean, it actually physically hurts, like a punch in the stomach that you weren't ready for. It hits me so hard I buckle forward a little bit. The crowd loves Genevieve and Andrew because it's their show. Not mine, not anyone else's. *Theirs*. Every attendee in this tent has been snacking on propaganda since before we planted a single peg in the scabby Fort Worth ground. Who do they see on the flyers? Genevieve and Andrew. The posters that are nailed to every wooden post in town, who do they show soaring through the air, hand-in-hand, with a matching set of 'fuck you, Mister Newton, what goes up stays up' smiles? Genevieve and Andrew. The people eat that junk up, and by the time they walk through the flap, they have it in their heads that Rowland's Circus is nothing more than the Genevieve and Andrew show. Correction: the Genevieve and Arkady show. Can't forget about his stage name, can we? Arkady, the renowned Russian acrobat who fled his native Saint Petersburg (St. fucking Louis, in fact!) to escape the crushing grip of communism and come to glorious America, where he can be free, free, free as a bird in the sky! My God, how they eat it up! Grab a bib and a pile of serviettes, because Rowland's Circus has just cooked up a heaping batch of bullshit for you to feast on. Don't be shy, there's enough for everyone!

I look out at the drooling citizens of Fort Worthless and it dawns on me that no matter how great I am, I'll still be nothing more than another opening act. You want some more popcorn? Another soda? Maybe a beer? You need to take an elephant-sized piss? Well, do it now. Do it now while the clown tosses his pins in the air. Do it before the headliners take the stage and the real show starts.

So I'm watching this enthralled kid in the front row when all this hits me, and that's when I think of it. That's when it occurs to me that choking the life out of Genevieve and Andrew would probably be about the nicest thing a guy like me could treat himself to.

CHET ROWLAND'S FACE LOOKS LIKE A SHEET OF TINFOIL that had been squished into a tight ball and then flattened out again. The guy isn't even that old—fifty-two or fifty-three or something—he just has one of those faces that wrinkles love to live on. Maybe a couple found their way onto his forehead years ago and then decided to send a telegram to every aunt, uncle, and twice-removed cousin in the family: Hey everyone, there's prime real-estate on this Rowland guy's mug! Spread the word! Load up the jalopy!

Since Wally Jakes made his grandiose exit, Rowland and I don't really talk much. He gives me my space, which I think is another way of thanking me, and for the most part, it's usually just the occasional nod here and handshake there between the two of us.

I think I hate him. But doesn't everyone hate their boss at least a little bit?

I'll say this, though: Rowland respects my talent, and for as long as I've been whiting my face, he hasn't had a single thing to say about how I do my act. He trusts me—he has good reason to—and he knows that whatever I do in the big top will be what's best for the circus.

So, you can imagine my surprise now, as I stand before him in his cluttered office/living-space, and he tells me, "There's something we need to change about your act, Toby."

Our eyes lock. Once his words finally seep their way into my brain, I don't know what to say. I flinch, but I don't know what to say, so I just keep staring at Rowland.

"Toby? Did you hear me? I said there's something we need to change about your act," he repeats.

"Uh. I. Is it about my makeup?" I say, and I sure as flaming hell don't know why I said that, but Rowland caught me offguard and, well, that's just the first thing that came out.

His forehead wrinkles rearrange themselves, probably because I've confused him, but who knows, maybe they just wanted to try something new. He folds his arms and leans back into his chair, which creaks like it's suffering beneath him.

"No, Toby, it has nothing to do with your makeup. The makeup looks top-notch, as always. What I need to discuss, though, does pertain to appearances."

"Oh?"

"It's your smile, pal."

"My smile?"

"Yeah. I'm wondering where it is. I'm worried that one day, the cops are gonna show up and ask me to come down to the morgue and identify an ice-cold smile with a John Doe tag clipped to it. You're a clown, pal. Would it kill you to look like you're enjoying yourself every now and then?"

I give him a phony laugh and tell him it must be that I'm concentrating so hard that I just forget, and I assure him I'll do my best to smile occasionally. After all, what's a clown without a smile? Rowland gives me an 'atta boy slap on the shoulder, then offers me a drink. I decide that my desire for a brandy (Rowland always opts for the high-end stuff) currently outweighs my desire to get away from him, so I take a seat and he pours me a glass. We make small talk over sips, discussing this-and-thats about the show and reminiscing about the so-called good old days, neither of us acknowledging just how bad the good old days were. I finish my brandy, slide my glass toward Rowland, and stand up. He takes the cue and reaches into his desk drawer and produces an envelope for me. I don't need to count what's in it. We've been doing this long enough. As always, Rowland's eyes stay on the envelope until I've stuffed it away in my pocket. Fucking guy. As if I'm going to storm out of his office waving the damn thing above my head. We've been doing this long enough.

MY SHADES ARE CLOSED AND THE DOOR OF MY TRAILER is locked. I don't think anyone would ever barge in here unannounced, especially at this hour, but it's a habit, something I do every time I reach under the bed and slide out my oldest travelling companion, my beat-up Samsonite.

Its hinges are stubborn, and for the last few years, whenever I open it, I feel like I'm prying open the jaws of a monster—a monster whose mouth is decorated in a very sharp plaid, but a monster nonetheless. There's not much in the main compartment of the suitcase; I have a few old issues of *Weird Tales* that I found in a junk shop in Minneapolis, as well as some more recent copies of *Galaxy Science Fiction* and *Line-Up Detective*, my emergency flask, some nudie pictures, and a couple meaty stacks of postcards that are held together with elastic bands. I used to buy a postcard every time we hit a town, but when you've done the circuit for as long as I have, well, you come to a point when enough is just enough.

I grab one pile, slide the elastic band off, and shuffle through them. "Greetings From St. Louis, Missouri,"

"Denver, Colo. The Mile-High City!" "Hello From New York, The Wonder City," "Seeing the Sights in the Windy City"— this one has a cartoon of a very excited-looking fellow hiding in the gutter, his nose poking over onto the sidewalk while he looks up the skirts of two ladies passing by—"Greetings From Niagara Falls, Ontario," and so on. I have hundreds of these things—mind you, some are duplicates, not only because I've been to the same cities so many times, but because if I saw one I really liked, I'd often buy two or three of the same card with the intention of writing someone back home. I've even gone as far as addressing some of the duplicates, but they've never seen a stamp. They just sit in my suitcase, postcard purgatory.

There's a zipper inside the top half of the suitcase, and that's where Rowland's envelopes go. Normally, I just stuff them in there without even opening them, but there have been times where I'll break a seal and grab a few extra bills for myself to play around with. Most of the time, when we have a few days off and I decide to trek to whichever city we're nearest to, I'll just treat myself to a picture or two, so I don't need to dip into the suitcase. But every now and then, I'll get the urge to sniff out a good card game or hit the track, and that's when I'll need a few extra bucks. Yeah, I've lost my fair share, but most of the time, I know a smart bet when I see one, and I've been pretty disciplined when it comes to reimbursing myself for whatever I take out. For the most part.

I return the Samsonite to its hiding place and hop on my bed to enjoy a cigarette. It's almost lunchtime, and there's muffled chatter leaking in from outside, a disappointing reminder that I'm not the last man on earth and that if I want to eat, there's a mandatory side dish of socialization. I've become suddenly aware of just how hot my trailer has become as well, but I don't want to leave quite yet, so I decide I'll have one more cigarette before I step out and grab some food.

Tonight will be our last show in Fort Worth, and then we make our way to Dallas, where we'll stay for three days before heading to Louisiana. We used to do longer stays, but things have really changed in the last few years. I'm not saying we're a stick-and-rag show by any means, but big shows like Ringling have mean appetites, so where we go, when we go there, and how long we stay has everything to do with timing. If we arrive in a town a week or two after one of the big guys has done a lengthy engagement, we're not going to get a great turnout. If we set up somewhere that, say, Ringling is going to be in the near future? Same deal. The big guys are like a band of rival anacondas, slithering across North America on different paths, and circuses like Rowland's are their favourite meal. All we can do is watch where we step and keep moving.

When I finally give in to the pressure of a hot trailer and a vocally displeased stomach and step outside, I see that it's pretty much business as usual for this time of day at Rowland's World Class Circus, which is to say the whole back yard is a mess of varying levels of activity, ranging from mending costumes and practising acts to throwing dice and wolfing down food.

There are only five or six people ahead of me in the food lineup because I've arrived so late into lunch. The Sycs are doling out corned-beef sandwiches with potato salad on the side. One of them spots me at the back of the line and stops what he's doing and waves, which triggers a domino effect of waves from the others. I nod and give them a salute, and then Eddie, the guy in front of me, turns to face me.

"Toby, how are you, my friend?"

Eddie and I aren't friends.

"Fine, Eddie, how are you?"

"Great, Toby, great. You grabbing seconds, too?"

"I'm grabbing firsts, Eddie," I say, emphasizing *firsts* because I can see that there aren't too many sandwiches left, and I know that counting isn't really Eddie's bag, and when he says *seconds*, he likely means he's on his second or third round of seconds.

"Firsts," Eddie echoes in a flighty voice that suggests it's been so long since he's been there himself that the concept of firsts is now foreign to him. "Well, bone-appa-tit, Tobe."

Like me, Eddie is a clown, but if you think that means he and I have anything in common, then I'll remind you that duck-billed platypus and man both sit under the same mammal umbrella. Eddie is part of the act Biff and Boppo. I don't know which one of those two Eddie is. The act has the two clowns sitting at a table playing poker. When the time comes for both Biff and Boppo to reveal their hand to one another, one of the clowns lays down a full house and the other reveals that he's got five kings. Then both clowns jump up from their seats and put on a pair of over-sized boxing gloves, while Cecil—a chimpanzee in a referee's shirt, who I consider to be the most talented participant in the act—comes rushing out to monitor the two clowns as they punch one another in the face several times. Apparently, it's a riot.

Once I've got a plateful, I head over to the Pie Car and buy myself a Coca-Cola. The Pie Car is a trailer that sells things like soda, cigarettes, chewing gum, and newspapers (which are usually a day or three old because we need someone to go to town to get them, so often, when a night rider goes to poster, he'll stock up on newspapers, comic books, whatever reading material he can find for cheap, and bring them back to sell to us at a slightly inflated price). One of our guys who used to work for Ringling claims that their Pie Car is like a diner on wheels and that you can actually go in and have a slice of pie and a coffee, but I'm not sure that I believe anyone who used to work for Ringling.

The sandwich is passable, but I don't think I'll help myself to seconds. I guzzle what's left of my Coca-Cola, which, I have to say, on a scorching day in death-dry Fort Worth, is divine, and then head over to the water buckets. Every performer is designated two water buckets for drinking each day. Sometimes you can get a refill, but it all depends on how much fresh water is available. The buckets are labelled, to prevent scrapping and to keep things square. Years ago, Susan, a woman of many talents—just one of which happens to be not getting hit by flying knives—painted one of every set of buckets with a picture of the performer they belonged to in action. The extra-personalized buckets are a way of telling who's been here longer than most; they're sort of like a badge of honour, or maybe an indication of rank. And Susan is no Manet, but she sure can paint. On my bucket, I'm depicted as an aerialist. She has me in my old sleeveless leotard, a bold scarlet number, and my black boots streaked with silver flashes of lightning, flying through the air. My face isn't very detailed, but the few lines that Susan's provided make me look almost angry—defiant—and my coppery hair is being swooped back by the wind. The paint has faded and chipped over time but still bears a hint of old glory. Some days, it stings looking at that painting, and some days, it stings a bit more.

I'm hauling my two buckets back to my trailer when I spot Gloria standing with four other spec girls, all of them watching Lana and Helena—two sisters from Thailand—practise their balancing act. I don't know how, but Gloria seems to feel my gaze right away. We lock eyes and she waves to me, and I smile, shrug, and crane my neck to one side, gesturing to one of the buckets I'm carrying. Gloria nods and laughs. By the time I've stashed the buckets in my trailer, she's made her way over to me. She lets my hello float right past her and gets to what's on her mind: "I saw you had another one of your meetings with Mister Rowland this morning."

"I didn't peg you for an early riser."

"Oh, you know I'm not. I sleep like a rock, but I sure couldn't sleep last night. I don't know what it was, but nothing I tried—and I tried everything, Toby—could get me to sleep. I was tossing and turning all through the night, and at some point, it must have been two or three, Camille, the girl who sleeps in the bunk below me, had had about enough. She climbed out of her bed and stuck her face in mine and said that she'd be damned if she lost another wink on account of my not being able to stay still, and if she had dark circles under her eyes for our performance, she'd be sure to give me a matching set."

"Christ. I hardly know Camille, but it's hard to imagine her as the confrontational type."

"You know how the quiet ones are, Toby. They're always the quickest to go off."

Looking at her bare arms and noticing the amount of sun hitting her pale skin, Gloria takes a step toward me, into the shadow cast by my trailer. "Anyway," she says, "I knew what was good for me, so I threw on my sweater and went for a walk outside. That's when I saw you going into Rowland's trailer."

"Well, how about that," I say, and I'm wondering what she's getting at. I don't say anything else because I don't want to accidently lead her some place she wasn't already planning on going. A few seconds drip by like molasses, and just when I begin entertaining the thought of giving in to the uncomfortable tightening sensation coiling its way around my body and saying something, Gloria starts up again.

"I don't mean anything by mentioning it, Toby. I hope you don't think I was spying on you. It wasn't that. I just thought I'd bring it up because I didn't think you and Rowland were pals or anything. I always thought you didn't really care for him, what with the way you speak about him sometimes when we drink."

"Nah, he's not so bad," I say. "I mean, yeah, he gets on my nerves from time to time, but we have a decent working relationship, you know. We might not always be on the same page, but we respect one another's opinions when it comes to the show. After the barbecue last night, he pulled me aside and asked if I wouldn't mind swinging by his trailer later to discuss a couple of things that'd been bothering him about a certain performer. He knows I have a better eye for technique than he does, so sometimes he'll ask for my input. I forgot to go see him, but I woke up early and saw that his light was on, so I went on over. And you know, while I had his ear, I put in a good word for a certain spec girl I know, one who's destined for bigger things."

She crosses her arms and shifts her weight to one side, jutting her hip out. I don't know if her smirk means she believes me—sort of a "you're damn right I've got bigger things coming" smirk—or if it means she knows I'm lying, but I don't think I really care. I offer her a cigarette. She nods and I pop one into my mouth, one into hers. Once I've lit my smoke, I pluck hers from between her lips and bring it to the burning end of mine, but I stop when I notice we have an audience.

If I had a trailer as swanky as Genevieve and Andrew have, I know the only way I'd come out was kicking and screaming, but while Genevieve has no problem shutting herself away, the amount of time Andrew spends in the sun lately makes me think he's trying for a Charles Atlas shade of orange. Every day we've been in Fort Worth, I've seen him sitting in his fold-out lawn chair, nothing on but his under- shorts, soaking up rays like he'd just scored a hot tip that the sun was going to burn out by the end of the week. You believe that? Rowland gives me shit about my lackluster smile; meanwhile, our fake Russian's skin is about two shades away from being a Christmas turkey! Anyhow, I spot that bastard eyeing me from across the yard, so I put Gloria's smoke back, step aside, and light her cigarette the way I'd light one for a nun I'd just met for the first time. Andrew cranes his head back and exhales his own plume of smoke, then looks back to me, sticks his tongue out one side his mouth, and rolls the invisible dice a few times down by his shorts. He gets a good laugh out of that, then leans further back in his seat and commences crisping.

"What's eatin' ya, pal?" Gloria asks in her goofy version of a New York accent— her go-to when she's kidding around.

"Nothing," I tell her, my eyes still fixed on Andrew.

She gives me a friendly punch on the arm. "Hang in there. Only one more night and then we're off to Dallas. I'm sure it's just as miserable there as it is here, but, hey, after a few shows, we get three days off before heading to Marshall."

"Great. I'll get a ride into Dallas, look at some skyscrap- ers, and get myself a giant doughnut. It'll be a gas." I take a lengthy drag—the kind that ends with your eyes going to slits—and turn to Gloria. Her eyebrows are angled in a steep frown, her mouth a sickle, and she's hunched forward slightly and sticking her neck forward, giving her the posture of a vulture. A few seconds pass before I realize she's imperson- ating me, and then I crack right up, a flash flood of laughter spilling from my face. Eventually, my smoker's cough butts in, but by then I've forgotten all about that rodent-faced fuck, his judging eyes, and his phantom dice. At least for the time being, that is. And hey, I'll take what I can get.

THE DALLAS CROWDS WERE AN IMPROVEMENT.

Two nights, two beyond sell-outs. The big top's gills were oozing. Rowland keeps a bunch of red envelopes in his desk drawer—Fire Marshal Blind-Eye Insurance—but I don't think he needed to dip in during our stay. Typically, the farther outside of city limits we set up, the less people care about regulations. Capacity is in the eye of the beholder.

When we first rolled in, if you'd asked me what I was looking forward to the most, I would have told you the three days of hibernation that would follow the shows. I don't know what internal switch got flipped and changed that, but here I sit, bouncing along in the backseat of a Syc-driven Ford. The way this kid drives, Christ, I'll tell you this: In the six years that I was a flyer, two of those years I performed without the safety of a net. Every night I ran the risk of plunging fifty feet to my death—but I've never been more scared for my life than I am right now in the back of this fucking Ford. When this kid's not busy straddling the centreline—commanding a chorus of honks from oncoming drivers who are all quite aware of their own mortality— he's acquainting his tires with the edge of the ditch. So, I figure I'll either die instantly in a head-on, or I'll get a topsy-turvy somersault that'll land me in a wheelchair, in which case I'd hope that Gloria has the decency to smother me with a pillow.

"Holy hell, kid! Do your clone brothers share your unique interpretation of a straight line? Or is this zig-zag shit your problem alone?"

"What's that, Toby?" he shouts back at me, and when he turns his head, the wheel follows suit, bringing us to the brink of the ditch.

"Fuck! Nothing! Forget it! Just keep your eyes on the goddamned road!"

He whips his head forward, "Whatever you say, sir!"

If we make it to Dallas, I fully expect my favourite brown suit to have finger imprints on each bicep from my white-knuckling.

"What do you plan to get up to in—"

"Do not talk! Please, for the love of God, just focus on getting us there in one piece! When we get to Dallas, lunch is on me. You can talk my ear off then, but until then, eyes on the goddamned road, understand?"

"Yes, sir, I do!"

About fifty Our Fathers later, we pull in curbside and screech to a stop. I don't even know if this is a proper parking spot. I don't even care.

Once, years ago, I stayed in the King James Hotel, and given that it was the kind of place that lets patrons pay by the hour, I wasn't expecting much from the tavern at its base. But if you think my socks were knocked off by its swank, you should see the face of the Syc I walked in with. Hat in hand, mouth agape, eyeballs sponging up the dark oak-paneled room, its stained glass lamps collectively emitting just enough of a glow to give the place that perfect level of warmth, the elaborate shelves of liquor behind the bar, so tall you'd need a ladder to reach the top-tier—you'd think the kid had walked into the Sistine Chapel.

I clap him on the back. "Hell of a place, ain't it?"

"I'll say," and I'm glad I got his mouth moving before the drool started leaking out.

The tavern is nearly empty. We slide into the booth farthest from the one that the other two patrons are sitting at. The bartender throws a nod, I catch and return. He steps out from around the bar, then turns right back around when I holler "Two bourbons!" at him.

He comes back with our drinks and places them in front of us. "The men know what they want," he says, as if he were talking to someone beyond our view.

"These men sure do," I say, and that gets a polite chuckle out of him.

"And will you be dining today as well?"

"Yeah, I think we will."

He nods so deep it's practically a bow, flaunting his friar-like bald spot. "Julia will be right over with some menus."

"Say," I get him before he turns to leave, "this is a helluva place."

"Thank you, sir."

"I stayed at the hotel up top a few years back and, well, no offense, but I didn't really picture anything like this at the bottom."

He closes his eyes and smiles knowingly. "Ah, the *old* King James."

"The old King James," I echo.

"The old King James was quite a different establishment. About five years back, the original owner passed on. The place was bought up and fixed up, but they decided to keep the name."

"I guess if you've got a regal name, might as well try and live up to it."

"Perhaps that's it," he says. "I've been here for years. Sure don't miss the old place. I started as a bellhop when I was fifteen. You want a fast dose of reality, get a job as a bellhop in a crummy hotel. My God, some of the people. There are things you can never un-see, know what I mean?"

"Do I ever."

I raise my glass and take a sip that turns into a gulp. The bartender eyes the new vacancy. I give the glass a tap, and he nods. "Well, welcome back to the King James, sir," he says with a smirk.

Staccato rasp-heavy coughs come jittering out of the Syc across from me, reminding me he's there at all. He buries his mouth in the crook of his elbow and rides the mini fit out. "Excuse me," he says once it stops. He's looking at me all apologetic.

"Not a bourbon man?"

"I love bourbon," he insists, then downs another mouthful to prove it. This time there's no cough. "The first sip of anything hard always gets me, though. Gotta give my system a second to get used to it."

I nod like I understand, and right then my second drink arrives. I clink glasses with the Syc and we both take a sip. "Look," I say, "I feel like an ass asking, but what's your name again, kid?"

"Rupert."

"Rupert. Right. God, I'm awful with names."

"No need to apologize, Toby. Guy like you, everyone at Rowland's knows you or wants to know you. Can't blame ya for forgetting the odd name."

"And it *is* an odd name, Rupert."

He exhales a laugh and nods, fidgeting with his glass, eyes ricocheting around the room, the poster boy for social awkwardness.

"But then again, I always thought Toby sounded like something you name a lizard, so you're in good company." That gets a more sincere laugh out of him and gets him to stop the nervous glass antics for a second.

He says, "I bet a Claudius or a Melvin is gonna come walking through the door any second and join us." The joke catches me by surprise, right when I've got a mouthful, and I have to put my hand to my mouth for spill insurance. I instigate another clinking of glasses, and next thing you know, I'm signaling the booze-friar for another round. He's about to leave his post and walk the drinks over when this waitress, who I assume is Julia, shows up and snags the drinks.

"Good afternoon, gentlemen," Julia—her name tag confirms it—says. She's all perk and point, right up to the tips of

her cat's eye glasses. I return her greeting and flash a smile.
I'm glad that the bartender's been demoted to wallpaper. Julia
places our drinks on the table and gets us a couple menus. It
takes me about two seconds to decide on stew, and Rupert
the Syc opts for a plate of French fries. I remind him that I'm
buying and insist that he get a real meal, but he's not having
any of it, so French fries it is. I also order us a couple of iced
teas because I have no idea what Rupert's booze tolerance is,
and a great way to get kicked out of a nice place like this is to
do an impromptu puke paint-job.

Rupert and I are now the only customers, so our food
comes pretty fast. Instead of pouring ketchup on his plate
and dipping his French fries in it, like a normal human might,
Rupert keeps the open bottle in his hand for the entire meal,
and every time he picks up a fry, he lets a little bit of ketchup
drip onto it. It's fucking weird, but I decide not to ask him
about it because the kid seems self-conscious enough as is.

When I'm done, my bowl and spoon look cupboard-ready.
Julia comes to take everything away, and I ask her to tell whoever made the stew that they've got an admirer. Rupert crams
his remaining French fries—about a quarter of what was
there to begin with—in his mouth and grunts to get Julia's
attention, then points to his plate to indicate that he's done as
well. I pay the cheque, and as I start to get up, Rupert, who's
still chewing, reaches across the table and puts his hand on
my arm. We meet eyes, and he does the most forceful swal-
low I've ever witnessed, then gasps: "Whaddaya say to one
more drink, Toby? On me." My first instinct is to say no. I was
planning to walk to the theatre a few blocks from here and
take in a picture. But he has this pleading look in his eyes,
and eating habits aside, he seems like a nice enough kid, so I
say sure, why not one more, and sit back down.

We've got a couple more drinks in front of us in no
time, with another two in hot pursuit. Next thing I know,
me and Rupert are chatting away like a couple of old pals.
He's slumped forward, one eyelid looking the slightest bit
heavier than the other, ragging on everyone at Rowland's,
but getting distracted mid-rag in the same way a dog
gets distracted when it goes to the park; one second he's

complaining about the other Sycs sticking him with all the grunt work, then another thought will zip past him, so he'll ditch what he's talking about, nab the new topic, and run with it. Anyway, this guy's got a lot of guts to spill, and, to be honest, I don't mind a mess. I'm getting a real kick out of it, actually.

"She's got the nicest ass," he tells me. "An' normally… *normally*, Toby, a ring don't mean a thing to this boy, you get me? But, well, when the guy she's hitched to has a talent for throwing knives with excellent accuracy," he drunkenly pronounces it *ex-lent ack-eracy*, "well, that changes things a bit, don't it?" The most ignorant volume of laughter bursts from his face before I can get a word in to tell him he ought to watch how he talks about Susan. And right as he starts to wind down, another topic gets picked up. "That Rowland seems like a real degenerate, you know…" So he turns down that road, and I just smile and nod along with him, laughing when he laughs, and so on, but inevitably my thoughts and attention begin to drift. Before long, I find myself wondering how soon I can sever this slanted conversation and shake Rupert so I can go catch a picture. I'm wondering if I can make time to hit the track and get the few extra bucks I have on me to spawn. I'm recalling Gloria telling me that she and a few other dancers were heading to Dallas earlier this morning, and I'm wondering what she's up to right now and if there's any chance I'll run into her. I'm wondering if that little bookshop I visit every time I come here is still in business, or if it's been shut down for distributing indecent material. So my wondering is really enjoying wandering, but then Rupert says something that pulls me back to the moment.

He goes, "…nothing wrong with that at all. You like 'em tight, not a man alive that'd fault ya for that." He punctuates it all with this stupid grin-shrug combo that I think is supposed to be comical but is sure as fuck not, and then leans forward, takes a sip from his glass, and gives me a triplet of eyebrow jumps, as if we're on the level. As if we know one another at all. As if me sitting down and having a few drinks with him propels him into some realm of privilege where he can go and say something like that to me. I'm right about to set him straight and tell him where he ought to go, when Julia shows up with two more drinks for us.

"These ones are on the house, gents. I think you're a couple doubles away from putting Max's kid through college."

The bartender, who I guess is Max, sees us accept the drinks, then gives a nod. Rupert is over the moon. You'd think no one had ever given him a thing in his life. He's doing that thing people do when they want to seem as if they're refusing a gift. "Oh, we couldn't possibly," he says. Then, "That's completely unnecessary. You tell Max I *insist* that we pay for these. I *insist*!" Julia humours him for a bit, then slowly backs away.

The interlude has cooled me. Rupert's comment is nothing worth getting riled up over. He's just a fucking drunk kid. And he's wrong. And if I lose my cool, one of the only memories his sober self will have of this late afternoon will be: I suggested that Toby was sticking it to Gloria and he flipped his lid! Grab the giant scissors and cut the ribbon, this new rumour mill's sure to stabilize the local economy and create a fuckload of jobs.

He and I go at our free round, and while Rupert is finishing his last sip, I rush to kibosh our meeting before he has time to order us another. "Holy hell, it's nearly three o' clock, pal. I've got things to do. I'd better make this drink my last."

Rupert indicates understanding with a nod. I think that last drink was the push over what must have been his third or fourth cliff of the afternoon. I tell him that there's a drugstore around the corner and that he ought to get himself some Aspirin for tomorrow. I don't realize how tipsy I really am until I stand. The fresh air will sober me up, and I'm sure I'll run across a hot dog stand or something. The two of us leave our money on the table, say our thanks to Julia and even Max, and step outside. Rupert tells me that he has plans to meet the other Sycs, and that they're all spending the night at a friend's place. He assures me that he's going to get that Aspirin and then head over there and catch some rest before the bunch of them hit the town tonight. All I can think is, lucky friend, having this guy show up on your step in the state he's in. We say our goodbyes to one another, Rupert gives me a dead-fish handshake, and then we go our separate ways.

48

It takes me maybe two minutes of walking before I find a hot dog stand. I get the chubster operating it to give me a loaded dog and a lemonade, and the first couple bites have got me feeling better. The track will be open for a while, so right now my plan is to take in a picture, and then maybe try and find that bookshop.

I get to the Majestic Theatre too late for the three o' clock showing of *Strangers on a Train*, but I grab myself a ticket to the four-thirty show and take off in pursuit of the bookshop. I can't remember the place's name, but I remember exactly where it is, and it's only a short walk from the Majestic.

I walk the few blocks and see that it's right where I left it last time I was in Dallas, and to my disappointment, but not my surprise, the bookshop's windows are boarded up, its sign gone. On the door, a staple-riddled notice reads, Closed Indefinitely. I guess they sold smut to the wrong fella.

I need a good spot to kill some time, so I wander until I find a little bakery that serves coffee. I buy a newspaper and make myself comfortable in a corner booth. There are a couple locals scattered about the place, so it's not quite dead, but given the amount of vacant seats, I'd say it's time to consider last rights. The waitress—a blonde girl with the wide eyes of a Walt Disney cartoon forest creature—is on me before I've read the first headline. I order a cup of coffee and a doughnut and work my way through the news. Every time I get near to the last mouthful of my coffee, the waitress zips over and makes sure I don't see the bottom of the mug. Maybe there's something crude written there, and she doesn't want to offend the polite man who's now become her only customer. I finish what must be my fourth cup, pay my bill, go take a piss, and then start walking back toward the Majestic. I'd gotten used to the air-conditioned bakery, so walking through the streets now feels extra hot, and I can hardly stand it. I could never live in a place this hot, this dry. When I finally spot the large red-and-white sign sticking out from the side of the Majestic, I've got my jacket slung over my shoulder and my shirt is clinging to me like a needy lover. It dawns on me that the theatre will be air-conditioned, too, so I quicken my pace.

The first thing I do once I walk through the front doors is go to the concession and get myself the biggest, iciest soda a man can buy. Before even stepping away from the concession counter, I take a gulp so big it leaves me desperate for oxygen. I'm catching my breath when I notice the crater-faced kid who gave me the soda is looking at me like I'm from one of Saturn's moons.

I say, "What? You been outside at all? Or were you conceived, born, and raised behind this counter?" He gives a nervous smirk, then turns and starts pouring kernels into the popcorn machine.

I grab a seat in the centre of the first balcony row. The place is aptly named: regal red seats, pillars capped with gold, wall fixtures that look like they were lifted from a European palace. The lighting of the room—sparse but deliberate—makes it feel like a Hollywood set, and as I let my gaze drift around, I start to imagine what I must look like right now, in this vast and grandiose room, from a dozen different camera angles. A couple necking on the lower level disrupts my fantasy just as the opening score in my head starts playing.

When the lights dim, I sink into my seat and put my feet up on the rail in front of me. A stupid cartoon about a skunk that wants to screw a cat plays, and then the feature starts. I'd seen Farley Granger in a couple flicks before, and I like him okay in this one, but, my God, Robert Walker, what a performance! The guy plays a great creep. He's this rich mama's boy type who meets Farley Granger by coincidence on a train and then goes and kills Granger's wife with the expectation that he'll be owed a murder for it. Walker's got these icy psychopath eyes that always look pained, even when he's laughing and having a good time. He actually kind of reminds me of Andrew, but just superficially, because Walker seems like someone with a great deal of depth to him, whereas Andrew is more the shallow end of the swimming pool—the end where all the necks get broken.

I quickly find myself smitten with the girl who plays the murder victim. I think the credits said her last name is Elliot. I haven't seen her in anything before, and I'd sure as hell remember if I had. They have her fixed with these thick glasses, and she kind of looks like a goody-goody bookworm, but as the story progresses, you see that that's not the case at all. I'm disappointed when she dies so soon, because I love watching her, but I can sure see why Granger's character hates her so much—she's downright cruel!

The show ends where it started—on a train—and when the Warner Bros. logo flashes on the screen, I feel a little pang of sadness because the experience is over and I love the movies so goddamned much and I hardly ever go.

When I step outside, the Majestic's nocturnal neons are glowing and the temperature, while still warm, is bearable. I light a cigarette and find a good spot on the wall to lean. The locals have come out of their heat-induced hibernations and are buzzing about in the streets. Taking a taxi to the track seems less appealing now, for some reason. Maybe it's all the activity surrounding me, making this area seem a lot more desirable than it was earlier when it was just hot, dry, and dead. I approach a few people who look like they might know where a game of cards is happening, but each of them brushes me off and tells me they don't know about that sort of thing. One guy asks me if I'm a cop, and I tell him that if I'm a cop, I'm about as deep undercover as a cop can get.

I throw in the towel and decide to head back to the King James. I'll get myself a room and then kill the rest of the night at the pub.

I move through the nighttime crowd, walking against the grain. There's lots of shoulder-bumping and pardon me-ing, but everyone is so friendly. People are tipping cowboy hats as they walk by, men's mouths bulge with chaw, women's smiles are Texas-sized, the air is filled with chatter and laughter. The cordiality proves contagious. Next thing I know, I'm wishing everyone I pass a good evening, substituting hat-tips with nods and two-finger salutes; my delight isn't content with behind-the-scenes stuff, so it forces its way to the surface. I think maybe I like it here.

The flow of people slows to a drip the further I distance myself from the Majestic. I pass three giddy teenagers doing a terrible job of hiding a flask. I move aside to let an old couple by. Maybe I could reach the King James by continuing straight, but I turn right because it looks familiar, so I figure I came from there earlier on my way to the theatre. The drip has become a drought by the time I reach the King James. All the night's action is either on other streets or shut away behind closed doors. I feel a push coming from the other side as I pull the tavern's door handle, so I step back to let who-ever it is out. She's better at sweeping her surprise under the rug than I am.

"Why, hello," she says as if she were expecting me all along.

"Evening, Genevieve," I manage after a couple seconds.

For a moment, we just stand there, seeing who can hold their stare longer, but then some drunk stumbles out of the tavern and Genevieve has to step closer to me to avoid his graceless line. Now, the two of us sharing the same gash of streetlight, she looks almost spectral—her pale skin, glowing lunar in stark contrast to her bottom-of-the-well black hair, her burgundy evening dress and matching halo hat—as if she were a photograph brought to life, but they ran out of colour somewhere in the transfer.

"Are you staying here?" she asks.

"No. I might be. Yourself?"

"Yes, we're on the tenth floor."

I nod. I look down at the ground and kick a couple of pebbles onto the street. "Where, um, not that it's any of my business, but where are you off to?"

She snickers at that and then digs a cigarette out of her purse. I go to offer her my lighter, but she rushes to whip hers out. She displays it with a ta-da gesture, then lights up, blow-ing smoke out of one side of her mouth as she stands there, making no effort to hide the fact that she's regarding me.

"Well, you're right that it's not any of your business, but I don't mind telling you. Andrew spent some time at the track today. We're going to meet up at a bar near there."

"Pretty nice place in there," I say, nodding to the tavern she'd just stepped out from.

"It's not so terrible. I had a cocktail, but one felt like enough."

"One's never enough."

"For you, Toby? You're damn right it isn't."

The moment I notice the silence returning, I walk—almost push—past her and into the King James. The person who terminates an uncomfortable conversation like that is usually the one who leaves with the most dignity. With Genevieve, I always walk away with less, but you can't blame me for trying, so I won't blame me either.

It's packed in the tavern. The air is high voltage; I can almost hear Victor Frankenstein screaming, *It's alive! It's alive!* Clinking glasses, slamming glasses, uproarious laughter, a thick layer of chatter poured onto a foundation of screeching chair legs, throats clearing, flint wheels sparking, and matches hissing through flame-births. I head for the bar. Julia, the waitress I had earlier with Rupert, has a full tray raised high above her head. Noticing that the liquid in the glasses barely quivers as she and I dance around each other, I can't help but think of the circus and wonder how Julia would take to the nomadic life. I squeeze onto a stool at the bar (the only empty seat in the place, as far as I can tell), and Max the Bartender nods in recognition.

"Bourbon?" he shouts above the din.

I mouth 'Yup' at him, feeling that I don't need to add to the noise myself. A second later, he slides a coaster my way, all smooth, as if he's got an ounce of finesse in him or something, and then places my drink on top of it.

I take a big gulp. I've got Genevieve on the brain. I'm about to take a second gulp when the guy sitting next to me swivels around on his stool to face me. Like half the people in here, he's got a cowboy hat on. His jacket is this goofy beige-plaid and brown-leather crossbreed; I'm tempted to ask him if he dabbles in clowning. He's quite a bit older than me—grey dominating black in the hair poking out from the sides of his hat—and he's got one eyebrow cocked, as if he's puzzling over something. At first, I think maybe he came to one of our shows and he's trying to determine where he knows me from. This doesn't happen often, on account of me performing in makeup now, but it has happened once or twice since I started the Freddy Folly shtick.

"I know you from somewhere?" I ask.

"Doubt it," he says, more to himself than to me.

I shrug and turn back to my drink. I can see him in my periphery, not moving, just staring away. I take another sip, then another, then I notice I'm gripping my glass maybe a little too hard, so I turn to face him.

"There a problem, pal?"

He mutters, "Shouldn't be," though I can hardly hear him over the clamour.

"Then may I ask just what the hell you're gawking at?"

"Ain't gawkin'."

"No?" I slam my glass down on the bar hard enough to get a few looks shot at me. "Because it sure looks like you're gawking at me."

"I'm just trying to figure something out," he tells me.

"Yeah?"

"Yeah. I'm trying to figure out if you actually apologized to me, and maybe I just didn't hear it on account of it being so loud in here, or if you didn't say nothin' to me at all."

"Apologize for *what*?" I shove the words through my teeth.

"When you grabbed that spot," he says, gesturing at my stool, "you caught my back with that bony elbow right as I was sipping my drink. Sent about half of it spilling down my chin. So, like I said, I'm trying to figure out if you apologized and I just didn't hear you, or if you just carried on like you're the only one in here who matters at all."

The funny thing, I'm told, about me being rather pale and bald is that when I start to get worked up, you can see the red rising through me, making me look like a human thermometer. I can feel it now, that growing internal boil, as my mercury climbs past my shirt collar, up my throat, onto my chin. But looking around the bar, a noisy tapestry of unfamiliar faces, I realize that this is a bad place to pop. Anger loves a struggling victim. But that's the key to beating it when you feel it coiling itself around you. Don't thrash out at it, don't tense up, simply breathe and keep yourself loose and it'll get bored and move on. This heaping pile of melodrama sitting next to me really wants to feel like a big man. He wants me to protest and tell him where he should go, so he can slug me with one of his meaty old fists and walk out of here feeling like he just told the world that while he may be getting older, he's sure not getting any softer. That's what he wants, but there's something powerful about denying someone else's wants, so I say, "Shit, I'm really sorry about that, pal. I hadn't even noticed. Let me buy you a drink."

He's taken aback. Maybe he's disappointed, but the outcomes for him were either hit me and feel like a tough guy, or, failing that, get a free drink, so either way, he's sitting okay.

"Thank you kindly."

Christ, he even tips his hat. What a ham.

I wave to get Max's attention, point to my new friend, then hold up two fingers: one for each of us. Max gets our drinks fast—maybe he's got another kid on the way and he figures that a man with two college graduates in the family is pretty set. Putting on the kind of smile that Rowland would love me to bring into the big top, I raise my glass to the man next to me, getting a raised glass back. We both take a drink.

"Jay Holden." He extends a hand and I shake it. The man's got a gorilla grip.

"Freddy."

"No last name?"

"Freddy Truman. I'm Harry's handsomer kid brother."

That gets a howl out of him. He slaps one hand on the bar, commanding a round of looks, and then claps the other hand on my back. I guess we're pals now. We get chatting, and I soon learn that Jay is the kind of man who likes to talk at people, but not necessarily with them.

By the time our fourth set of bourbons arrives, I've had about enough of Jay Holden. He's got a whole lot to say about Koreans, local politics, certain Hollywood actors and actresses who are *definitely* communists, and his late wife, who he's certain is the only woman he will ever love. The booze seems to really be getting to him. And as if he weren't hard enough to understand to begin with—with all the noise in here and his thick Texas drawl—the lake of alcohol sloshing around inside of him has given his voice a sort of sluggish, melting quality. I pay my bill, and as I stand up to leave, he grasps my arm and says something I can't make out. It takes three strained repetitions (drunk or not, his gorilla grip remains, so I'm forced to stay until he lets me go) before I'm able to decipher his words.

"Tell yer brother, the president, Jay Holden from Texas says hello!"

I assure him that I will, and his laughter follows me to the door that connects to the hotel lobby. I pass through, shutting the door behind me, sealing away the tavern's buzz. It's likely the fresh quiet that makes me realize that the steps I'm taking to the front desk feel a little funny—I'm half drunk. Maybe a little more than half, but measurements can be tricky when you've had a few. The lobby floor is covered with a checkered burgundy and gold carpet, and I use its pattern to aid me in walking a straight line to the desk. The guy manning the place has a waxy look to him. For the job, he appears a bit young, but maybe he's just well preserved. I tell him I'd like a room. He gets me to fill out a form, and then he takes my money and gives me a key to room 616. Anything that's not on the tenth floor is fine by me.

"I wasn't sure if I'd be staying the night, so I'm short one toothbrush and one razor," I tell him.

"That's not a problem, sir. We supply our guests with such amenities."

"Geez, what a place."

He smiles and nods at that. "Thank you, sir. Will there be anything else?"

"Nope. Have a good night," I tell him.

"You as well, sir."

I turn and start walking across the lobby toward the elevator, but as I pass the door to the tavern, I peer through one of the panes and notice that Jay Holden has gotten up from his stool and looks to be heading toward the men's room. I walk back to hotel's front desk, patting my pockets as if I'm looking for something.

"Did I leave a cigarette case up here?" I ask. "A silver case with a golden fleur de lis on it?"

The man behind the desk looks up at me with well-practised urgency lighting his eyes. He eyes the top of the desk, then bends down and checks the floor behind the desk, then pops back up and peers over to my side of the floor. "I don't think so, sir. If I come across it, I'll be sure to set it aside for you."

"You know, maybe I left it in the tavern there," I say, still fumbling through all my pockets except for the breast pocket of my jacket, where my cigarette case actually is.

"Perhaps. The bartender's name is Max. If one of the waitresses found it, she would have brought it to him."

"Max? Thanks."

I walk back into the tavern, moving quickly past the bar. Max is reaching for a bottle, so his back is turned to me. The men's room is at the far end of the place. I push the doors open and slide in. Jay's standing at the urinal, one hand on the wall for support. The other one appears to be trying to manoeuvre his dick out. He's muttering to himself. There are two stalls in the room and both have their doors open—it's just the two of us.

I hear piss trickling into the urinal now as I walk up behind him. I cradle the back of his head with my hand, and before the old drunk even has time to get one syllable out, I shove his head forward into the wall, leaving a spider-web crack in the tile. He falls to his knees, and—poor son of a bitch—smashes his mouth against the edge of the urinal on the way down. A couple of yellowing teeth drop from his mouth onto the floor. He's lying on his side, looking up at me, all wide-eyed and clueless and pathetic. His mouth is bloody, the little gash on his head is just beginning to seep, and his shaking hands are frozen into two harsh, gnarled claws, as if rigor mortis were setting in.

He's trying to say something to me, but I could barely understand him earlier, so my chances now are pretty scant. I reach down and pluck the cowboy hat off his head.

It's a little big on me, but I have enough postcards from Dallas.

HIS SHADOW FELL OVER ME WHEN I WAS SITTING ON THE front step of my trailer, trying to rip a loose thread from my sweater without unravelling the whole thing. It was a trailer I shared with two other boys—Chester Ames and Paul Frum, both part of the Sledge Gang, a group who took care of pounding stakes into the ground during setup and, when nothing needed pounding, would be called upon for any sort of labour that needed to be done—the more mindless, the better.

I wasn't content staying in the trailer and playing another round of cards. Paul had no shame when it came to squeezing his pimples in front of others. During our last game of poker, when I picked up the Jack of Hearts, I noticed it had an extra bit of red smudged on one corner. Paul, whose face and neck were oozing in about five different places, tried to deny it was him, but I'd had it by then. I threw my cards down and told them both where to go.

I had the thread coiled around one finger and angled sharply upwards, ready for amputation. I put my thumb in lowest point of the V and gave a brusque tug, but the thread pulled further out, leaving me with a good four inches sticking from my sweater. That's when Wally came and, quite literally, darkened my doorstep.

"Here," he muttered, offering me his pocket knife. The knife was a faded piss-yellow with red writing that said, DRINK COCA-COLA (TRADEMARK) IN BOTTLES 5 CENTS WORLD FAIR CHICAGO, 1933. The blade made a peeling sound as I pulled it out of the handle. It was filthy, all mucky brown and Halloween orange, any remaining silver herded to its dull edge.

"Thanks, Mister Jakes," I said, without looking directly at him.

He cleared his throat, spat, then pulled a cigarette from his pocket and popped it between his lips. "Mister Jakes was some asshole from Sheboygan who didn't know when to pull out. You call me Wally."

I nodded.

With the thread severed, I closed the knife—having to really force it shut, which produced a sort of scraping crunch—and handed it back to Wally.

"Better be more people tonight. Weather ain't *that* bad. Bunch of fuckin' chickenshits. If a little chill scares you, move to Australia." His gaze was fixed on something in the distance. Or maybe it was on the distance itself. I just remember that he was staring off at something, and I wasn't sure if he was talking to me or not, so I kept quiet. Once he had puffed away half his cigarette, which took about half the time it would take anyone else I knew, he turned to me. "Fuckin' elephant's sick again. Shitting swamps."

"Which elephant?"

"The grey one," he chortled, then said, "Chuck, the smaller of the two. He's always fuckin' sick. Rowland should let me put him out of his misery."

I agreed, Rowland should have let Wally put poor Chuck out of his misery, but I didn't say so. It wasn't because I was afraid to speak ill of my boss, nothing like that. Granted, I had a lot more respect for Rowland then than I do now, but I've never been one to keep my opinion leashed. Back then, I didn't know Wally very well. He was always cordial to me—or at least his take on cordial—but for some reason, I used to get nervous whenever he and I were alone together, and I'd always do as little speaking as possible in hopes he'd get bored and move on.

A couple minutes walked by with neither of us speaking. I wanted to get up and leave, maybe head over to the big top and see if I could catch anyone rehearsing, but I stayed put, for some reason feeling as if I needed to be dismissed.

Naturally, it was Wally who cut the quiet. "See those new folks who joined us?"

I shook my head no.

"Fuckin' hoity-toity bunch. Family of acrobats. From *France*."

Of course, this was incorrect. Genevieve and her family were from Montreal, but Wally wasn't the type who'd worry himself with knowing the difference between a European French accent and the French-Canadian accent that Genevieve's parents had. To Wally, anyone who spoke French was a Frenchie, anyone who was English, Irish, Scottish, Welsh, or Australian was a limey, anyone with dark skin was a jig, and pretty much everyone else was either American or Chinese.

He stepped closer to me, then placed one foot on the middle step of my trailer—the same step I sat on—and bent forward, resting one elbow on his knee. The thick tobacco smell was the most pleasant odour wafting off him. At this new range, I could smell the whole bouquet: the dehydrated booze-breath from last night's binge, and his lived-in-for-a-month clothes—that yellowing collared shirt of his and those overalls smeared with a chronology of food and probably-not-food stains. Paul Frum's pimple popping didn't seem so bad all of a sudden. But I still felt I should stay put.

"Hoity-toity or not, they're probably a good thing for the show," Wally continued. "No offense to you, naturally. I seen you out there. You're a fine acrobat, but you're still an amateur. And that other kid you perform with?"

"Clay," I said.

"Yeah, whatever the hell his name is. That kid, he's fuckin' awful. I've talked to Rowland about him a couple times. You ought to ditch that hack. Or maybe you'll luck out and he'll have a bad landing," he laughed. It was a laugh that rattled, though I don't know what would produce a rattle quite like that. The first thing that came to mind was pebbles of gravel bouncing around in his lungs the way popcorn kernels leapt about in a hot pot.

Something—maybe my eyes widening, or perhaps a more subtle gesture—must have happened then, because I could see in Wally's face that he regretted what he had just said. Not regretting having said it, mind you, but regretting having said it to me. He wiped his nose on his hand, then rubbed that hand on the side of his overalls and turned away for a moment.

Once he started up again, it appeared he was addressing both me and his old friend, The Distance. "Yeah…you're good, but you're not putting asses in seats. People come and see you, and they like what they see, but they ain't coming here *for* you. We got a circus full of sick animals and hack performers. That trapeze pair that top the bill aren't half bad, but you gotta have more than that to bring the money in. And, hell, when you do something wrong, word gets around. Some folks come to a show and see a lion take a piece out of his whip man, or see some drunk clown with a hard-on handing balloons out to children? Nails in the coffin, that's what those are. Nails in *our* coffin."

"And you think this new act will be a big ticket item?" I asked, lured out of my shell by a mix of intrigue and Wally's brutal honesty.

"Better be, for what Rowland's forking out. I'm not gonna give you a number, but you can trust me, they're doing pretty good. Folks like that, they wouldn't be here if the money wasn't right."

Wally stepped away from my trailer. He shoved his hands in his pockets and stretched his back in a way that reminded me of a bow having its string yanked. I heard a couple of cracks. His face told me the cracks hurt, but maybe it was a good hurt. He met my eyes and nodded at me, in agreement what what, I'm not sure, but right after that, he turned and walked away.

One week after that conversation with Wally Jakes, Chuck the sickly elephant would be gifted two bullets to the head. One should have done the job on its own, but Wally's aim was a little off that day, so more lead was needed to put an end to the poor elephant's hysterics. Putting hopeless creatures out of their misery was something that had to be done every now and then at Rowland's World Class Circus. One day, I'd even have my hand in such a task, although I certainly didn't know that at the time of poor Chuck's mercy killing. It's not the kind of thing a person enjoys doing, but it's something that has to be done. That's why you do it. You do it because you have to. You do it because you care.

"HI-HO, SILVER." SHE POINTS AT MY HAT.

I give a tip. "You like it?"

"Sure. You must have made some impression in Dallas if they went and made you a ranger that quick."

"Yeah, they know a good thing when they see one."

She takes a seat next to me on the wooden curbing surrounding the ring. We've ended up in Baton Rouge a few days early because bigger names were hamming up San Antonio and Houston. Had it been another circus of about our size, we might have planted our pegs and dealt with a couple nights of half-capacity crowds, but the giants in those last two Texas towns were the type that eat shows like ours without stopping to chew. We have guys in Baton Rouge right now, plugging tonight's show at half price in hopes of undoing the self-fucking that comes with an ahead-of-schedule arrival like this. The crew had to work through the night to get the tent up. They're all sleeping like bricks now, but Rowland was good about making sure us performers, talents and hacks alike, got a decent rest. Gloria's not usually up this early, and it's nice to see her. She looks like she's still half asleep herself: no makeup, heavy-lidded eyes, hair tied back, sporting pink-and-green-patterned pyjamas and a cardigan sweater to fend off the morning chill. She motions her hand at my cigarette and I hand it over. Why not?

"I met Clayton Moore once, you know."

"Who?"

"Clayton Moore," she says, pointing again to my new cowboy hat, "the guy who plays the Lone Ranger on television."

"No kidding."

"No kidding," I'm assured. "It was a while back. He was at a fair in San Francisco dressed in his Lone Ranger outfit. The television show was just starting, so I guess it was a publicity thing. He signed autographs for me and my two girlfriends. I remember he was very generous with his time. There was a pretty big crowd—well, bigger than you'd think for a relatively unknown actor at a local fair—but he still took the time to chat with us. I don't remember how it came up, I guess one of us must have asked him how long he'd been in show business or something like that, but he told us he'd been performing since he was a child and that he started as an acrobat."

"No kidding."

"No kidding."

The morning glow melting in through the tied-open flap has this uncanny beauty to it. It knifes through the middle of the ring toward us, inching ever forward but being discreet, which I appreciate; it's my kind of intruder, the non-intrusive type. I haven't seen Gloria since before I went into Dallas after our stint there. The last couple days during our trek here, I stayed in my trailer as much as I could. Whenever we'd stop, I'd wait until there weren't many people around before I'd sneak out to grab food and relieve myself. I wasn't feeling very social after my trip to the city.

I don't know that I missed Gloria, but I think I was used to having her around, so maybe I missed that consistency.

She tells me about her time in Dallas. She says that her and a couple other spec girls spent the day wandering the streets, seeing sites, looking through shops. She tells me about this toy store she came across and how she'd hoped to find something for her nephew back home. She got the kid this toy chimp that has a couple of cymbals attached to his hands—I'm sure that won't get on the parents' nerves in the first five minutes. "I also found a board game I thought you might like," she says.

"Oh yeah?"

"Yes. It's a crossword game called Scrabble. You get a bunch of tiles with letters on them and you try and build words to score points. I thought we could play it together sometime. I've played it with some of the other girls in my trailer, but they didn't really care for it. But you're always reading, so it's probably right up your alley."

"That sounds like a ball. And I didn't even know I had my very own alley, so that's good news. Let's give the game a whirl tonight."

"Sounds perfect."

I don't notice I'm staring until Gloria points it out. Her inhibition clearly unaware of today's new wake-up time, she gestures with her head in the direction of the acrobat's platform and says to me, "You come in here to get some quality time in with your misery and that platform, or what?"

"What the hell are you—? Me and my *what*?" I don't mean to raise my voice, but, Christ, what a blindsiding. I'm sitting here enjoying the morning mellow, enjoying my own company but still willing to scrap that and have a friendly conversation, and she goes and says something like that. "I'm not miserable," I say. "I come in here to be alone. I come here to get a few goddamned minutes to myself. Is that so hard for you to understand?"

"I'm…I'm sorry, Toby." She looks afraid, afraid and fully awake now. She goes to put a hand on my shoulder, but then withdraws and covers her mouth, as if touching me would trigger something, something worse than my bark. A whisper comes from behind her palm. "I didn't mean to…I'm so sorry."

I can't find a response. Yeah, maybe I'm not really looking, but if I can't find one, then I can't find one.

"I was only trying to kid. I didn't…I wanted you to know you can talk to me, that's all. We're friends, Toby, right? You and me, we're friends. I know you like to come in here when it's empty and take the place in, but if you come in here and you're feeling awful or something…I only wanted to come and chat, see if you were okay, that's all. I don't know the full story—"

"You're damn right you don't," I tell her.

As if it's suddenly become colder, she pulls her cardigan closed and wraps her arms around herself, then stands up to go. Her gaze stays in the dirt. I can feel my heartbeat in my forehead. Holy hell, I'm quick to boil. Always so quick to boil! I suck in my cigarette and let my eyes drift around the room. They go back to their favourite place. The platform towering just a few feet short of kingdom come. The trapeze rigging bobbing like uneasy ocean water. I know that really, it's barely moving, that the light breeze ghosting in from outside can hardly touch it, but when the place is this still—this silent—that shadow-drenched web bounces with an eerie frenzy to it.

"When you came in here, I was thinking about seconds." I don't look to her as I speak; even if I did, I know her back is to me, but I hear her eggshell walk go mute. "I was thinking about trapeze, and I was thinking about seconds. Remembering how to cut seconds up into a hundred pieces, and then choose the right piece for the job. The slice of second you use depends on what you're trying to accomplish. I was trying to remember my slices of choice."

I hear the slight sound of her shifting, perhaps turning back to face me, but I'm still locked on higher places, grander places. "That time…that one time, I chose the wrong piece of a second," I say, talking to myself as much as Gloria. "No one died. The world kept turning. But I chose the wrong piece. A hair early, a hair off. She broke a cheekbone and her nose— no. No, that's not right. *I* broke her cheekbone and her nose. I did that. The bad landing, though, that wasn't me. Whether you're in pain or not, you hit that net right, you fall like a professional. I won't argue that the net was tighter than it should have been that day—there's no doubting that. But when you fall, you make damn sure to correct your form, and you hit the net right. The nose and the cheek, that's on me, but the landing was all her."

"W-what happened when she landed, Toby?" Gloria asks in barely a whisper.

"Well, she didn't fucking *die*." It's such a ridiculous thought that I almost laugh, but I catch myself. "She landed wrong. Not headfirst—thank God—but almost. Those ropes were tight. Too tight—not the kind of embrace you hope for at the bottom of a plunge. She broke her wrist, messed up her shoulder, and tore some muscles in her neck. But like I said, that part's on her."

"I believe you, Toby."

"Of course you believe me. I'm not asking for a leap of faith! It's all facts!"

"I'm sorry. I just meant that I agree, the wrist, the shoulder and neck, that's on her. And she's fine now, right? All healed up. She's still performing, still headlining."

"Yeah," I say, unable to hide my disdain. "Yeah, she sure is."

TAKE BREAKFAST IN MY TRAILER. I KNOW THIS LONE-WOLF

shtick has a finite lifespan, but it can hang on until noon.

Once I'm done eating, I do some push-ups. When I go down for number thirty, I decide that multiples of ten are over-rated, so I stay down. Too much too fast—my beating heart, pressed to the floor, sending tremors through the trailer. It's nice down here, though. A fresh perspective is always nice. I see I need to dust under the bed. Dust and replenish my booze. I should have got one of the guys going into town to pick some stuff up for me, but I'm not too worried. I'll be fine for at least another day or two. For some reason—maybe the overexertion has made me a bit light-headed—the stitching on my Samsonite is just about the most interesting thing in the world right now. I trace the lines over and over with my eyes, counting each stitch and going, "Tk, tk, tk, tk," as I follow them around the front of the case. Because it's still early, I have no intention of stepping out for at least another hour, so I'm down on the floor, staring at that case and thinking, Toby, you really ought to know exactly how much money you've got stashed away in that thing; that's the sort of information that's just plain old good to know.

I pop the hinges, open the case, and tug the zipper open. I stuff my hand into the compartment and dig out every single envelope. I decide I'm not going to take the actual money out of the envelopes. There's so much, a few bills would be bound to drift off the bed and get lost somewhere. And besides, I know how much is in each envelope. I stopped counting after the first year when I realized Rowland would be stupid to rip me off.

There are thirty-two envelopes in total. I lay them out on the bed in eight rows of four. The math isn't difficult. Thirty-two envelopes of $125 gives me four thousand big ones. Whenever I take a few extra bucks to go play with, I always take from the same envelope, and it's that same envelope—the one with a big X penciled over the seal—that I add to when I win or when I make a point of reimbursing what I owe myself. I open that envelope and count what's in there: $75. That makes one envelope short $50, leaving me with a total of $3950 stashed away.

Not bad. Not a fortune, that's for sure, but definitely a nice hunk of dough. A decent rainy-day fund. A decent ditch-this-hole-and-start-fresh-somewhere fund? Yeah, maybe.

I gather everything back up and return it to the zippered compartment of the suitcase. Every buck. Now, I'm not usually the self-congratulating type, but I'm pretty damn proud right now. All those envelopes and I only blew $50 of it over the last two and a bit years. Not too shabby, Toby-boy, not too shabby at all. And you know, I'm actually glad I held off on counting it until now. I'm glad that all this time, I'd just taken the envelopes and stashed them away and then hardly ever thought about them except for when I needed a few extra bucks for a card game or to go to the track. It makes for a nice surprise. $3950—Christ, I wouldn't have guessed it'd be that much by now. I wouldn't have guessed it'd been that long since I started getting these little treats.

Time flies when you leave it unattended.

I spend—I don't know—maybe a good five minutes just pacing around my trailer, all proud, then I sit down on my bed and flip through some of the magazines in my suitcase, realizing that if I were to walk out of here now, with this irrepressible smile plastered on my face, people might think something was going on.

The cover of an old *Weird Tales* grabs me. The issue, which I'm sure I found in a junk shop somewhere, is all tattered and beat up—creased paper, once-sharp corners worn down to curves, staples holding on for dear life. On the cover is a woman wearing a mask. The mask is shaped like a bat, its wings spread, ready for flight, its face pointing upward, creating a pose that reminds me of the crucified Christ you sometimes see in old paintings. Even though most of the woman's face is covered by her INRI bat, you can tell she's beautiful: long-lashed, twenty-thousand-league-deep blue eyes, pale skin with flushing cheeks, and blood-red lipstick that looks about three seconds fresh. She's looking either right past me or right through me, but definitely not at me—something more interesting has caught her eye, so I won't flatter myself. An idiot might think she looks vacant, but that's not the case at all—she's entranced. The story's title, which sits conveniently just below her breasts, reads, "The Vampire Master," so maybe that's whose spell she's supposed to be under, but looking at her now, I think maybe she's the master. She's the master and she's under her own spell, mesmerized by herself and no one else. And looking at her, who can blame her?

Staring at the cover, it occurs to me that I can't recall any details about "The Vampire Master." I know I've read it—I've read every story in every one of these magazines, some of them twice, but I can't remember a damn thing about "The Vampire Master." The painting on the cover always gets me, though. There's something about it, about her, something foreign but familiar, that makes me want to stare for hours.

ABREEZE MUST HAVE CARRIED ME HERE. OR MAYBE The Vampire Master hypnotized me and sent me over, and I've just come out of my trance. POOF! I snap out of it and find myself in one of our three shaded lounging areas at this table with Julian and Eddie. We've all got a cup of coffee in front of us. Eddie is a slurper. Slurping irritates me, so it's only fitting that Eddie the clown—Biff, Boppo, Rocko, Jocko, whatever his stage name is—has a genuine talent for it.

"You fellas know when lunch is happening?" he asks, concern lighting his eyes.

Julian takes a sip of coffee, then puts his hand on his chin and looks off like he's contemplating something. "I think it's at noon, Eddie," he says. "And do you know why I think that? I think that because it's precisely the time lunch has been served every other goddamned day."

I put a calming hand on Julian's shoulder. "Easy, easy. You can't expect that much from a guy who was replaced by a wooden sign."

"Aw, fuck the both of you! Go to hell!" Eddie slams his fists down on the table, gets up, and slides his chair away, fast and gracelessly so it falls on its back.

That wooden sign jab drives Eddie crazy. We try not to bring it up often on account of one time he actually burst into tears when we were razzing him, but there are times, like today, when it can't be helped. What had happened was, years ago, before Eddie joined our circus, he worked at a carnival. His job was to measure the heights of children who wanted to ride The Jumpin' Jack Rabbit, an attraction that took riders high in the air and spun around so fast that a hose needed to be installed by the gate because someone would vomit at least once every hour. One day, Eddie—whose real name, I should add, isn't Eddie—was getting a little lazy with his measurements. He let a boy on The Jumpin' Jack Rabbit who was a little small for the ride, and wouldn't you know it, the kid flew out of his seat while his car was at its highest point. The story was all over the news: Child Dies After Being Thrown From Amusement Park Ride. Operator Responsible Flees. Eddie and Rowland, an old carnie himself, had worked together years back, so after his monumental fuck up, Eddie hopped a train in Saint Paul and found his way to us. Go figure, Rowland, saint that he is, saw an opportunity in having a fugitive working for him. He agreed to take Eddie in on the condition that Eddie would only be paid half of his earnings (which, if you ask me, is still a bit much). At any rate, the amount Eddie eats almost makes up for his loss of wages. Apart from Rowland and Eddie himself, Julian and I are the only ones who know Eddie's deal, and, honestly, as much as we like to bug him every now and then, I know neither of us would ever let that information out of the vault. Now, Julian's got a sister out in Minneapolis, and wouldn't you know it, about three years back, this sister was visiting a friend in Saint Paul, and she found herself at the very carnival that had Eddie run out on. Her and Julian keep in touch, and after her visit to her home city's fraternal brother, Paul, she wrote Julian a letter, which she's done every month for as far back as I can remember. She mentioned that The Jumpin' Jack Rabbit had been repainted and renamed The Astro Swirl, and that now all the rides with a height restriction have a wooden sign with a goofy-ass cartoon character painted on them telling you exactly how tall you need to be in order to take a ride. This cartoon character—I think it's a moose in overalls or some nonsense—has one arm extended, and as long as you're taller than his arm, you can go for a ride. So anytime Eddie's getting on our nerves or saying something so goddamn stupid it just can't be ignored, Julian and I will throw a wooden sign jab his way. 'Hey, Eddie's getting suited up to perform, did a wooden sign call in sick today?' Stuff like that.

With Eddie gone, Julian and I drink our coffees—mine black and his tainted with cream—and chat. I ask him how Susan is doing with her no-longer-secret pregnancy and if they've discussed baby names at all, not so much because I'm interested, but because I know people who are spawning really like it when you ask them about how their spawning is going.

Julian's yammering on and on about what names he likes for a boy, but right before he's about to put the n on the end of Martin, he stops abruptly, looking over my shoulder at something behind me.

I guess there is a God; He's the vengeful type, though, and He must not have appreciated me making fun of Eddie, one of His simpler creations, earlier, because Andrew—a living, breathing slab of penance if there ever was one—has walked into our patch of shade.

I accidently make eye contact, which appears to be enough for him to alter his route and make a stop at our table before grabbing his coffee.

Next time I make fun of a dimwit I'll be sure to drop to my knees and rattle off ten Hail Marys and ten Our Fathers right away.

His cocky smirk has already clocked in. "Toby, how's my favourite clown?" he says, as if it's the cleverest bunch of words ever to tumble out of someone's face.

"Bozo?" I say. "How would I know? If you miss his voice, go listen to one of the Capitol Record Readers you've got in your trailer. I hear the one where he goes under the sea is pretty educational."

He slaps me on the back like we're pals and does a phony laugh. "That's good, Toby. It's nice that you can joke around a bit. Laughter helps people through tough times, doesn't it?"

"Eat shit."

"Here for coffee, but thanks," he says, moving past us.

On the far table sits one empty coffee pot and one close to full, a faint tendril of steam writhing up from the black. Paper cup stacks, Domino Sugar packets, and two porcelain jugs of creamer are laid about the red-and-white checkered surface. Andrew's back is to us, but I know he's still wearing that smirk. He's the most complacent person I've ever come across, and I know from experience that that smirk has the forced work ethic of an orphan in an Industrial Revolution-era factory.

Me to him: blatant dagger eyes. I see no sense in hiding their points—a stab or two in the back is about all Andrew deserves. And looking at his back, I realize that even his posture pisses me off. There's proper posture, and then there's bow-down-to-me posture.

He helps himself to a cupful, turns around and leans into the coffee table, facing me.

I force myself back to Julian. I say, "Martin, then? I think Martin is a swell name."

Julian nods. "Yeah, Martin," he says. "Susan's grandfather was named Martin. I really like the name."

We go on talking about baby names, both knowing it's become the type of in one ear, out the other chatter used to bide time. Andrew is still leaning against the table with the coffee pots on it, sipping away, looking at us as if he's waiting for something. By the time Julian has exhausted names for a baby boy and started with names for a girl, I've had about enough of Andrew's lingering. Julian's going on, "Margaret, or Louise, or Linda, or maybe Betty—I've got a cousin named Betty. Or maybe Pa—"

"Are you just going to stand there all day?" I bark at Andrew over Julian's shoulder.

"I'm enjoying a cup of coffee," he shrugs. "Can't I enjoy a cup of coffee?"

"Maybe you could enjoy it somewhere else," I tell him.

"We're trying to have a private conversation here, get me?"

"Sure, Toby, I get you." He stands up straight and steps away from the table. "I was thinking maybe I could help with name suggestions, but—"

"If the baby needs a Russian alias somewhere down the road, I'll find you," Julian says, getting a whisper of a laugh from Andrew and a full-on haw from me.

Andrew goes to leave, but as he approaches our table, he raises his right hand and whips something at my head. I jerk to one side, so it misses and lands on the ground a few feet beyond me.

A scrunched-up packet of Domino Sugar.

"Now, what the hell was that?" I shout at Andrew.

He winks at me—the bastard *winks* at me!—and says, "I thought drafts were all that you dodge, Toby," then continues past our table.

Andrew's back to me, I jump up from my seat and lunge at him, my arms catching around his waist, thrusting him face-first to the ground. Before he has time to catch his breath, I roll him over and plant one right in his mouth—that damn smirk of his can take a day's leave. Paid.

I raise my hand and go to give him another, but he manages to shove my forearm away and lands one on my jaw. It hurts like hell. It comes with a rattle. The impact sends a shooting pain up the side of my skull, and I fall backwards off of Andrew.

He's on his feet while I'm still trying to find some stability on my hands and knees. That punch of his, he really made sure it counted.

From my knees, I clumsily grope at him, but he gets a grip on the collar of my shirt and pulls me up just high enough off the ground to hit me with another one.

He makes that one count, too.

Same with the third one. But if anything counts after that, I hope someone else is keeping track, because number three puts me out.

OPEN AND CLOSE.

Open and close.

Each blink dusts a few specks of spacy grain away. Consciousness is being filtered to back to me.

My head feels cold. My head feels wet. Beads of water rolling down from my temples.

Or what I hope is water.

Open and close.

Open and close.

The ceiling—I'm in my trailer, in my bed, looking up at the ceiling. Those familiar planks, eight of them in all—God knows I've counted them enough times on sleepless nights—are peppered with the grainy specks that have placed themselves under my supervision.

Open and close.

My heart is beating in my brain. My face feels like it's burning. I lift one hand up from under the covers and touch my forehead—a cold washcloth. Water, not blood, wetting my head.

I touch my face with the tips of my fingers, delicately, the way you might touch a pricy glass ornament in a you-break-it-you-buy-it shop—the slightest bit of extra pressure and everything crumbles in your hands, and there goes your beer money for the next month.

I've been tenderized. I've got a bandage on my left cheek and a bandage covering my right ear, sticking it to the side of my head. The skin above my right eye and part of my lip are marshmallow-puffy.

Open and close.

Less than a handful of specks remain, toughing it out. Otherwise, a couple more heavy blinks gets my vision back. Someone has placed a glass of water on the stand next to my bed. I take it and drink. All of it in one breath.

Two knocks from outside. Before I can say, 'Go away,' or, 'Who is it?' or whatever I might say if someone were to come to my trailer, the door flings open and there he is: recently smoothed-out tinfoil face and the proportions of a snowman, Mister Rowland himself.

I only wish I'd had time to tidy up and make a pot of tea.

"To what do you owe this pleasure?" he asks me—helluva guy, hey? Able to anticipate a question like that.

My voice comes out sandpapery. "I'm wondering that myself."

Rowland steps in and closes the door behind him. He walks to my bedside and cocks his head back, eyeballing me. "What? You've never seen a horror flick?" I ask him.

"Ha! Julian pulled him off you quick enough, so I don't think we need to worry about Universal snatching you up for *The Return of the Hunchback of Notre Dame*, or anything like that."

"Movies pay well."

He drags a chair over and plunks into it. "Yeah, Toby they do. But in your case, I pay well, too."

"Don't act like it's out of the goodness of your bleeding heart, Rowland. I'm worth every penny."

"I won't argue that," he says, turning his attention to a dangling piece of skin around his thumbnail. He twists the skin round and round until it comes clean off, then places it on his knee, flicks it away for me to find later, and looks to me again. "So, what happened?"

"I don't know how long I've been out, but—"

"A few hours."

"Right. Well, in that few hours, I'm sure you've managed to get the story from someone."

"I have," Rowland nods. "But not from the person who got beaten to a pulp."

"Well, what do you want to know? Andrew was hassling me—"

"What about?"

"Jesus, are you going to let me finish a damn sentence here, or do you somehow enjoy the sound of your own voice even more than I thought you did?"

"I'm sorry," Rowland says. He waves an 'after you' gesture at me. "Please continue."

"Thanks for that." I pick up the water glass, forgetting it's empty, then set it back down and clear my throat. "So, he's hanging around, eyeing me while I'm having coffee with Julian. The way he stood there, I could just tell he was up to something—trying to get under my skin. I tell him to beat it, and as he's leaving, he goes and makes this crack about me dodging the draft. I've got no patience for that shit. I don't know what Genevieve's told him, but you and I both know I'm not a damn draft dodger."

Rowland stays silent.

"Christ, how's it my fault if I'm out of the country when they *happen* to be drafting people? Hell, I would have enlisted in Canada if they'd let me. And that chump, Andrew, did he hit himself on the head practising his garbage routine and fuck up his memory? What, does he think he was on Normandy Beach? From what I hear, that son of a bitch was a civil defense trooper, spent his war days on American soil. Probably spent his time with the service getting good at solitaire."

What Rowland does with his hands reminds me of a conductor hushing his orchestra at the end of a tune, like he's pushing shut an invisible trunk lid with uncooperative hinges. I don't care much for the gesture, but I suppose I could try and calm down a bit, at least lower my voice a hair.

"All right, so he made a comment about you dodging the draft—"

"Which—!"

The invisible trunk pops back open—cue conductor hands. "Which you and I both know wasn't the case, yes."

"Right. So he makes that crack and I lose my temper a bit and go and sock him. Once, mind you. I only hit him once, and he sure deserved it. Then, as I'm walking back to the table, he sneaks up and punches me in the head. And he keeps going, swinging away until I'm in dreamland, and, well, I guess you know the rest of it better than I do, because next thing I know, I'm here."

The two of us sit without speaking for a moment. Gently, I trace my fingers over my bandages. Even the faintest of touches makes me wince. Whatever is underneath that gauze and tape isn't going to vanish after a good night's rest.

"You know, come to think of it, I'm curious as to how exactly I ended up in here," I say. "I'd locked up when I left earlier."

"Oh, for God's sake, Toby, you paranoid son of a bitch. Julian fished the key out of your pocket and he and one of the Sycs carried you here. It was Harriet who patched you up."

"Harriet?" I say.

"Harriet Lane. You know her. She directs the chorus girls. She's a trained nurse—worked in a military hospital over in England during the war. She knows what she's doing, if that's your concern. Patched up worse things than you, no doubt."

"And what was Miss Lane's professional assessment after bandaging me up?"

"Diagnosis: walloped. You took a real beating, Toby, but you'll be fine in a few days, *if* you take it easy. You'll miss all the Baton Rouge shows, but I'm sure you'll be fit to perform by the time we hit New Orleans."

"*New Orleans*?! That long? What the hell am I supposed to do it the meantime?"

Rowland shrugs. "What do I care? Play Tiddly Winks, do whatever you want. Just make sure whatever you do, you're taking it easy." He stands, gives his lapels a quick tug, and buttons his coat. "You're here because of you, Toby, understand that," he says. "I feel bad that you took the pounding you did, but this," he points at my face, "is on you. You've got to keep yourself in check. You can't be pulling this kind of shit. Picking a fight—come on, man. This place is hanging by a thread. You know that, right? We're hanging by a thread, and the last thing I need is having my top performers tearing strips off each other."

"You wouldn't have a fucking thread to hang by if it wasn't for me," I growl. I'm careful not to raise my voice, but unable to keep the venom in.

Rowland says nothing, just turns from me and heads for the door, moving with the pathetic lumber of a man who's had enough.

Just as he reaches for the handle, I say, "Too bad Julian was there at all, hey?"

"I'm sorry?"

"I said it's too bad Julian was there to pull that animal off me. A few more hits to the head and maybe we wouldn't be having this conversation right now. Think of the bread you'd save."

He gives me this look like he feels sorry for me or something, then opens the door and leaves without speaking another word.

Bad rubbish, good riddance.

I stay in bed for another minute or two, then decide I should wash away the residual sand in my throat. A sharp pain in my lower back catches me by surprise as I get up. Maybe Andrew took a few kicks at me when I was down and out—something he would do—or maybe I landed funny after that third punch knocked me into the dark.

My bed is in the corner opposite the door. The headboard sits against a wall that extends halfway across the trailer, partitioning the room. The jug of water I normally keep within reach of my bed is nowhere to be seen, so I assume that Harriet Lane left the jug on the other side of the partition, since that's where the cupboard I keep my glasses and dishes in is.

I walk around the partition, empty glass in hand, but the second I turn the corner, the glass drops and explodes across the floor, sending a hundred little bits of shrapnel in every direction. Maybe I gasp or maybe I scream, I'm not sure which, but holy hell, am I startled.

"I didn't mean to intrude."

"Funny to hear that coming from an intruder, Gloria. You scared the shit out of me!"

"I'm so sorry. When—after Miss Lane left, I thought I should come check on you. The door was left open, so I came in. I…I know I shouldn't have, but I was so worried for you, after hearing about what that bastard did." She reaches to touch my face, but I jerk away. "When I came in, I noticed the cloth on your head wasn't cold anymore, so I soaked it in cold water and filled the glass for when you woke up."

I say nothing.

She's looking at me with wide, wounded eyes, her fingers laced as if caught mid-prayer, her mouth pulled into an anxious downward curve.

It's then, noticing her unease, her hand-in-the-cookie-jar demeanour, that a question occurs to me. A question that I know the answer to, but a question I need to ask: "How much did you hear?" I ask her.

Wider eyes, tighter fingers. "Everything, Toby," she says. "I was right here. And I heard everything."

THERE WAS LOTS OF SHOUTING. PEOPLE SHOUTING AT each other and people shouting at the radio. Mostly the radio.

A hockey game happening on the other end of the country was being broadcast, the Toronto Maple Leafs against the New York Rangers, and the way everyone in the tavern was hollering, you'd think they'd all bet their mortgages and maybe a couple kidneys each on the big matchup.

It didn't matter what city—or, I suppose, even what country—you were in, Wally always knew where to get the cheapest drinks. His spidery red nose could sniff out cut-rate booze anywhere and any when, and that night in Calgary, his bulbous beak led us to the King Edward. Both of us having only the slightest interest in hockey, we sat at a table near the back, glasses clasped, hunched forward, like a pair of gossiping vultures.

From September until mid-March, the circus stayed in the southern half of the United States on account of the weather. Once March hit, we'd begin making our way up the west coast, stopping in Portland, Seattle, and Bellingham, zipping up to Vancouver, from there moving to Spokane, Butte, and Great Falls, and finally heading north again, into Alberta. Timing was always important when it came to Calgary, because the city has a big Stampede every July, so if we get there any later than mid-April, we'll see a drop in attendance, since a lot of people will be hanging onto their money, saving it for the Stampede.

A couple days earlier, the Nazis took Denmark. Food was being rationed in Britain. The world was on the edge of its seat, but that night in the King Edward, for a couple of hours, you got to forget all about humanity's hell-via-hand-basket expedition. Heated chatter about Hitler, Stalin, conscription, and death were on a temporary hiatus, having been replaced by remarks like "Alf Pike's a bum!" "That Kerr is a goddamned brick wall!" and "Lynch the referee!"

Wally and I were gulping our beers down because that's what we did whenever we had time to spend in a Canadian city. Cheap dollars, cheap booze—we always made it count. Wally, of course, made it count a little more. He didn't have to worry about maintaining a headlining aerialist's physique, or really maintaining any particular physique beyond simply being Wally-shaped, so he went at booze and food and pretty much everything else with the most ravenous of appetites. Before we came to the King Edward, Wally went to a tobacconist and bought himself a bunch of nice cigars, the kind that, whenever I had one myself, always made me puke before I reached the end. The game was just beginning when we took a seat and ordered our first drinks. After the Rangers and the Maple Leafs switched sides for the first time, I realized that Wally seemed to have set a one-cigar-per-period quota for himself—something that would be both ambitious and nauseating for most men, but was, for Wally Jakes, just another night out.

I cupped my hand around my mouth and leaned forward across the table. "Aren't those pricy ones the sort of thing you want to take your time with?"

"Take my time with?" Wally plucked the cigar from his mouth and held it in front of his eyes. "Who's got time to take their time with anything? All this shit happening in Europe," which he pronounced *year-up*, "bombs dropping, folks being rounded up and killed, entire countries falling to the feet of that Chaplin-lookin' pansy—the hell do I know how much time I've got to do anything, Toby? As far as I'm concerned, I find something I like, I enjoy it as fast as I can...and then I enjoy it again." With that, he popped the cigar back in his mouth, crossed his arms, and leaned back in his seat. He angled his chin upwards and blew a thick, dark cloud from his mouth, then turned toward the bar and barked, "Another round over here!" loud enough to cut through all the cheering and the yelling that filled the air.

"One minute, pal," the bartender hollered to Wally, staring, with most everyone else, at the radio and raising a hushing finger at us.

"Hell, you, the bartender...where is everyone getting all this time from?" Wally grumbled.

The game ended in overtime with the New York Rangers taking the victory. The radio's sound was cranked down, and after a few minutes of groaning and cursing, we watched a handful of patrons file out of the King Edward. Those remaining in the bar went back to their quiet conversations or their solitary drinking.

"How's that twist you're flying with these days? You make it with her yet?" Wally asked me, with the same volume he'd been using when the bar was full and noisy.

"Wally, keep it down a bit, would you?" I said in a whisper that I hoped Wally would aspire to. "I don't need everyone in this hole knowing my business."

"Who gives a shit?" Wally said, just as loud as before. "You know anyone here?" Christ, you couldn't take the guy anywhere.

I picked up the matchbook sitting between us and lit myself a cigarette. "No, I haven't *made it* with her," I told him. "Why do you have to ask me stuff like that?"

"I'm curious, Toby. Can't a guy ask? She's gorgeous. I figured you two working together, those tight outfits, all the touching that goes on—something's bound to happen eventually."

"I'm not saying Genevieve isn't a looker. She is. But we're professionals. When we're together, we're working. That's it." Of course, that wasn't it. In the few months that Genevieve and I had been working together, something had started to develop between us. At the time, I wasn't quite sure what that something was—though I sure knew what I hoped it would become—but even if it were anything more than a flirtatious remark here, an ardent glance there, the last person on earth I would talk to about it was Wally. I liked the guy, sure, but he had this habit of digging into other people's business. He was a dirt hoarder of sorts, and very much a leverage man. He was the last guy you'd ever want to have anything on you, anything to hold over you, good or bad.

"So, what you're telling me is you're a free man?"

"I'm always a free man."

Wally grinned. His grin was spaced out in a way that made me think of a rural community and coloured in a way that made me think of candy-corn. It was a conniving grin, the only kind he knew, a grin that reminded me he was always a step or two ahead, always thinking. Despite appearances. "Then can we get out of this dump and find us some fun?" he asked, but the way he said it, I knew it wasn't really a question.

We finished the round, paid our tab, and left the King Edward, me staggering, Wally lumbering. He always lumbered, but when he was drunk, his lumber was more pronounced, almost exaggerated. We made our way up the street, me following Wally and Wally following either his heart or some other organ of equal importance. We didn't have to walk far before we came across what he was searching for.

She told us her name was Dot. She said, "More than you could afford," when Wally first asked, but then she looked from Wally to me, then back to Wally and said, "Who are you asking for?"

"For me," Wally told her.

"Yeah," Dot nodded, "like I said." She turned from us, eyeing a trio of soldiers who had just rounded the corner and were stumbling toward us with their arms around each other.

She hooked a couple loose strands of hair behind her ears, smoothed her blouse down the front, and pushed out her chest. "Have a nice night, boys," she said, making a shooing motion with her hand.

Wally stepped closer to Dot, into her periphery. "How much for him?" he asked, nudging his head to me and fanning out a wad of cash to show he meant business. "For him, with me watching."

"Jesus Christ, Wally!" I said. "What's wrong with you? I never agreed to—"

"Shut your mouth, Toby." He snarled and shot me a glance that left an exit wound. "I said, how much for him with me watching?"

Dot half-faced him. She looked to the bills in his hands and then met his eyes. "I don't like the idea of you being involved at all, mister," she said. "Watching, listening, smelling, anything…The answer is *no*."

Wally reached into his coat, pulled more bills from his breast pocket, and started counting them out. When he got himself into these drunken states of unwavering determination, the only way to get him to back off was to distract him with another of his vices. I reached an arm around him, pulled him close, and tried to steer him away from Dot, figuring I'd try, as delicately as possible, to let him know this wasn't something anyone else wanted to pursue. "Come on, Wally," I said in the calmest voice I had, "she said no. Let's quit wasting our time and get out of here, pal. The night's young. Let's grab some more drinks, get real sauced."

"I said *shut* your *mouth*, Toby! *Shut it!*" He shoved me so hard I landed flat on my ass. "Now look, dolly," he said to Dot, waving his fistful of bills, "I got another fifteen here. You and the kid, and I get to watch. I'm not your cup of tea? That's fine. You ain't gotta lay a finger on me. Just let me have my fun."

Dot ignored the offer and took a step away from Wally. She was quick to ditch the look of irritation that he brought out in her in favour of a 'why, hello there' face for the approaching soldiers. As they neared, she waved, fluttering her fingers in a way that was probably supposed to look girlish and flirtatious, but from where I sat looked like someone checking for paralysis after a bad fall. "Evening, boys. Anyone looking for a little fun tonight?"

The soldier in the middle—a slick, square-jawed fellow with the kind of irksome smile normally reserved for salesmen—clapped and rubbed his hands together, then elbow-nudged his pals. "Yeah, sweetheart, we're lookin' for some fun, ain't we, boys?" The boys seemed to agree. They were looking for some fun. "Yeah, some fun, fun, fun," he continued, pacing around Dot, stopping behind her with his hands on his waist, looking her up and down, his mouth going mmm mmm mmm.

"I know where you could find some fun, fun, fun," Dot told him over her shoulder, punctuating each 'fun' with a shake of her hip.

"Do ya, now?" the soldier looked to his pals and gave them a wink.

Dot assured him: "I do."

She screamed as the soldier then swung his hip hard into her hip, forcing her off balance and sending her tumbling to the sidewalk. "Because you look like you only know where to find some syph, syph, syph!" the soldier shouted, eliciting a howl from his friends and, naturally, himself.

"You bastards!" Dot shouted. "You lousy bastards! I hope you're blown to hell out there! You hear me? I hope they ship you out and the first Nazis you meet shoot you to shreds and piss on your stinking carcasses!" But the soldiers were already moving on, continuing up the street. Their laughter only seemed get louder the farther they got, compensating for the swelling distance between us, until the distance opened wide and swallowed them right up.

The makeup around Dot's eyes had become blotted and runny. She was catching her breath and staring in the direction the soldiers had walked, as if, by staring long and hard enough, her stabby eyes might find them and teach them a lesson. The hurt on her face was almost masked by her burning anger. But only almost.

Wally slapped his bills against the palm of his hand and Dot looked up to him, then over to me. "How much you got there?" she asked. That pleased Wally.

Dot and I dusted ourselves off and the three of us made our way to a nearby bridge. The bridge stood over a river whose edges were still thawing out. It was dark, but if you looked over the side and gave your eyes a few seconds to adjust, you could make out the form of ducks gliding across the water's surface. Wally gave the steel a knock as we crossed. "Camelback truss," he said. "Nice and sturdy." No one responded or, for that matter, said anything at all for the rest of the walk.

You couldn't tell from the outside of the house that it was that kind of place. Not only did it appear well maintained, but it had an old-fashioned, elegant look to it—I'd call it Victorian, but what do I know? We walked up the steps onto the porch, Dot leading. She grabbed the door knocker and gave it three stern pounds, then paused and gave it another pound, followed by two soft knocks and then another three pounds. A moment later, the door squeaked open a crack. Dot held up two fingers and the door opened the rest of the way. Dot entered, and when Wally and I tried to follow, a colossus stepped in front of us. This wall of a human made no attempt to hide the fact he was sizing us both up. I found I was unable to look him in the eye. And it wasn't because I didn't feel like craning my neck that far back.

"You don't pull any shit here, you understand?" His voice was the sort of thing that came out of a deep pit and ate your first born if your village didn't meet its sacrificial quota. "The ladies call the shots. What they say goes. What you say means shit. Understand?" Wally and I both nodded. "We're not gonna have any trouble from you two, then?" Wally and I shook our heads 'hell no,' and after another few seconds of consideration, the big guy stepped aside.

A burgundy carpet adorned with golden trim and an explosive floral pattern covered the mahogany floor of the foyer and continued up the stairway in front of us. To our right was an arched doorway that led to what looked like a drawing room where I could see a few men who looked maybe a little better off than Wally and I sitting in cushy chairs, drinks in hand, mesmerized by the lingerie-clad women orbiting them. Dot emerged from the room with a bottle of scotch in one hand and two glasses in the other. The makeup around her eyes had been fixed, her face a veneer of composure. She walked past us and headed up the stairs. Once she was about halfway up, it dawned on us that we ought to follow. So we did.

"I don't like this, Wally," I whispered. "This whole thing creeps me out. I-I don't want to…I can't do it. I've never paid for it before and the whole—I mean, you watching? Hell, Wally, this just isn't right."

"Shut it," Wally, who had now found his whisper, replied. "We do each other favours, kid. I'll owe you one. Think of it like that."

"*Owe me one*? For Christ's sake. This isn't the sort of thing you just owe someone for. This is sick, Wally. I-I'm out." I turned around with every intention of walking down the stairs and marching right past colossus and out the door, but Wally grabbed a fistful of my collar, whipped me around, and pulled me close.

"You're doing it," he hissed. "We're here, and I said we're doing it, and that's that. Partners in crime, you and me."

I said nothing in reply, but something in my eyes must have told Wally he'd won because he loosened his grip, turned from me, and continued up the stairs.

Partners in grime.

We followed Dot down a dim corridor, passing three closed doors before reaching our room at the end of the hall. She stopped at the open door and motioned for us to proceed. My heart was thrashing against its bars. I felt queasy, I felt weak in the legs. I wanted to be a hundred miles in any direction from here.

Without noticing, I halted in the doorway, but Wally was quick to remedy that. He gave me a hard shove, sending me stumbling into the room. "Come on, Toby," he said, "you move any slower, you're gonna go backwards in time." And, boy, what I wouldn't have given to do just that.

Dot closed the door behind her and brought the glasses and scotch over to the nightstand. She poured two generous drinks and handed one to me. She was about to take a sip from the other glass, but then Wally said, "You forget about the paying customer, dolly?" so she handed the glass over to him and took a long pull straight from the bottle herself. I followed her lead and knocked mine back in one gulp, feeling it right away.

"The money now, please," Dot said. Wally handed it over and she counted it quickly, then placed it on the dresser. "Now, you stay over there in the corner and try not to make a mess," she said to Wally without looking at him. When I'd first laid eyes on Dot, I put her at around my age, twenty-one. But the way she conducted herself and the way she seemed to have each step in this bizarre scenario all mapped out as if it were nothing more than a familiar routine told me that she wasn't all that new to the world's oldest profession. "You give me any trouble and I'll holler. One holler and Marty will storm up here and punch you so hard your eyes will shoot out the back of your head." Wally nodded, indicating that he understood, and then backed into the corner. I looked away from him when he started unbuttoning his pants. Despite everything, I felt bad for the guy.

I noticed Dot undressing, and so I started undressing too, and that got me feeling bad for the both of us, too. Christ, what a sad room.

Once everything was off, the lights were killed, and she and I got to it pretty quick. I didn't get much out of it, and, given the circumstances of it all, who could blame me?

I finished with a whimper, and Dot pretended to finish with a groan. I don't know if or when Wally finished, but there were certain unmistakable sounds coming from the darkness throughout the whole ordeal, so I know he was keeping busy. Dot rolled off of me almost instantly. She dressed hurriedly in the dark like she'd done it three hundred times before. I heard the sound of her hand sliding across the surface of the dresser, collecting her pay, and that followed with the creak of a door opening. "Take a few minutes, but don't get it in your heads that this is a hotel," she told us before she left.

We took her up on that few minutes, Wally and I, lying in the dark, letting our pulses find their footing as we digested the experience. Neither of us spoke, but I think Wally had enjoyed himself. The softest bursts of laughter detonated in his corner and drifted over to me. It was faint, that laughter, so faint and ghostly that I had to concentrate to hear it at all, but it was definitely there. It was odd for Wally, who was normally so loud and boisterous, to be laughing like that—all clandestine. And there were a couple times, only a couple, that the laughter became so muddled it sounded a bit like weeping.

Or maybe it was the other way around.

GLORIA IS SITTING ACROSS FROM ME, FIDGETING WITH HER dress and looking at the floor. I believed her when she first said she was sorry, so the other five or six times have just been for good measure. The problem is I don't know what to say to 'sorry.' I don't know what to say, so I stay zipped. I don't like seeing her sweat like this, being crushed under the silence growing around us, looking more and more anxious by the second, but no words come to me, and I can't say what I don't have.

"Do you want me to leave?" she whispers, shifting her eyes up to me but keeping her head hung.

"No," I respond. "No, I don't think I want you to leave."

"All right, then. I won't leave."

I get up, kneel down, and grab the bourbon that's under my bed. "You want a drink?"

"I-I don't think I should. Not when I still have to perform."

"I'm not asking you to pound half the bottle," I kid, getting half a smile from her. She reaches for the bottle, takes the shyest of sips, then hands it back to me. "Well, if I don't have to worry about performing later…" I raise the bottle in a toast and take a deep swig.

"Should you be drinking anything? I mean, after getting knocked around like that?"

I shrug. "I don't know, Gloria. That's a good question. But I'm betting that's not the most pressing question you've got on your mind, is it?"

Her cheeks redden. Eyes back to the floor.

"Maybe that's the best way to go about all this," I say to her. "Maybe you ask me some questions—whatever's on your mind—and, if I can, I answer. No anger, no hostility, just one person asking another some questions."

"You don't have to tell me anything," she says.

"I know that. But I want to. I can't take back whatever you heard me and Rowland discussing. If I send you out of here without saying another word, well, whatever questions you have will only grow. They'll grow and they'll grow, and before you know it, you'll have a bunch of new questions—your questions will have questions of their own—so I think it's best if we address whatever is on your mind right here and right now, don't you?"

"I…I guess so, Toby. I mean, if that's what you want, I'll ask you some questions."

I assure her, "That's what I want."

Gloria sits up in her chair and crosses her arms. Her gaze ricochets around the ceiling. She's wondering where to start. "Okay," she says to me after a moment, "I know you told Rowland you lost your temper with Andrew because he called you a dodger, but why'd that tick you off so much? You *weren't* a dodger, were you?"

That's as good a starting point as any. "I wasn't a dodger," I say. "I didn't fight in the war, I didn't enlist, but that doesn't mean I was consciously avoiding it. In late '42, Genevieve's old man got real sick. He and her mother used to perform here—The Fly De Lis, they were called—but when they threw in the towel, they moved back up to Quebec. So Genevieve and I, we went up there because he was in a bad way and Genevieve's mother was so worried about him that it was taking a notice-able toll on her health. About a month after we got there, the old guy croaks. Her and her mother were really torn up about it, as anyone would be, so we stayed for a few weeks after the funeral, just to make sure her mother didn't go and drink a bottle of bleach or something. A few weeks went by, and it looked like we were clear to go. I'm not saying the old lady had finished grieving and moved on, but she was a hell of a lot better than she had been, and besides, we needed to get back to the show. On what was supposed to be our last morning in Quebec, I went and got us two tickets on the night train to Baltimore, where we'd meet up with the circus and get back to our act. I walked back to Genevieve's mother's house, ready to start packing, but when I arrived, no one was there. There was a note waiting for me, though, written by Genevieve, telling me her and her mother were at the hospital. Wouldn't you know it, the old lady went and had herself a heart attack. She was dead by the time I got to the hospital. So, Genevieve got stuck with another funeral to organize and, on top of that, she had to figure out the family estate—the selling of their house and all that shit—which tacked even more time onto our stay. By the time everything was sorted, Rowland's World Class Circus had made their way up to Canada. Me and Genevieve met up with everyone in Ottawa, then we did the Canadian circuit—the same order we still do it in today, which, you know, takes some time. So, no, I didn't get drafted, because I was in Canada for so long during the draft. When we finally got back on this side of the border, there was still a draft, but no one came knocking, and I didn't go out of my way to enlist. Genevieve had been through so much and she needed me there. The draft missed me, that's all there is to it."

"And you got so angry at Andrew because—"

"Because not only did that bastard accuse me of being a certain disgraceful something I'm not, but the reason I was in Canada at all is because I was with Genevieve—who's now his Genevieve! I missed the draft because I was doing the respectable thing, making sure she didn't have to face all that garbage alone."

Gloria nods, indicating that my answer is a reasonable one. "I see."

"I'm glad you do. Next question."

"Oh. Um, I-I guess I was wondering, when you told Rowland that if Andrew had just killed you, then Rowland would save a lot of money—or something to that effect—what did you mean?"

She's pushing into meatier territory now. I take another sip to buy myself a few seconds, then clear my throat. "What I meant was, even though I'm not a headliner anymore, Rowland still takes care of me. He knows what I'm worth, and as stupid as the guy can be, he still knows talent when he sees it. That's all that was." It's close enough to the truth, and close enough is good enough for me right now.

"Oh. All right. I figured that. I only wondered if there was more to it, since, well, I know you and Rowland meet in his digs pretty often—it must be once a month—and—"

"And, like I told you before, we talk business. We talk about the show, what's working, what's not. He consults me about certain…things."

"I see," she says, then after a lengthy, pondering pause, "Have you mentioned me to him at all, Toby? My dancing, that is. I like being a spec girl, but the longer I do it, the more I start to think I might be destined for something bigger." And there you have it, the most transparently veiled ulterior motive.

"I'll keep on him, Gloria. Don't good things come to those who wait?"

"I'm not sure. I've only ever done the waiting part, so I'll have to keep you posted."

"Yeah," I say, "you keep me posted all right."

Before she leaves, she assures me that she'll come by after tonight's show so we can try Scrabble. "I'll even see if I can buy a few beers off Sal," she says. "He sent someone to town with a huge order earlier today."

"That sounds good." I light a cigarette and ease back into bed. "Break a leg tonight."

"It won't be the same without you," she says. "Get some rest now."

I nod and assure her I'll do just that, and she blows me a kiss and leaves.

I don't know how much she knows, but I know she knows too much.

What I told her about the draft is all true. I've got no worries there. But I'm certain she suspects there's something more than I'm telling her going on between me and Rowland. If I can trust anyone else in this place, it's Gloria. She's on the level, no doubt about that, but I don't feel I can tell her everything, especially not about my money. The line I fed her about Rowland knowing what I'm worth probably has her thinking I'm just getting paid more than all the lower-tiers around here, which isn't too fishy, but I'm worried she's got more on her mind than she's letting on.

The area above my right eye seems to have swollen further. I touch it with my fingers. It's so puffy, it feels like something that should pop. I poke it and pain forks out in every direction. I'm tempted to pull the bandage on my cheek aside and take a peek, but I send that thought packing. Let yourself heal, I tell myself. If the starving Christ could resist the Devil's mountain of bread, surely the suffering Toby can resist a look at the nasty gash on his cheek. Perspective is everything.

Still, all the pain that had sulked away to accommodate the shock of finding and the stress of dealing with Gloria in my trailer is beginning to find its way back to me. My head and face took the cake, but the pain I'd first noticed in my lower back is starting to branch out across my entire body; it appears I'd received a full working over.

Over the course of two cigarettes, I knock back enough bourbon to get me good and woozy. And the second woozy happens, I plant my head on my pillow and let sleep flood in. I dream about the Vampire Master and her depthless gaze.

GLORIA OFFERS THE VELVET POUCH TO ME. "TAKE SEVEN. And no peeking. What you get is what you get."

I dip my hand in and palm a few tiles, then mix the contents of the pouch with my fingers and grab a couple more.

"Hurry up!"

"I want to get a good variety," I tell her.

Once I've got my seven, I place them on my wooden tile rack. NUPKOLC. Now what the hell am I supposed to do with NUPKOLC?

It's warm, despite the sinking sun. Warm and muggy. I've got my electric fan going, but I need to keep the windows open so the air can circulate, which I'm not too happy about since noise from outside tends to hitch a ride in on the air's coattails. A syrupy flow of laughs, shouts, chatter, music, motors sputtering to life, and God knows what else passes through my trailer, in one window and out the other, steady and endless. I peek outside and see the garbage joint—the stand where we sell souvenirs and balloons on sticks and shit like that—is being swarmed by locals. We usually clean up pretty good at the garbage joint, but the crowd there now is larger than normal. I look closer and I'm just able to make out Genevieve and Andrew standing near the little shack, signing autographs for an onslaught of eager children. Their signing is briefly interrupted when the two stars stop to pose for a photograph by a man in a garish yellow hat who I assume works for the local newspaper. The night is only in its early stage of darkness, but the explosion that comes from that rag-man's flashbulb is so bright it's like glimpsing a supernova, a flash so bold it splashes the whole scene in light for a slice of a slice of a second.

I take solace in Genevieve and Andrew's temporary blindness and then sit back down and return my focus to NUPKOLC. Across from me, Gloria is staring intently at her own tiles. She rearranges them, takes a sip of her beer, pauses, and then rearranges her tiles again.

She'd rushed over here right when the show ended, so she's still in costume. Peacock feathers, flesh to boot, and a Hollywood do only showing the slightest bit of distress after her performance. "How's your head feeling?" she asks, still focusing on her tiles.

"About the same as the rest of me: miserable. But I feel a bit better than I did a few hours ago. Time heals all wounds, doesn't it?"

"Right. And fingers crossed that in Andrew's case, time wounds all heels."

I get a pretty good laugh out of that.

"That's a Marx line," Gloria tells me.

"Karl Marx?" I ask, surprised that she's familiar.

"Groucho," she says. "I don't think there's a Karl, but they come from a pretty big family, so who knows." She looks back down to her tile rack then back up to me. "I've always liked that line, though. It's funny, but it's clever too. I mean really clever, not like some Bob Hope gag about Democrats or pushy wives or any of that."

I nod. "Groucho can be pretty sharp."

"I think it has some truth to it," she says, her head angled to one side and her eyes moving over her tiles like eyes do when the mind is working through something. "That's why it's clever, because it's the truth. Or at least it's the kind of thing you hope is the truth. That's it. The best jokes—the ones that don't just drift away after you've heard them—have a bit of truth to them, don't you think so?"

I raise my beer. "To time wounding all the damn heels."

"To time wounding all the damn heels," she echoes with a laugh, clinking me to make the toast official. "Now let's give this game a try before we've drunk so much that we can't remember how to spell."

She starts the game placing SAINT in the middle of the board. I shuffle NUPKOLC around a few times, and I can't come up with anything too flashy, so I add PUN above her S and get a pretty sad number of points penciled under my name.

For a few moves, I can only put down short three-letter words, so I start to get a bit frustrated. At one point though, I put down QUASARS, which I thought would basically give me the most points you can give a guy in one go. But then Gloria bursts my bubble. First, she scolds me for not maximizing what she calls my point potential by putting my Q in a worthless spot. I tell her there was no other place to put QUASARS, and she tells me I should have been more strategic and added to other words instead, giving me a bunch of examples of where I could have placed tiles if I wanted more than the eighteen points QUASARS got me. After that she takes three letters—U, I, and Z—and puts them under my Q, getting herself *forty-four* points because her word landed on a space where you get to double the amount you'd normally get.

"You're ruthless, Gloria!"

"What? Did you want me to go easy on you?" she laughs.

The first game ends quickly, and we decide to play a second game. Noticing the time, Gloria goes out to get us both some food before we start round two. We've both become a little tipsy, but there's no beer left. While she's out, I pour us a couple of bourbons. I also throw on the cowboy hat I got back in Dallas; I guess I'm in a goofy kind of mood.

Gloria bursts out laughing when she walks in the door with our plates. I've got the hat pulled low over my face and

I'm pointing two finger-guns at her. "Freeze, ma'am. Hand over the food and no one gets hurt," I say in my best John Wayne voice, which is pretty much the worst John Wayne voice.

"Oh, you're terrible, Toby!" She passes me my plate and takes her seat, immediately noticing the bourbon waiting on her tray. "Well, thank you," she says and takes a sip.

"Well, thank *you* for retrieving our dinner," I say.

We make quick work of our meals, then get back to Scrabble. Scrabble and drinking, that is. We divide our attention between the two, but drinking soon starts to take more than its share, which it has a tendency to do, I've noticed. Our second game of Scrabble dissolves without a proper finish, but it's pretty clear Gloria has me beat. I get up and light a few candles. Outside, full dark is closing in. Thick clouds like aggressive graphite rubbings draw across the sky, diminishing the moon's relevance, leaving only its trampled halo untouched. The usual circle of boozing silhouettes mingles around the bonfire, their voices bleeding together into one monotonous murmur.

Gloria notices my gaze drifting out the window. "Don't worry about them," she says.

"I don't." I assure her, then realize, "Wait, don't worry about who?"

"You know. *Them*," she says, as if it adds any clarity. I look at her blankly. Maybe slightly irritated, but also blankly. "Genevieve and Andrew," she says. "Don't worry about them. They're nobodies. Hacks. So what if they're headliners? The public wouldn't know a good act if it kicked them in the ass. They're nobodies, so don't let yourself worry about them, Toby."

I'm about to protest, to tell her she's way off if she thinks I give a damn at all about those two, but I keep quiet. The way Gloria spoke, her assuring tone, the way she said Them as if it were the most obvious thing in the world, I realize if I'm fooling anyone, it's not her. The ensuing scowl is almost a relief to my beaten face. Turns out optimism is a taxing expression to wear when you've been smacked around a bunch. "I wouldn't say I worry about them," I tell Gloria after thinking for a moment. "Worry...worry isn't the right word. I mean, I worry about the commies nuking us, but I don't worry about Genevieve and Andrew." I reach for the bottle and pour what's left into my glass. I take a long drink. "Hope," I say, raising a lecturing index. "Hope is the right word. I hope for Genevieve and Andrew."

Gloria considers this for a moment and then shakes her head. "I don't think I understand you, Toby."

"When they climb that ladder to the trapeze platform, I hope that the last step breaks just as Andrew commits all his weight to it. When they swing out into the air, I hope for the sound of a snapping wire. Whenever I head to the city like everyone else does on our days off, and I hear a siren— police, ambulance, firetruck, the fucking national guard, *anything*—I hope to God it's something to do with those two. So, you see, Gloria," a chuckle escapes me, "as miserable as I must seem whenever I watch a dumbfounded audience eat out of Genevieve and Andrew's grubby hands, I'm still a hopeful guy when you get right down to it."

"Well, look at that," Gloria laughs, "I've had you pegged all wrong. You're just a ray of sunshine, aren't you Toby?"

"Sure am."

She wiggles her eyebrows in a manner that's equal parts nefarious and hammy, then she hunches forward over our Scrabble game and brushes some tiles off the board. At first I think she's cleaning up, but then I realize that while she's taking some tiles off, she's keeping others on the board, shifting them around meticulously.

All but a small handful have been removed, and once she looks satisfied with what's on the board, she stands up on booze-wobbly legs and plucks the cowboy hat from my head, placing it on her own. She pulls it down in the front, like I did earlier, like a vigilante, and picks up the Scrabble board, turning it carefully, as if it were a crowded tray of brimming teacups. "Ya know, pardner," she begins in a low villain's register, "if hope ever feels like it just ain't enough," she places the Scrabble board before me and gestures to the words she's arranged, "you could always" KILL THEM, it says.

KILL THEM

Seventeen points if it were all one word.

Our eyes lock. Hers eyes have a glassy, drunken shine to them. The flicker of a candle is encased in her large pupils. We sit in silence for a moment, and then I open my mouth to speak, but before I get a word out, Gloria cracks. Laughter pours out of her. She tosses the hat off, leans back in her chair, hysterical, shooting off her own finger-pistols.

"I'm sorry, Toby," she manages to get out. "I couldn't resist, but, oh, what a terrible thing to joke about!" She laughs it up for a while, and just as tears begin to well up around her eyes, she manages to get the laughter down to a containable snicker.

I chuckle along with her. "You know, you really had me there for a second," I tell her, my laughter climbing. "I-I mean, the hat, the seriousness of your face—you really had me there, Gloria!"

"I thought I did!" she shouts, falling back into her fit. "You—you looked so panicked! Oh, hell, Toby, I'm awful! What an awful thing for me to kid about."

I assure her that she needn't be sorry. "If anyone around here appreciates a good dark joke like that, it's me," I say. And as the two of us expel any remaining laughs from our systems, I'm thinking, yeah, the best jokes really are the ones that have some truth to them.

GLORIA LEAVES EARLY IN THE MORNING. DISCREETLY.

I didn't sleep much.

KILL THEM.

What a terrible thing to think of. What a terrible thing to consider.

Terrible, but still…something magnetic about the idea. Sure, I've thought about it before. Often. But it's as if, by actually saying it, by speaking the idea out loud, Gloria breathed life into it. Joke or not, that thought was up and walking.

All night, I let it roll around in my brain, and now, dawn cracking the sky, another thought—one that's perhaps felt a little neglected lately—joins in: $3950.

What if? I'm thinking. *What if?*

What if not *them*, but *him*? Yes, only him. I loathe Genevieve, but to kill her? That would be too much. Granted, in my memories of her, the bad far outweighs the good, but recalling our good times, I realize I couldn't off her. Those good times haunt me enough with her still above ground. Dealing with those memories if she were to die? When you've loved someone, you leave a piece of yourself with them, a piece that they keep forever, even if you both hate each other's guts. I know I could never harm her. But *him*... him? What if?

And the money? *My* money? What if I went ahead and did it and then took the money and left? Got a fresh start in a place where I wouldn't be plagued by petty jealousy and shitty memories. No more Freddy Folly, no more face paint, and no more shaved head. No more having to deal with talentless hacks like Eddie, no more Rowland. I could put a beefy down payment on a house somewhere. I could buy a car and still have a couple thousand left over. I could get myself on a bigger show—The Ringling Brothers and Barnum and Bailey? They'd be thrilled to have someone of my calibre working with them. Hell, I could even forget about performing altogether and hit the track and see if I could get that $3950 to breed.

What if?

SHE GLIDED TO ME, SEQUINS SHIMMERING. A GLINTING blur of red, she tore through the air against a blasting spotlight and propelled herself off her bar and into a double full twist, completing two full somersaults and a body twist midair.

No one breathed until I caught her. And I always caught her.

Together, we moved flawlessly like a clock built by an old master, a thousand tiny gears and springs operating as one machine with the most elegant synchronicity.

I can't explain why or how, but after her parents died, the act Genevieve and I put together was better than anything we had ever done. Before we came up to Canada for what ended up being a much lengthier stay than either of us anticipated, we were renowned aerialists, not just admired within Rowland's World Class Circus, but seen by many rival acts as a team whose skill was something to aspire to. Our act was always very good, but in the Great White North when we rejoined our circus family, we somehow found a way to turn very good into incredible.

We'd do our usual stuff: a knee-hang here, a layout half-twist there, a backend planche, a double angel return, things like that, but we also tried to add some more daring tricks to our repertoire. As a catcher, I was normally situated on one bar throughout the act, with Genevieve, the flyer, alternating between her bar and my bar, where I would receive her. But with this new act, we got a little more adventurous, adding a bar-to-bar passing leap, which is normally a manoeuvre done only between two flyers. It involved Genevieve leaping over me while I swung beneath her. Letting go at the same time as she, I would fly to the bar she had just left, with both of us airborne for the same flash of an instant. That really got the crowd going, but the double full twist that Genevieve pulled off was act's true *pièce de résistance*. We always finished our set with that double, and I swear, the rapturous applause that followed that trick—an explosion of praise you could set our watch to—was the most beautiful sound I've ever heard.

The days of moving the whole show by train were slowly creeping to an end. Many of the big shows had already turned their backs to the tracks, but Rowland's was a circus that embraced change the way a stepchild embraced his new father's rules; you hold out until you're whipped into submission. That night in Ottawa was our last engagement before yanking the pegs and hauling off to Toronto. And while Genevieve and I autographed photos and told children that if they drank their milk and listened to their parents, they too would someday be able to fly through the air like we did, the ring crew was scrambling to take down the big top and get everything loaded onto a train car so we could all split.

Everyone who wanted an autograph got one. Genevieve would sometimes go a little further and stamp a big red kiss next to her signature, but she'd only do that for the younger ones. She said if they looked old enough to diddle themselves, they didn't get a pair of lips on their photograph or their programme.

Hand in hand, we walked back to our trailer, navigating through a buzzing throng of riggers. Wally was normally in the thick of everything, barking orders and insulting the work ethic of everyone in earshot, but that night, he wasn't tearing down with the rest of the crew. Being the multitalented guy he was, there were about a hundred different places he could have been at that moment (I wondered if maybe he'd spotted a new guy not pulling his weight and decided to drag him away from the group and tear a real strip off of him— an occurrence not at all uncommon), but as we neared our trailer, I spotted Wally and Rowland standing off to the side, in the shadows. I could only catch a bit of Rowland's profile, but he was clearly very angry. His face was all scrunched up and his hand motions were vehement and accusatory. Wally, on the other hand, oozed complacency. He stood with his arms crossed, a toothpick rolling from side to side between his smirking lips. I did my best to look straight ahead while we moved past them, watching them in my periphery in the voyeuristic way you watch a bickering couple have at it in public. Rowland was whisper-yelling, but I couldn't quite make out what was being said. Whatever they were going on about was something to be filed under hush-hush.

As we passed them, I caught Wally shooting a glance my way. I didn't turn to face him, but I could tell he was looking at me. From the corner of my eye, I saw his smile grow just a little.

"I don't care for that man," Genevieve proclaimed the instant I shut the door behind us.

"Rowland or Wally?"

"Both, I suppose." She shrugged. She kicked her boots off (we only wore our boots when we were grounded—always performing in our bare feet), and walked over to the kitchen area, retrieving a damp sponge. So many of Genevieve's manoeuvres depended on her ability to grip with—or to be gripped by—her legs, and she had recently taken to chalking her calves as well as the area behind her knees. She took a seat on the edge of our bed and with the sponge began wiping the chalk from her legs. "They both give me the creeps," she said, looking up at me, "but more Wally than Rowland. Rowland is an oddball, but he's always been good to me. But that Wally? What a vile individual."

"He's a bit much sometimes," I agreed. "But when you get to know him, he's not so bad. And he's always got the show on his mind. Always doing what's best for the group. Hard to hate a guy who's got your best interests in mind."

"I never said I hated the man, Toby. There's just something about him that bothers me. He's got this look in his eyes all the time. I see it whenever he's talking to someone. It's like he doesn't just look at you, he sizes you up...like he's trying to spot a weakness. It's so...unsettling."

I shook my head noncommittally, then went to fetch a towel for her legs. I didn't think she was right about Wally. It wasn't necessarily a weakness he was searching for. The look Genevieve was talking about was probably nothing more than a creepy stare, something he was either born with or developed over so many decades of poor socialization. What Wally was after was dirt. The guy was like a damn vacuum cleaner. He collected dirt as if it nurtured him. Any dirt he could get was an angle he could work, something to keep up his sleeve, to exploit when he best saw fit.

She made quick work of towelling her legs and then untied her hair and rolled onto her side. Against her cream pillowcase, her freed hair looked like a whirling well of India ink. I took a seat on the bed with her and rested my hand on her hip, on the border between her costume and her bare skin. Genevieve's costume matched mine in colour, but stylistically it was entirely feminine. It was cut similar to a woman's bathing suit, leaving her legs, arms, and shoulders exposed. She opened her mouth to let out a lioness's yawn and nestled further into her pillow. "I wonder what Wally and Rowland were going on about," she said, closing her eyes, her voice the resigned mutter of one who has given in to the nagging persistence of sleep.

Slowly, I rubbed my hand up and down her bare leg. "Yeah. I wonder that myself."

She replied with the faintest murmur, and I imagined my voice falling as a whisper from the swirling skies of her dreams.

WE HIT TORONTO AT AROUND FIVE THE FOLLOWING morning, leaving plenty of set-up time for the crew. If the circus arrived in a city any time after seven a.m., you could count on a horde of locals waiting at the tracks, eager to watch the erection of the mighty cathedral of wonders. Five was too early for even the most eager of beavers, but I figured a bunch of folks would show up in an hour or two and get the eyeful they deemed themselves entitled to.

I hopped out of our trailer as soon as the train whined to a halt. I'd been tossing and turning all night, and around three, I figured I'd give up on sleep and just bide my time until we arrived. The fresh morning air felt almost too good to be true, so I lit a cigarette and brought it down a notch. Genevieve smoked as well, but she couldn't stand it when people smoked indoors. She liked the smell of a burning cigarette but hated the resulting stale stench that made its home in upholstery and pillows and blankets. Sometimes she'd let me get away with smoking by a window, but those times were rarer than a proper steak, so that morning, my first smoke was nothing more than business as usual. A couple others had trickled out of their living quarters, but they were farther down the track and I couldn't quite make out who they were. Once I finished my cigarette, I snubbed it out on the bottom of my shoe, making sure it was really dead before I discarded it in the ankle-high grass.

The sun had begun its ascent. I reveled in the temporary placidity the scene offered. There was a cluster of fir trees huddling at the far end of the field. They stood together in a tight circle, like a group of boys who'd stumbled across a dead animal and were taking turns poking it with a stick. I started walking toward the trees because it seemed like a decent spot to sit down and have another cigarette in private. If it somehow wasn't as decent as it looked from a distance, I thought, I could at least pick up a stick and take a poke for myself.

I only made it about halfway there when I noticed a cloud of dust rolling up the road that led to the field. As the cloud drew nearer, I saw that the car responsible was one I recognized: a beat-up silver Ford covered in a rusty rash that made me itch just looking at it. I forgot about the trees, lit my second cigarette of the morning, and headed for the car.

I got there as Wally was stepping out of the passenger-side seat. He buried his mouth in the crook of his elbow and took off his hat and started fanning at the surrounding dust. I wasn't sure if it was because he felt satisfied with his fanning or if he'd realized the futility of using a hat riddled in holes to shoo away a cloud, but after three good swings, he returned his hat to his head, coughed, then spat out the glob of whatever the cough had shaken loose. A twig of a man named Clowes got out of the driver's side of the Ford. Like Wally, Clowes was a do-whatever-needs-to-be-done type, but his primary job was to work with any vendors who wanted to set up outside our show. We had our junk shop and a couple of carts that sold popcorn and Coca-Cola, but Clowes was the guy who'd bring in locals to sell corndogs and pink lemonade and cotton candy and whatever else people liked to stuff in their faces while they watched us perform.

"Howdy, kid," Clowes said, tipping his hat to me. The dark bags swelling beneath his eyes told me he'd been doing all the driving, but he looked more than merely sleep-deprived. Clowes looked sickly, or perhaps rattled. Before I could respond to his greeting, he turned and walked away from the car, forgetting to close the door behind him and leaving the keys in the ignition.

"Jittery fuck," Wally grumbled, placing his hand on his hips and shaking his head in Clowes's direction. He walked over to the driver's side of the car, plucked the keys from the ignition, and slammed the door shut, then walked to the trunk and opened it up. From the trunk he pulled a satchel made of brown leather. The leather was so faded and lined that it looked as if it would flake into nothingness if you gave it a good flick. When the satchel's strap settled on Wally's shoulder, I heard a faint clanking sound come from inside it.

"Shit, Wally, I thought you were taking the tracks like the rest of us. What'd you need to take Rowland's rolling scrap heap out for?"

He slammed the trunk shut and walked around the car to where I was standing. "Coleman's Circus was due here two days after we left," he said. "They got tigers. We're down to a bunch of dogs running through hoops."

"Yeah," I nodded, "our animal section isn't what it was. No disrespect to Jenny and her dog act, naturally."

Wally snorted. "You kidding me? *Plenty* of disrespect to Jenny and her stupid dog act! They run around in circles, they jump through hoops—who gives a shit?"

I laughed politely. "So, you and jittery old Clowes out tearing down opposition paper? Handing out rat sheets?"

Wally shook his head. "Nah. Got to do more than that to balance things. Coleman's got a pair of world famous acrobats. The Flying Franellis. Big draw. Lucky for us," he hoisted the satchel's strap further up his shoulder, producing another clank from within, "Mister Franelli went and broke his hand in about five different places last night."

IT WAS JUST AFTER SIX A.M. WHEN I GOT BACK TO OUR trailer. The smell of roasting coffee hit me the instant I opened the door. Our Silex had volcanic aspirations, so you had to keep an eye on it. I always thought it looked less like a coffee maker and more like something you'd see in a mad scientist's lab, but it made a great pot, so I made peace with its bizarre aesthetic early on. Genevieve was awake, dressed, and made up, ready to be seen by the locals who would begin their descent upon the circus any moment now. She wore a cornflower-blue dress with short sleeves and a thin lace ruffling around the collar and down the front, and she had even gone as far as fixing a white rose clip in her hair. Her beauty had a sly way about it. She always looked stunning, but there were times when some small gesture, like a slight tilt of her head, elongating that milky neck of hers, would illuminate something about her that seemed new, and would magnify her radiance. It would catch you off guard, and the beauty you thought you were used to would sink its fangs into you, making you question everything you trusted as you winced and brought the fresh wound to your lips. Whenever this happened—and it happened that day—a picture would flash in my head of the two of us walking together, like I was someone else, watching us from a safe distance. The picture barely lasted a second, but the contrast it revealed to me would tattoo itself onto all three levels of the iceberg in my brain. I grabbed the mirror on Genevieve's nightstand to make sure my hair was still slicked and check if there was anything lodged in my teeth, even though I hadn't yet eaten. I wasn't much to look at by comparison, but I was groomed enough to pass as a civilized human being.

She placed a kiss on my cheek and then took the mirror from my hand to make sure my face didn't mess up her rouged lips. "Anything interesting out there?"

"Nah. I couldn't sleep so I went for some fresh air." I'd decided not to tell her about Wally and Clowes because that sort of thing bothered her, even though she knew damn well that it happened every now and then.

The coffee was ready a minute later. I poured us each a cup and we took a seat across from each other at the kitchen table. The table sat against the wall that, from the outside, faced the field where everything was being set up. There was a window directly above the table. Rays of light leaked in through the Venetian blind slats. I gave the string a tug and let it all flood in, feeling the warmth on my face right away. Genevieve got up and retrieved her sunglasses, but I was fine with having to squint slightly.

We sipped our coffee and watched the big top go up. A steady procession of cars from the city rolled up the road, and the face of every man, woman, and child that poured out was brim-full of wonder.

THE SUBTERRANEAN FAR OUTWEIGHS THE SURFACE-level stuff. I end up with two tiny scars: one barely the length of a thumbnail above my right eye, and another only slightly longer across my left cheek. Sure, I'd rather have walked away totally unscathed, but when I first woke up after the beating, it felt like someone had tried to cut a jigsaw puzzle out of my face, so, all things considered, I think I can deal with two small scars.

And who knows, maybe a couple well-placed scars could come in handy. Once I ditch this place, I could go straight to Hollywood. I bet there are a handful of pictures that'd need a dangerous, rugged leading man. Like a show about a lightweight boxer who gets tangled up with the mob. They want him to take a fall, and he says he will but he changes his mind at the last minute, so he's got to fight his way through a bunch of hoodlums to escape the mob's clutches—what a riot that'd be!

I mulled over the thought of killing Andrew for a short while after Gloria joked about it, but I quickly did my best to push the thought away, blaming its contemplation on the pain I was in, the booze I was drinking, and the sleep that was avoiding me. I told myself, that kind of vengeance was all right to fantasize about, but it wasn't the sort of thing you actually go ahead and do. Not in real life. So, like I said, I did my best to push the thought away.

And it went away. Or at least it backed the hell off. For a bit.

I think it was all the isolation that did it. First, there were those three nights in Baton Rouge, lying in bed, thumbing through my old magazines and doing pretty much nothing else. Sure, I'd occasionally get up and walk around outside. It's not like I was crippled, but I needed my rest if I wanted to be back in tip-top shape. And I had visitors here and there—Julian, Susan, Eddie, Rupert the Syc, Sal, and, of course, Gloria. She'd come by every night after the show. She'd bring me my dinner and we'd play Scrabble and drink and talk until our legs dangled over the edge of unconsciousness. But even with all those visits, the days really found a way to drag on. I'd read and I'd read, but there's only so much of that a person can do before their eyeballs start to throb, so sometimes I'd just lie there in my bed, thinking.

When we arrived in New Orleans, I still wasn't feeling my best, so I didn't perform on the first night, which is too bad because I love playing in New Orleans. I maybe could have pushed it, but the last thing I wanted was to lower the calibre of my act, so I figured I might as well give it one more day and make my return show one for the books. So that's three nights in Baton Rouge, one travel day between there and New Orleans, and another day and night once we arrived here.

Five days of nothing much at all.

A person's mind can do a lot of thinking in that time. You can lie there and think about the past; you can wonder about the future; you can dwell on the tedious present. And after a while, lying there for hours on end with nothing but your own thoughts, you start to think about things you ought not to think about. You sometimes find that the thoughts you did your best—*your absolute goddamn best*—to push away had really never left at all. They merely slithered into a dark corner, hid behind an old trunk, and waited there for the right moment to come back out and reintroduce themselves, like an old acquaintance you maybe started off on the wrong foot with. And after chatting with that acquaintance for a while, you realize the two of you actually have a lot in common.

"LAZARUS FINALLY EXITS HIS TOMB!" SUSAN PROCLAIMS.

She struts over and squeezes my arm. "I must not have paid attention in Sunday School, because I could've sworn it was only supposed to be four days."

I point to her protruding belly. "Forget the tomb, when's the exit from the womb?"

She laughs and gives me a playful slap. "Glad you're back amongst the ranks of the living, Toby. This one here," she cradles her stomach with her hands and gives it the tiniest of shakes, "she's still going to be cooking for a while yet."

"She?" I say. "You think it's a girl?"

"No. I *know* she's a girl," she says matter-of-factly.

I get stopped about three hundred times on my short walk to the big top. You're out for a few days and suddenly everyone's got to get their hellos and their nice to see yous in. Julian catches me and insists I join him for coffee, but I tell him I need to get to the big top and practise my act, see if I'm really all right to perform tonight. When I'm almost at the tent, I spot Gloria. Her back to me, she's huddling with her usual crowd—a few other spec girls, some whose faces I recognize, and some who, for all I know, could have started with the circus this very morning. I'm not sure if it's telepathy or some sort of sixth sense, but she always seems to know when I'm near. As I pass by, she turns and looks over her shoulder at me. Not missing a beat of the conversation she's occupied with, she flashes one of her warming smiles at me, no doubt glad to see me not only up and about, but to see me making my way to the big top, my way to work.

I do my stretches. The bit of ring rust I feel when I first sit down on my unicycle vanishes the instant I put my feet on the pedals and give a push. I'm able to pull off every unicycle manoeuvre I know. Even the more complicated tricks, like jumping onto the curbing backwards and dong a full circle in reverse, are landed without a flaw. Juggling is its top-notch usual, and after running through my acrobatics—frontwards and backwards flips, somersaults, cartwheels, twists and the like—I find I only have the slightest note of pain lingering in my right kidney area. It's not anything that would impact the quality of my act, though, so I deem myself fit to return to professional astonishing.

And astonish I do.

If Wally Jakes still had a mouth to say it with, he'd tell me I bounced back like a rubber ball with fangs. My evening performance is transcendent. I earn my crowd. My movements are fluid and, my God, these Louisianans are a thirsty bunch. A rolling snare and crashing cymbals punctuate my final set of manoeuvres: a combination of improvised acrobatics from one end of the ring to the other, performed at a machine-gun pace.

When I land my last flip and go down for a bow, I feel a wave of exhaustion streaming through my muscles, accompanied by a sudden shakiness in my limbs. It's got nothing to do with my having been hurt or this being my first performance in five days. No, none of this is a consequence of rust or my body crying out for further healing time. What I'm feeling comes from me pushing myself even harder than I normally would. And making my exit from the ring, sending panoramic waves to the wowed masses, it dawns on me that tonight I operated like a man with something to prove.

The moment I step out of the big top and into the night, I'm ambushed by a swarm of congratulatory pats, caresses, and handshakes.

"Helluva comeback, Toby!"

"Can't keep a good man down!"

"Ya knocked 'em dead, buddy!"

Being what it is, routine takes hold. I start walking back to my trailer, like I always do, the holy trinity—tobacco, bourbon, and solitude—beckoning me. But tonight, for some reason, hearing Rowland's voice boom out of the big top as he readies the crowd for Genevieve and Andrew has the opposite effect that it would any other night. Tonight, when I hear "…without the safety of a net," "…fled the vile Communist clutches of his motherland to come to America," and "…with the woman he loves and be as free as a bird in the sky!" I stop, turn around, and walk right back to the big top, like an ant to an open bottle of honey.

Why not watch the damn act? I'm thinking. I've only seen it the once, and that was how long ago now? Two years, or close to. Yeah, it must have been between two and a bit years since I was grounded and Rowland dragged my inferior replacement out of the woodwork. But why not take in their act? What harm can come from watching? Susan made that Lazarus crack earlier, but maybe she wasn't that far off. I don't feel like I've come back from the dead, mind you, but something does feel different. And come to think of it, I think the change happened about the time I decided to go ahead and kill Andrew. It was like a crack had broken in a wall that I never knew was there in the first place. And I peered through the crack and glimpsed the infinity waiting for me on the other side, away from Rowland's. I looked through that crack and I saw what was out there, and what was out there was a hundred different roads to the rest of my life.

As I'm returning to the big top, a few people are looking at me like there's something wrong. One man whose face I recognize but whose name I'm not sure of says, "I'm pretty sure your trailer's the other way, Toby," pointing his thumb back where I came from.

"Good to know," I clap him on the shoulder like an old friend. "Spare a cigarette?"

He hands one over. I light it, take a good, long drag, then go find myself a decent vantage point to catch the show.

Their act is as useless as I remember it. Of course, the crowd goes bonkers for it, but I can't blame them. They don't know any better. Any other time, the gasps, cheers, and applause would really cut into me, but not tonight. Tonight, the crowd's love for Genevieve and Andrew has a calming effect on me; I hate them for the undeserving accolades they receive, and their reign as the royal couple of this circus is a constant reminder of my own fall from grace, but I've finally allowed myself to accept that nothing will change on its own. If you're freezing to death, you can stare at a pile of wood until you go blind, but it won't turn into a fire until you go ahead and pick up two sticks and rub them together yourself.

I laugh when think back to Baton Rouge, to long those days when I lay in my trailer, stewing in internal conflict, worrying that committing another murder would destroy me. But looking out on Andrew as he stands on my former platform in my former light with my former woman, I realize that this murder won't destroy me. No, it won't, not at all. This murder will be the much-needed period on a sentence that's gone on far too long here at Rowland's World Class Circus. This murder, I'm sure, will be different.

GLORIA WAVES WHEN SHE SPOTS ME IN THE WINDOW. The hood of her red raincoat is pulled up over her head, its strings tugged tight. She falters in the mud, but catches her balance right away. Once she's regained her footing, she throws her head back and laughs, giving the skies the opportunity to bathe her face in rainwater. I think she yells, *So close but so far!* but it's difficult to hear over the rain. It's been coming down heavy since early morning. The road leading to our circus has turned to soup, so it looks like yesterday was our last performance here in Pensacola.

I open the door to greet her, holding out a kerosene lamp so she doesn't trip on her way up the steps. With the door open, the rain sounds like a thousand drawers of cutlery being shaken, an off-time percussion section from hell. I can see the shape of the Scrabble board tucked away, safe and dry, under Gloria's coat. I help her in and shut the rain out. All four of my kerosene lamps are going, placed strategically to ensure there is an abundance of light at the table where we play Scrabble.

I'm getting better at the game. I still haven't won, but our matches lately have been neck-to-neck, a far cry from the crushing defeats I suffered nightly when we first began. I'm finally coming to terms with it being a game that's more about strategy than it is about knowledge. I play as tactically as I can now, always sure to keep the numbers in mind, especially if I'm lucky enough to get a Q or a Z, but my mind is also busy working on other strategies.

How do I kill Andrew? I've been sitting on it for days, and of the half-dozen scenarios I've conjured up, I can't come up with a single plan that doesn't have *at least* one gaping hole in it. But while I've not yet found the right setup, I'm coming to realize that as far as method is concerned, the less complex the delivery, the better. I've narrowed the deed down to being committed either by strangulation or by knife, leaning towards the tidier of the two. What I'm having trouble with is the where and the when. I've got to do it in such a way that no one would be able to place me—the guy he recently beat into unconsciousness, the guy with a motive—anywhere near the crime. The nomadic life of a circus performer can come in handy if you're like Eddie and you've gone and done something awful and you need to stay on the move, but what do you do when the guy you want to do something awful to is always on the move with you?

She points to the two glasses I've set out for us. "I appreciate that kind of portioning, but if you think all it'll take to throw me off my game is a few mouthfuls of bourbon, you've got another think coming."

I pull a chair out for her and she slides in, giving me a taste of her rainwater and perfume scent. She smells good wet. "Nah, I wouldn't do a thing like that. A little bourbon on a night like this keeps you warm."

Since Baton Rouge, these gatherings have become an almost nightly ritual. I'm going to miss her when I leave here.

"It's awful for business being rained out, but between you and me, I'm glad to have a night off from performing," she says.

"You could have fooled me. Whenever I watch, you look like you're having a ball out there."

She sighs. "In that case, maybe I should have become an actress."

"What's the matter with being a spec girl all of a sudden?"

"Aw, nothing, Toby. I get frustrated with having such a small part sometimes, that's all."

She unfolds the Scrabble board and the two of us grab our seven and place them on our tile racks. We get on with the game, but Gloria won't stop griping about her newfound dissatisfaction with being a spec girl. She tells me that she's good enough to be more than a supporting player, and that some of the other girls are holding her back because they don't have the skill to take the routine further, and so on. I nod and agree and say things like That's too bad, and You're better than that, and You've got a face made for the movies, but my thoughts are elsewhere.

It occurs to me that if I kill Andrew here at the circus, I might as well telephone the police beforehand and ask them to make sure Old Sparky's wiring is up to snuff so he doesn't take fifteen tries to fry me. If I'm going to go ahead with it, it needs to be done on one of our off-days, away from everyone else. Earlier, I had considered doing it here and making it look like a suicide, but I figured that there's too much to cover in staging a suicide and I'd be sure to overlook some thing. That, and it would be inconceivable to think that someone who loves himself as much as Andrew would ever pull their own plug. Yeah, an off-day in a big city—that's the way to go. No need to cover anything up there, no sir. But one glaring problem—one that sticks out at me in every scenario I can think of—is catching him while he's away from Genevieve. The Royal Two are damn near inseparable. If either of Genevieve's parents were still alive, or, really, if she had any living family she was close with, I could send a wire saying 'come visit, so-and-so is on their deathbed,' but as far as I knew there was no one she cared about enough to travel and visit, deathbed or not. She had an uncle in Nova Scotia, but she always had terrible things to say about him, and, if I remember correctly, the uncle was her father's much older brother, so for all I know he's worm food now, too. Plus, even if I could use someone from her past or anything remotely personal to lure her away from Andrew, I would in turn be making myself a suspect since I was one of a select few who knew anything about her private life.

And I won't even consider offing her as well. It would make the whole thing much easier, mind you, if I could get rid of them both and make it look as though one killed the other, but I could never go through with that. Still, there has to be some way to separate the two of them long enough for me to pull off the one.

"You have a death wish tonight or what?" Gloria says, shaking her head at the tiles I'd set down. "You could have put the S on the end of my THWART and put the H-E down that way and got a double word score on top of THWARTS. Geez, Toby, it's no fun when you don't try."

"I'm sorry," I tell her. "I was thinking about my act. Something I could maybe add to it."

"Well, maybe we should play another time if you can't devote any attention to anyone other than yourself." She stands up and smooths her dress, shoots me a disappointed look, and then walks to the coatrack and grabs her coat, which is still sopping wet. I know she won't make it as far as the door before she turns around and tries to hook me with another tactic. Some nights I'm all right with letting it all play out. I sit there and look disinterested and let her run through all her boo-hoo bits until she gets tired of her own routine and returns. Tonight isn't like that, though. Tonight is one of the rare nights where I find myself compelled to play along and reel her back in.

"Oh, come on now. Put that coat back where it belongs and come back here." I sit up and give her vacant seat a pat. It's nice and warm. "I'm sorry, Gloria, really. I shouldn't let myself drift like that. I'll stop, I promise. I prefer your company to my own any day."

She walks back to the table, her lips pursed, her hips moving with the slightest sway. When she sits back down, she looks me in the eyes. Some might call the smile Gloria flashes me half-assed, but I'd call that fraction naïve.

"Thin ice, Toby."

I nod and reach across the table and give her arm a pinch. I point to her empty glass.

"Sure. But you have anything other than bourbon? Anything lighter?"

I make her a rye and ginger ale. She ends up drinking those for the rest of the night. After kiboshing our first attempt, we get two more games in before heading to bed. Gloria's out pretty quick. My body is tired, but my mind is buzzing, making up for lost time. Before leaving Pensacola for Montgomery, we have two off-days. There will be a lot of people heading to the city tomorrow if the weather lets up.

Eyes on the ceiling, I recall my run-in with Genevieve in Dallas. She was alone then and she told me Andrew was off at the track. I'd never seen him at the track before in any city, but maybe he's just beginning to take an interest in the races. The two of them go to the city on every off-day, regardless of where we are. I decide that I need to take every chance I can get to go to the city as well. I'll hit the track, see if I run into Andrew, see if he makes a pattern of leaving her for a few hours at a time or if Dallas was a one-off.

ONE OF THE THINGS I LOVE ABOUT THE TRACK IS YOU SEE

all sorts there. Monocled men and pearl-throated women who puff through skinny ebony cigarette-holders; crumbling ancients; fresh-faced college brats trying to make tuition in a single afternoon; thrill-seeking housewives on a grocery store detour; desperate working stiffs whose wettest pipe dreams involve flipping their boss a nickel and telling him to shove it up his ass because they're through. I've met some interesting folks down at the track, but you have to be careful there, too. Some really shady people spend their time down at the track.

I GOT A LIFT TO THE CITY FROM A LOCAL NAMED BUD WHO

was keen on learning about the circus. After catching what ended up being our last show in Pensacola, he drove back up to Rowland's in the rain yesterday afternoon in hopes of befriending a performer who would regale him with wild circus tales. He didn't find one. I noticed him sniffing around the place this morning and I told him if he gave me a lift to town, I'd talk his ear off. He had a ghastly green 1945 Studebaker truck and a right eye that thought every day was Sunday. He hung on my words like they dangled over shark-infested waters, and he didn't ask me to chip in for gas.

There are a couple of cars and trucks that the circus owns, but they're normally not enough to accommodate everyone who wants to go to the city. The crew will sometimes pay a few locals to chauffeur, but usually someone (a Syc, in most cases) will drive to the city and back until everyone who wants to go has been dropped off. Because I'm a respected veteran around here, I usually get dibs on the first rides in, but today I didn't feel like sharing a car with anyone I knew.

Bud got his truck in gear the second Genevieve and Andrew's ride took their first inch, and he was able to follow discretely, like I asked him to, until we hit the city. Their car stopped at the Hotel San Carlos. I had Bud drop me off at the end of the block, and once they went in, I waited a few minutes to make sure they were staying and then went and got myself a room at the Lighthouse Hotel, which was a cheaper joint only a short walk away.

I decide to make six my new lucky number when a beauty named Bartholomew wins me thirty-eight dollars. I wasn't going to come all this way without placing a single bet. I've been here for a couple hours, since 4:00 p.m., figuring that if Andrew were to come here it wouldn't be first thing after arriving in the city. It's a crowded place, but I've been vigilant and I'm pretty sure he isn't here yet. The next races start at 7:00—an hour from now—so I head back to the entrance and find myself a good spot to stand with a newspaper and watch people without being spotted myself.

The Pensacola Journal has a pretty good funny pages section. I've missed the last few installments of Dick Tracy, but it looks like Crewy Lou is still working at turning over some stolen diamonds. I don't want to invest in any real news, since losing myself in even a short article could mean missing Andrew.

6:30: No sign of him. Four men have asked me for directions to the restroom. The first three got them, the fourth one had this entitled way about him, so he got his question answered with another question: "I look like I work here, pal?"

6:52: Nothing. Still. Betting is closed, so it's unlikely he'll come through the front now. And though I'm positive he hasn't walked through the entrance since I've been here, I do a couple laps of the place just in case, checking the restrooms and all of the food stands, to be sure he didn't slip me by.

He's nowhere to be seen.

Tomorrow I'll come back.

Maybe he and Genevieve are enjoying the city and the track is only a place he goes when he gets bored? Or maybe that time in Dallas was a one-off; he tried the track, went and lost a bunch of money because he doesn't know shit about picking a winner, and left, never to return. That may very well be the case, but I have to check again tomorrow. If I'm to go through with it, it has to be in the city, and it has to be when he's away from Genevieve. So where do I do it if not the track?

THE NIGHTTIME BAY VIEW FROM THE SECOND FLOOR OF

the Mockingbird Bar and Grill almost makes up for the place's drab décor. The walls, which look like they were built from wood salvaged from five different barns, are covered in porcelain enamel signs advertising beers, cigarettes, and extra cheap, stiff drinks for ladies every Thursday night until ten p.m. Flashing neon from outside—a profile of a blue-and-pink bird with its wings flapping up and down—flickers in the top corner pane of our window. The dimness of the room seems strategic, and I wonder how my beer glass would look in more honest lighting.

Gloria doesn't seem to mind the Mockingbird's dinge. She sips her gin and tonic, excitedly recounting her day in the city to me. Her and two other spec girls got a room to share down by the Saenger Theatre. They took in an early show and spent the rest of the day at the beach. She's got the colour in her face to prove it. Any lulls in her telling are filled with her humming the tune of "On Moonlight Bay."

"You should have come, Toby," she says. "At least to the picture."

"I don't like musicals. They're not realistic. People breaking into song and dance at the drop of a hat—who does that?"

"That's the fun of it! It's all one big fantasy world. And don't tell me you don't like Doris Day."

"All right, I'll keep that to myself."

She shakes her head. "You're no fun," she teases.

"Sorry to disappoint."

A waiter comes by and takes our order. Gloria gets deviled crab and I get swordfish, because how many chances do you get to eat a fish that's part sword?

"If you didn't go to the movies, what did you do all day?" Gloria asks me once our second round of drinks has arrived.

"I told you, I was at the track."

"Yes, but all day?"

"Yes, 'all day,'" I say, a note of irritation creeping into my voice.

"There's no need to be rude about it," she scolds. "And I don't mean to pry, but I don't see how a person can spend the entire day at the races. That sounds like such a bore."

I say, "Doris Day loves the races."

Gloria's eyes light up and she clasps her hands together. "Does she?"

I shrug and take a drink.

"Oh, you're just being mean." She reaches across and gives me a poke in the chest.

Our food arrives quickly. We dig in. Gloria seems impressed by her deviled crab, and my swordfish is okay, but I expected more from something that looks borderline mythological. It's a little tough, and a little dry, but maybe my palate isn't refined enough to appreciate such a creature. After eating, I go to the restroom and wash off the fish smell that climbed up my utensils and onto my hands. When I come back a moment later, some chrome-dome in a rumpled suit is trying to sweet-talk Gloria.

"Take a walk before your hand gets jealous, pal." I remove his hand from the back of her chair.

"Easy, mister. No need to get rude. We're just having a conversation. That okay with you?"

"What are you asking me for? She's the one you're talking at."

Gloria pipes in: "Toby, this slimeball told me he's been watching me all night and says I ought to ditch you and let him take me for a drink."

Baldy's demeanour jumps from calming to defensive. He raises his hands, two pudgy white flags, and takes a step back. "Apologies. I guess we had a miscommunication, me and her," he says.

My fist tightens around his tie. I yank him forward and ram my head into his face.

ARMS LINKED, WE WANDER THE STREETS OF PENSACOLA,
its balmy gulf air breathing over us as we search for the right

spot to grab one last drink before calling it a night. We've passed some dives and we've passed some ritzers, but that just-right spot has eluded us so far. Gloria is swooning. You'd think me head-butting that perv was the nicest thing anyone's ever done for her. She keeps going on about how shocked all the other diners looked when the chump crumbled. "Don't believe anyone who tells you chivalry's dead," I tell her, patting her arm.

After about a half-hour of walking, we've still found nothing decent, and I start to get a bit antsy. There's a liquor store at the end of the block, so I beeline over and grab us a quart of rum. We pass it back and forth, but we don't make much of a dent before we find ourselves in front of Gloria's hotel.

"Shoot, Toby, I can't believe I didn't think of it earlier—I'm sharing a room with Mary and Angela. You won't be able to come up. How far is your place from here?"

"Maybe we ought to take a night off," I say. "I'm beat."

"Oh. Well, that's fine." She sounds as disappointed as she looks. It's nice to be wanted, but I need my rest. I've decided I'll spend the whole day at the track tomorrow, sober, and I'll need to be as alert as can be.

Gloria points to my forehead. "You're bleeding a little bit."

I dab the spot and my fingertips come back red. "Shit. Bastard's tooth must have nicked me." It's nothing major, just a wet coin-slot in the middle of my head. Pop a nickel in and I'll do a little jig.

She gives me her handkerchief and I fold it into a square and hold it over the tiny gash as we say our goodnights.

I chuck the handkerchief in the first trashcan I see once I'm out of sight of her hotel. A cut like this heals faster when you let the air get at it.

THE FIRST RACE STARTS AT NOON, SO I HEAD TO THE TRACK

around eleven and grab myself a paper and a cup of coffee. People are still trickling in, but the place isn't too busy this time of day. The bigger crowds on weekdays will start to show after four o' clock, since a lot of regulars will be at work during the earlier races. Mind you, looking around the track, I get the impression that some of the folks floating around right now are at work, too.

I'd look extra fishy standing near the entrance with a newspaper when the place is this empty, so after I place a bet, I find a good leaning spot just inside the first entranceway to the stands. This way I'll have my back to anyone walking past me, so there's less of a chance I'll be spotted, and, in turn, I'll be able to scope the back of anyone who passes me by.

Easter Sunday lets me down. I put ten whole dollars on him, and the way he runs, well, maybe he should have been named Good Friday. Him and a chocolate-brown gelding named Young Goodman start the race looking like they'll be fighting it out over first, but after about fifteen seconds, Easter Sunday throws in the towel and decides he only wants to play for fun. When the race is done, I notice I've bit the hell out of the rim of my paper coffee cup.

Every time someone passes me, I peer over my shoulder to assess. 12:50 and no Andrew. I make sure to keep half an eye on the races so as not to appear conspicuous. I've snuck off twice, once to get another coffee and once to use the restroom, but I was quick about it, so there's only a slim chance I'd have missed him if he came by. And that's a big 'if.'

I only got here early as a precaution. I didn't really expect him to come so soon in the day. Still, by the time the 1:30 race starts, I find I'm beginning to get restless. I quash the feeling the best I can. I go and make another bet (my last for the day), and walk around for a bit, seeing if I can spot Andrew anywhere. The track is slowly getting busier, so it takes more and more time to scan the crowd. He's nowhere to be found, though, so I return to my post like a good little sentinel and continue to wait, doing my best to remain incognito.

Four o'clock hits and I'm really getting impatient. I've smoked all my cigarettes. I've binged on shitty racetrack food—a hot dog with mustard, popcorn, and soda—but resisted the urge to buy a beer. The food's not sitting very well, and I'm starting to feel nauseous. A couple people have tried to strike up conversation, but I channel my inner Wally Jakes (which isn't too hard when you're already cranky and feeling like garbage) and they split pretty fast.

I'm at a point in my day where I'm starting to lose my powers of discretion, so for the last little while, every time I notice someone coming through the front gate, I turn around to see who it is instead of being sneaky about it. Around 5:30, about twenty minutes after I told myself I was wasting my time and should only give it another hour, Andrew shows. I'm facing him when he strolls through. It doesn't register that it's him at first, so I continue to stare in his direction. Then, my brain decides it'll wake up and process some information. In the span of one or two seconds, I think, *I know that face, who is it? It's Andrew, I work at the same circus as he does. I don't like him. Why does his presence seem so significant right here and right now? Oh, shit! Because I've been waiting for him all damn day!*

Quickly, I turn around. He breezes right by without noticing me, which isn't too surprising when you consider who he is. I get a good look at his getup as he passes: a cheesy brown suit with a pink shirt, a striped red-and-white tie, and a matching pocket square. I move away from the stand entrance and cross the corridor, situating myself against the brick wall where I can blend in with the other congregators, and watch him walk to the wagering windows and place a bet. The clerk hands him his ticket and he stuffs it in his breast pocket and walks away from the window, heading back in my direction. I open my newspaper and cover most of my face with it, doing my best to look absorbed. It's a good thing I moved from my original spot at the entrance to the stands, because that looks to be exactly where Andrew's going.

Only it isn't where he's going.

He walks by me, again without noticing, then goes right past the entrance to the stands and continues down the corridor. For a second, I think maybe he's grabbing some coffee, but then he walks past the coffee stand, too. My eyes follow him as he strolls down the curving line of the circular corridor, until he's right back where he started—back at the entrance to the track.

He leaves the track.

Right away, I rush to the wagering window and elbow my way up to the kiosk that Andrew was just at. "That fella in the ugly brown suit that was just here—did he place a bet?"

"What's it to you?"

"Never mind what it is to me. If you want me out of your hair answer, yes or no. Did he place a bet?"

The clerk removes his glasses, closes his eyes and pinches the area between his brows. Maybe I'm the last straw on a particularly straw-heavy day. "The man in the brown suit with the pink—"

"Yeah, the pink shirt."

"Yes," the clerk says, "yes, he placed a bet. That's what people do here. They place bets. Now, do you want to place one, or—"

"Do bettors have to collect their winnings right after the race, or do you give them a certain window where they can come back and cash in?"

The guy sighs and smears his palm up his forehead and through his greasy hair like I'm the meanest thorn in his knotted crown.

"Bettors have a window of one hour. But we're very strict about that. We offer one hour and not a minute longer."

"And the man who I asked you about, he placed a bet on the next race? The one that starts at 5:40? Answer this one and I'm gone for good."

"Yes," he says. "He made a bet on Gray Ghost, who races," he consults his watch, "eight minutes from now."

I leave the window and rush back to my post against the corridor wall near the entrance. Why would he place a bet for a race that's about to start and then not stick around for the race? And who wouldn't want to watch a race he had money on? Maybe he knows about the time window and he's going off somewhere else for an hour, but if that were the case, then where would he go? There's nothing close by here that you could walk to and back from in the time of an hour. At least, nothing interesting, nothing worth leaving the track for. If he needs booze, cigarettes, some reading material, food—anything—well, they've got all that right here at the track. That and more, when you factor in the damn entertainment!

I wait there for a full hour, but Andrew never comes back.

A WAVE WOULD BE TOO MUCH FOR HER. A HAUGHTY GLANCE IS what I get. I'd been so wrapped up trying to figure out this

Andrew business that I didn't think to take the two-block detour to my hotel and avoid the San Carlos altogether. She's standing under a canopy raising a match to the tip of her cigarette when we spot each other. I'm caught off guard, so the first words that try to come up pertain to Andrew and his poor betting habits. Luckily, I choke them down before they escape my lips. "Evening," I say.

She shakes the flame dead and flicks the matchstick to the ground. "Well, isn't this déjà vu. Are you staying here?"

"No. No, I'm down a ways. The Lighthouse, the place is called. Where's lover boy?"

She almost winces at 'lover boy.' "He's off at the track. He's meeting me here shortly."

"On this particular square of sidewalk?"

She tuts and shakes her head. "In the hotel bar. I just came out to get some air."

"He, uh, he go to the races often?" I fumble out my lighter and a cigarette as I ask, trying to appear disinterested, like I'm on small-talk turf.

"Not really." She pauses, then adds, "Well, I suppose more often than he used to go, which would have been never. Why do you ask?"

"Just making conversation."

"I see. 'Making conversation'—something you feel obliged to do?"

"Christ, Genevieve, can't a guy have a goddamn conversation with his—aw, forget it!" I throw my hands up and turn to leave.

I walk fast, so I'm already halfway up the block when she calls, "I'm sorry that he hurt you," turning my square of sidewalk to quicksand. The clack of her high heels moves behind me. The clack stops when I feel her standing inches away. "I'm sorry that he hurt you," she repeats. "I wish he hadn't." Her voice is flat and matter-of-fact.

"A lot of good wishing does," I reply, keeping my back to her.

"He shouldn't have gone so hard on you. I know you started it—the violence, I mean…I'm sure he was doing something to egg you on—but he didn't have to take it that far. I told him that."

"He called me a fucking draft dodger." I turn to face her, and looking her in the eyes, as I say those last two words, my voice quavers the tiniest bit.

"You *are* a draft dodger."

"How can you of all people say that? I came to Montreal to—"

"To dodge the draft. You came to be with me at a time when I needed you, yes, but you also came—and stayed—to avoid being drafted. And there's nothing wrong with that. I don't think so, at least. If I were in your position, I'd do everything in my power to keep from being shipped off to the front lines. But try being honest with yourself for a change, Toby. Own up."

Neither of us speaks for a while. We stand together, there in the unsteady glow of the jittery bulbs that trim the canopy above us, avoiding each other's eyes and puffing away. As I flick my cigarette to the gutter and start another, I wonder what the hell fidgety people did in uncomfortable situations before smoking.

They probably sucked their thumbs, I suppose.

When she's had enough of the silence, Genevieve says, "Is that dancing tart staying with you at your Lighthouse?"

I shake my head 'no.' Maybe it's 'No, she's not a 'tart." Or maybe it's, 'No, she's not staying with me,' or 'No, you don't get to ask me that sort of thing.'

Whatever it is, it's no.

She's smiling when I turn and leave her.

I KILLED WALLY JAKES WITH AN EMPTY WINE BOTTLE THAT I found on the ground outside Rowland's trailer. I bashed his head with it.

That wasn't the part that killed him, though. It hurt him, no doubt, and it shocked him—his eyes told me that much—but it didn't kill him.

See, I was holding the bottle by its scrawny neck when I swung it, so a good chunk of it broke into pieces and went flying across the room once it hit his skull. After that, the part I was left holding looked like a chalice with a jagged, blood-dotted brim.

That was the part I killed him with, The Unholy Grail.

It was messier than I ever could have imagined.

"GRAVITY FEARS THEM!" WAS PAINTED IN RED LETTERS, slanting across the middle of the poster. I was depicted swinging with my legs hooked around the bar, reaching out to catch Genevieve, who was gliding through the air towards me. 'Mr. & Mrs. Angel' was written in calligraphy just below

'Rowland's World Class Circus,' which was up top. There were always lots of different posters. The idea was to have one for each of the bigger acts, but being headliners, me and Genevieve had two posters dedicated to us. The other one had a similar picture, but beneath Mr. and Mrs. Angel, it said, 'Not For The Faint of Heart,' which I thought was pretty generic, nowhere near as good as 'Gravity Fears Them!'

We were *the* act to see on the travelling circuit. Every night, we filled seats and left a lineup of asses standing outside, hoping to score a ticket for the next performance. Back then, if you were to step into the big top of Rowland's World Class Circus on any given night, you'd see a packed house of people who had forked over top dollar—and I'm talking Ringling and Barnum prices—to see our show. You'd look at all the smiling faces, and you'd crane your neck back and look at me and Genevieve soaring through the air, and you'd think: *All this looks pretty damned good*. And then I'd tell you that looks can be deceiving.

Despite receiving a great deal of acclaim and raking in hills of cash on a nightly basis, in 1948, Rowland's World Class Circus was a grandiose shitshow that was core-of-the-Earth deep in debt.

A number of animals that we bought without having the means to properly care for went and died long before they'd earned us back a fraction of their cost. A Bennie-loving lion tamer with poor whip control took out a young Cleveland man's eye and brought a hefty lawsuit down on us. And a train track fuck-up in Sacramento cost us three trailers and put seven dancers and eight crewmen out of commission for several months. Rowland, crooked bastard that he is, went and fired most of the remaining crew, hiring winos and buck-starved vagabonds as replacements and paying them only a fraction of the wages he'd have paid anyone less desperate. To take care of the lawsuit and keep the place afloat, he borrowed a pile of money from some mobsters in Boston, agreeing, as part of his repayment, to let any of their men join us on tour if they needed to lay low for a while. We'd take up to five men at a time. They'd usually stay cooped up in a trailer during the day and come out at night after the show ended. They'd get stir-crazy and drink themselves stupid and pick fights with the winos and try and screw with the women. Julian even got stabbed by one of them once. He'd caught a guy forcing himself on Susan, so he pulled the son of a bitch off and hit him a few times, and figured that was that. But the guy came at him with a shiv the next night and made a hole in Julian's arm. He was going for the heart, but Julian's too quick to get it in the heart by some stinko mob fuck.

Yeah, back in 1948, if you found yourself in our big top, you'd have been delighted and thrilled and astonished beyond belief. And at the end of the show, when you and your gawking date's beer bottles had been drained and your striped popcorn bags had been emptied save for a swishing subfloor of molar-cracking kernels, you would look up at the two acrobats waving at the adulating masses below them, and you would think, *Rowland's World Class Circus—pretty damned good, if you ask me.* But you know what I'd tell you? I'd tell you you're just a clueless rube. I'd tell you that you live a vapid life that's so vanilla-shit that you have to pay other people to get your thrills for you. And I'd tell you that a shimmering surface means jack, and you had to be a special class of naïve to think our fool's-gold tumour of a show looked pretty damned good, because at most, we were only pretty damned.

HISTORY REPEATED ITSELF IN MONTGOMERY, BUT NOT in Birmingham, and we didn't have any days off in Tallahassee. After all the time I wasted hanging around in Pensacola, I decided from then on I'd only stake out the track on the second of our off-days in any given city.

On day two in Montgomery, Andrew did the same thing as in Pensacola: showed up late in the day, bought a ticket, and left the track immediately after without watching a single race. Figuring that he might pull the same ditch, I'd stationed myself closer to the entrance. That way, I could pursue him from a discreet distance and see what the hell he was up to. When he left, I'd managed to stay on his tail for about three seconds before some half-blind yahoo with his nose practically poking through his race ticket knocked me on my ass. Andrew was gone when I got up.

I went to the Birmingham races with the same approach in mind, but he didn't show there at all.

I'm starting to think I'll need a new venue for the job. Still, I can't help but be intrigued by what's been going on—or *hasn't* been going on—at the race tracks with Andrew.

Atlanta's Piedmont hotel is classier than any of the places I'd stayed in the last three cities, but after Birmingham, I was getting sick of lodging in dives. Both Alabama and Georgia get seventh-circle hot this time of year, and if the cheaper joints have air-conditioning units at all, you can bet your ass they'll also have a 'TEMPORARILY OUT OF SERVICE' sign with at least a year's worth of dust on it taped over their controls. The signs are always written in capital letters like that, too. That's one of life's certainties right there—people who write 'out of service' signs love capital letters.

When I first rolled into Atlanta, I watched the Royal Two stroll into the Piedmont and then went off in search of a close-by spot for myself. I got about a block away, and after scoping some of the alternative accommodations thought, the hell with it! When did I sign up for a lifetime of suffering? I'm treating myself to a nice, clean room with air-conditioning!

The Piedmont was located on the corner of Peachtree and Luckie Street. It had a drugstore called Jacob's at the base of it and was a short walk from The Forsyth Theatre. To cut down the chances of running into Genevieve or Andrew in the lobby, after they walked in, I killed a few minutes by going for a sandwich at Jacob's before entering the Piedmont and booking my room. Knowing that the two of them wouldn't have taken something on the ground floor, I requested a room there myself. The desk clerk obliged, handing me the key to 101 and telling, not asking, me to enjoy my stay.

THE SHOWER IN MY ROOM IS TOP-NOTCH. THE TOWELS ARE

the kind of soft you can't help but bury your face in. Once I dry off, I lie on the bed for a while. The ceiling fan whirring above me was raised by a pack of helicopters. When I set it to its top speed, it spins so fast that I can't differentiate the individual blades and instead see only one circular blur. The cool air that it whips across my body has a lulling effect. I doze, bobbing in and out of consciousness, half awake, half alert, half real, and half vapour. Maybe in reality, maybe in my dreams, I rub my hands over my face, feeling the lines of my young scars. Memories of the beating and the ensuing indignity come rushing to meet me. They hold my eyelids open with sharp, bony fingers to make sure I don't ignore them.

I force myself awake and spring from the bed. They can't be ignored, those bastard memories, but that doesn't mean I have to let them have their way with me. I dress in such a hurry that I'm still tucking my shirt in as I walk down the hallway and into the lobby.

These days in Atlanta are everyone's last two off for a while. When we leave here, we hit Charlotte, Raleigh, and then Richmond without stopping. After that, we'll head to Baltimore, where we'll get another couple days off. If Andrew shows today at Lakewood Track, I assume he'll continue with his pattern of buying a ticket and leaving right away. If that's the case, I'll tail him—making sure not to collide with some clueless buffoon this time—and see if he goes somewhere that might provide me with an opportunity. I won't do it here in Atlanta, but if I'm able to tail him today, maybe I can come up with a plan as to how I'll do it in Baltimore. Maybe he goes to a tavern, in which case I could sneak in unnoticed, and follow him to the restroom and do it there. Or perhaps he goes to the movies—a big, dark room that, given the time of day, might be close to empty. Hell, for all I know, he goes to church and spends a few much-needed hours in a confessional booth, in which case, I'll throw on some robes, hear him out, and then shove a knife through the wooden grid—that'd be some penance.

If I don't catch him at the track and get the chance to follow him to wherever he goes, I'll have to wait until Baltimore, where I'll either spend another day waiting and tailing so I can come up with a plan for the change of venue, or I'll have to improvise and go ahead with it right then and there, which would be a risky way to go about it.

The desk clerk tells me there's a bus that does runs out to Lakewood Track. He sketches a quick map on a Piedmont notepad and hands it to me. The bus stop is only a fifteen-minute walk from the hotel.

There's a table in the lobby that has coffee and Danishes. I fill a cup for myself and take the last lemon Danish, leaving the late-rising suckers with a choice between apple and apple, and then leave the cool comfort of the lobby. It's around nine a.m., but holy shit, is it ever a scorcher out! I'm getting pretty damn sick of being on the Southern end of the country. I down my coffee as fast as I can because it's hot and I want to be rid of it. By the time I've found the block where the bus stop is, my shirt is splotched with sweat. There's a crowd of about twenty or thirty waiting for the bus. A handful of them are somehow wearing their jackets, and I figure they must be either native to the city or they're recently deceased and don't know it yet. The bus stop is outside of a beauty parlour. There's a rectangle of shade outside the place's window, so I go stand there. Inside, five women sit in a row on cushy pink leather chairs. Each of them is covered with a floral smock and has one of those metal Martian contraptions pulled over her head. One of them looks up from her *Life* and meets my wandering eyes. I smile and she smiles back and then returns to her *Life*.

The bus arrives after about ten minutes. Because I separated myself from the other commuters by standing back in the shade, I'm one of the last to get on. There aren't many seats available. Each seat accommodates two. A few people have already resigned themselves to standing and have found a good spot to hang on to. I spot a vacant seat near the back next to a coloured man. It's being blocked by a standing white fellow in a gator's-dick-ugly purple suit.

"You taking that seat, pal?"

Purple Suit dabs sweat from his brow with a polka-dotted handkerchief. "Be my guest," he says, in a better-you-than-me kind of way, stepping aside to let me sit.

I slide in and nod at my new seat-buddy. He returns my nod and then gets back to looking straight ahead. The bus gets rolling a moment later, and all the standers tip to one side and tighten their grip but pretend they're not tightening their grip as our ride pulls away from the curb and accelerates. Once we hit a steady speed, cigarettes are pulled out, followed by the sound of sparking flint wheels and the scraping of matches. Forgetting I'm not wearing my jacket, I reach where my breast pocket would be and pat absently, but then realize my cigarettes are back in my room at the Piedmont. The fellow next to me offers me his open pack. I take one of his Pall Malls and he takes one, and lights them both.

"Thanks, pal."

"You bet."

"I've got a feeling everyone on this bus bets."

A nod and a quarter-smile for my effort.

Purple Suit makes a disgusted face and shakes his head. He's towering above us, and I get the feeling there's nowhere else he'd feel more at home.

Twenty miles isn't far, but time sure likes to stretch itself out when it notices you're in an uncomfortable spot. A few of the bus's windows are jammed so they only come open a couple inches. The driver's got a small fan going at the front, but it might as well be a photograph of a fan for any of us who are seated more than a few feet behind him. And with the temperature climbing, a number of occupants are starting to smell, so there's a nauseating oniony odour permeating the already unfresh, stagnant air. To make things worse, an accident a few blocks up has got the roadway gagging. "I'd kill for a drink right about now," I mutter without even really noticing that I say it out loud.

"Don't go that far," my seat-buddy says. His coat is draped across his lap. He rifles through one of the inner pockets and produces a small flask. He passes it to me. "Gin," he says.

"Geez, pal, I'm racking up a real tab with you, aren't I?"

"Don't worry about it. And it ain't 'Pal.' My name's Horace."

"Well, thank you kindly, Horace." I raise the flask to him and take a drink. It's good gin, but right now, any gin would be good gin. Purple Suit winces. A few people around us make a disgusted noise. Some guy sitting across from me mumbles, "Fucking nigger lover." That ticks me off, so I take another drink from Horace's flask, this time smacking my lips as I hand it back to him. Horace is staring straight ahead. The attention has got him nervous. He takes the flask back without turning to look at me and returns it to his coat pocket.

As we approach Lakewood Track, I notice Horace is fidgeting with his hands. He's sliding the scratched-up wedding band on his ring finger up and down over the knuckle and his eyes are shifting back and forth anxiously. We pull up outside the track, and before we've come to a complete stop, I stand up and step to the side, letting Horace leave the seat and make his way up the aisle. Whispers scuttle through the bus as he makes his way to the front door. I'm about to follow him out, but Purple Suit pushes past me from behind. He walks hastily up the aisle, and just before reaching the door, collides with a man in a navy blue suit and matching hat who stood up from his seat without first shoulder-checking. Purple Suit pushes past the man the same way he pushed past me, only this time, he throws his shoulder into it a bit more, causing the man in the navy blue suit to spin around halfway. The half spin gets me a look at the guy's face—Andrew's face. He looks at me, and while I'm sure that I look shocked to see him, he looks more irritated than surprised to spot me. His hat is pulled down low in the front, like he's been trying to obscure his face. I must have walked right past him when I'd first boarded the bus, but I was probably too concerned with finding a seat to notice him at all. Without saying a word, Andrew whips around, turning his back to me, and promptly exits the bus. From inside, I see him rush for the gates and get swept up in the flow of busybody bettors.

I get off the bus and hustle through the gate and toward the wagering window, where I'm sure Andrew is heading. The place is busy for this time—around eleven a.m.—on a weekday. Lots of shoving and bumping of shoulders. I quicken my pace to the window, getting a bit pushy myself. The lineup is a couple dozen long at least. Andrew is about ten men from the back of the line. He's looking around like he's searching for someone. It was unexpected to see him on the bus; he never gets to the track this early on any day. And something about seeing me there seemed to piss him off—more so than laying eyes on me would have pissed him off on any other day, that is. I'm careful to avoid his darting gaze. I creep past the lineup and make myself invisible by standing in a blind spot next to a coffee cart opposite it. A few more men hop in line. I hold off for a few more to come, and then I find what I'm waiting for: a refrigerator-shaped fellow cabooses onto the horde of waiting bettors. I scurry over and stand behind him, peering around him every few seconds to see what Andrew's up to.

He's in the upper half now, still looking back and forth. I notice now that he's clenching his fists.

The lineup gets a little melty near the top, so I lose sight of him as he gets closer to the window. A couple of minutes later, he emerges, exiting with a ticket in his hand. If this were any other time, he'd leave the track right about now, but not today. Today, he heads straight for the bleachers, checking over his shoulder every few steps as he crosses through the crowd.

A HORSE NAMED HIGH TIDE LANDS ME FIFTEEN DOLLARS.

I take the fifteen and put it all on Duke during the next race. I drink beer and crunch peanuts and watch Duke turn my money into a memory. Andrew is sitting a number of rows down from me. I'd found a spot in a corner that allowed me a good vantage point. This high up, I feel like an eagle looking down from his nest. There's a couple who look to be in their late twenties sitting a couple rows ahead of me. They also won big on High Tide, and their method of celebration fits in with my eagle's nest motif—watching them go at it makes me think of the way birds feed their young. They remind me why isolated corner spots are usually vacant.

Andrew is still checking over his shoulder every so often. I can't figure him out. Every other time I've seen him at the races, he buys a ticket and then leaves before the race starts. I know from my one run-in with Genevieve back in Pensacola that she believes he stays at the races for at least a few hours whenever he goes. Today, though, he actually does stay for at least a few hours. But for all I know, his stay has something to do with him spotting me. Or, rather, him spotting me spotting him.

If I've been as careful as I think I've been at the tracks, today is the only day he knows I'm here and that I've seen him. I've got a hunch that if he goes to the track in Baltimore, he'll be extra vigilant. And if he doesn't go to the track in Baltimore? Well, it's clear he's up to something he wants to keep secret from Genevieve. Maybe he's having an affair, or he's got himself a habit and he spends his days in shooting galleries. Or maybe he just wants some alone time, some time with his favourite person: himself. Anyway, whatever he's up to, he wants it to stay hush-hush. And that means he'll need an excuse—a place he can tell Genevieve he's going. The track's worked for him so far, and it's probably worked well because he leaves with a ticket, with proof of his whereabouts. But now he knows I go to the track too, and there's at least a possibility that I could catch him buying a ticket and leaving before that ticket is of any use.

My guess is in Baltimore, he goes to the track, because switching gears would look suspicious. I could try following him from the track again, but it would be more difficult than ever if he's expecting to run into me. My best bet, then, would be to go to the track, but somehow convince him I'm nowhere near the track. If I can do that and lull him into a false sense of security, I'd have a better chance of tailing him to wherever he goes. And for all I know, that wherever could provide me with an even better opportunity for my cathartic goodbye. It could also not, but a little optimism never hurt anyone.

I notice my beer is nearly empty, so I scarf my remaining peanuts and wash them down with the last mouthful, then get up to refill and place one more bet. Ten bucks on Bayonet, a chalk-white thoroughbred with just the right amount of risk to him.

Don't let me down now, Bay. Duke screwed me, and I've got to at least break even today.

BACK AT THE PIEDMONT. I DIDN'T WANT TO RISK SITTING AT

the hotel bar and running into Genevieve and Andrew, so I had room service send up a couple bottles of wine for us. Gloria isn't very talkative tonight. She's been getting on my case about how often I go to the track, so I tell her I spent my day doing some sightseeing and taking in a couple pictures, which is what I'd told her I'd be up to before coming to Atlanta. I ask her about what she did during the day and she tells me, "This and that." Further prying gets me: "The usual, with the usual girls." I tell her about the movie I didn't really see. While I speak, she turns and stares out the window at the hanging sickle moon. She finds something fascinating to look at on the back of her hand. She becomes mesmerized with the way the red wine tumbles around her glass as she rolls it.

"Is something nagging at you?" I ask.

"Why would anything be nagging at me?" she says.

I shrug and refill my glass. Hers still has plenty in it, but when she notices me pouring, she walks over to me and holds out her glass for me to fill.

"What, are you worried I'm going to drink it all? If we run out, I can order up a couple more bottles."

"I'm not worried," she says, then brings the glass to her head and takes a sip that pretty much puts her back to where she was before I topped her off.

"It's a shame you didn't bring Scrabble with you."

"Why would I? I never bring it when we go to the city. I like to travel light. The last thing I'd want to carry around is a big box with a million little pieces rattling around inside it."

The window is open a crack, but it feels stuffy. I walk over and open it all the way. I light a smoke and blow a mouthful out into the night sky, narrowing my lips to make a dense stream. I exhale for as long as my lungs let me and watch the smoke coil into the darkness, seeing how far my cloud will go before vanishing. I shift my gaze to the moon. I think about how it's the same moon everyone's staring at everywhere that it's nighttime, and I wonder if in Russia, there's maybe some sort of cosmic hammer crossing its curve.

The tap of a glass brings me back to the room. Gloria has set her empty glass on the nightstand. The bottle of red—our second bottle of the evening—is empty.

"Is there a contest I don't know about?"

"No," she says.

"I'll get them to send another bottle up."

I pick up the telephone, but before I dial the front desk, Gloria says, "Don't bother. I think I need to go."

"Now what the hell has gotten into you? Apart from what I'd guess is about two litres of wine at this point."

"Nothing. I just don't feel well," she says. "And not because of the wine. I've been feeling…off all day. I should go back to my hotel and rest."

"You're welcome to rest here," I say. "Here is a lot closer than there. Always is."

"No. Thank you. I think I'll head back." She goes to fetch her coat off the rack. Her drunken movements border on clumsy. She's struggling to get one of her arms in its sleeve. I walk over and help her out.

"If something's wrong, let me know and I can—"

"I just don't feel well, Toby. That's all." She buttons her coat, leans in, gives me a peck on the cheek, and opens the door. "Goodnight."

"Goodnight. I'll call the desk and make sure they have a cab for you."

"Thank you. I'll see you back at the circus."

I go to pull the door shut, but she takes care of it before I've taken two steps.

WATER INVADES THE BOWELS OF A SHIP FIRST.
Cargo storage, boiler and engine rooms. The hot, dark, and dingy, uninhabitable spaces of a moving vessel, that's where the flooding starts, adding weight and fucking up the balance of a ship. Dragging it into the depths.

Wally Jakes lived in the bowels. He was the man who'd shovel coal and stoke fires. He'd monitor meter needles and crank wheels and make sure the steam kept on blowing. Rowland drove the ship, sure, but it was Wally who made movement possible. He was a doer. When he had to be, he was a manipulator. And dwelling in the bowels, you can bet he'd be the first one to spot a leak and plug it.

The thing about Rowland's World Class Circus, though, was that there were always a lot of leaks. Some of them could be patched up no problem, but some required a bit more work. Wally wasn't afraid to get a little wet if he had to, and he'd always do whatever needed to be done to keep things rolling. But when too many leaks spring up at once, you can bet that if anyone knows the ship is doomed, it's going be the man down below. Now, every ship's got an evacuation protocol, and that protocol has a thing or two to say about who hops in a lifeboat first, last, and all points between. I can guarantee you that there's not a ship floating today that says the first man to ditch is the man on the bottom. But I don't blame Wally for what he did, because protocol or not, I believe every man and woman has a certain self-preservation instinct that kicks in in situations like that. No, I don't blame Wally at all. And I don't think he would blame me either.

I USUALLY SLEEP JUST FINE WHEN IT'S COLD OUT. THE HEAT,

the heat is what gives me trouble. I have a bastard of a time trying to touch saw to wood on even a slightly warm evening. But the cold? That's easy. Falling asleep on a cold night as is formulaic as the blues. When you first tuck yourself under the covers, it's not the most pleasant place to be, enveloped in a cold cocoon of blankets like that, but once you're under, that's half the battle! Your body gets word that you're all wrapped up like a burrito and it goes, Hey, there's some potential here. You find your position—maybe it's up against someone else, or maybe you return to Position Number One and get fetal— and then your body radiates the warmth you're craving. For me, once I'm good and comfy, the second I hit the perfect temperature, I'm out like a broken bulb.

So you can imagine my confusion and irritation three years ago on that chilly late-September night, when I lay in bed next to Genevieve, as awake and as alert as I'm capable of being, long after I'd hit the sack.

I drank liqueur-infused warm milk.

I counted sheep, and then, when that got old, moved on to wool sweaters.

I chugged half a quart of rye.

I closed my eyes and imagined infinite nothing and stared at it until it crumbled and became infinite something.

Believe me, I tried. But come three a.m.—not a damn wink.

My last resort was to get up and go for a walk outside. The cold does things to your body. It has a way of wearing you down without you even noticing you're being worked. The small number of times I'd found myself in this rare predicament, a good walk in the cold did the trick.

I crept out of bed and put my jacket on over my pyjamas. I wiggled my feet into my shoes, but didn't bother tying the laces. Genevieve was a heavy sleeper, but I knew I still needed to use tact in dealing with our door. Its hinges had the whine of a suffering trumpet, and it was high-pitched enough to raise even the deepest of sleepers. The only way to keep it quiet was to push against it—as if you were shutting it—at the same time as you pulled it open, using only the tiniest bit more force on the pulling end in order to get the job done.

The door was cooperative that night. I opened and closed it behind me with only a muffled whimper expressing its dissatisfaction at being roused at such an hour.

The icy night air needled into me. It was cut-you-off-mid-breath chilly—much colder than usual for Seattle that time of year. I did up the top button of my jacket and shoved my hands in my pockets—I wanted to be chilly, not cold-blooded. One nearby trailer had a lamp flickering inside, but otherwise every window in sight was black. My feet swished through ankle-tall grass, frost-kissed blades wetting the cuffs of my pants and sneaking in an ankle caress here and there. I was wandering with no real sense of direction and no destination. I've always found that minimal structure is best when you're trying to coax yourself into fatigue. If you're doing it right, your mind starts to get hip to the whole wandering idea, and if you let yourself get tired enough, it will venture off and leave you behind. That was the goal for me. Get myself so weary that my mind would ditch and leave me with only enough sense to sneak back to my trailer and crawl back into bed.

The big top's peak poked up at the end of the maze of trailers. If I was walking toward it, which I may have been, I was doing so in the most inefficient path possible. I'd loop around one trailer and then cross over to the next row, circle one or two, and then return to the side I'd just come from, sometimes farther back than I had originally crossed from. I was like a Snakes and Ladders game piece, moving back and forth in no discernably logical manner, as if controlled by a guiding hand from above, or below.

I was growing more and more tired, but tired wasn't good enough. The goal was exhaustion or bust. I wasn't going to return to a night of tossing and turning. If I was going so far as to drag myself up out of bed to walk around in the cold, then you can bet your ass I wasn't settling for anything less than a deep, stones-throw-from-a-coma sleep that would leave me well-rested and refreshed—the way any headlining performer ought to be when he's got to deal with the pressure of getting a tent-full to pitch a full tent.

The booze I had pounded during my earlier efforts was finally beginning to grasp me. My legs got lighter and my swooshing steps brushed across the grass in loose, broad strokes.

Finally, my staggering brought me to the end of the trailer maze, facing the backside of the big top. No longer just a teasing peak, the cathedral beckoned.

I walked around it, tracing the canvas with my fingers as I went. When I reached the front, I lifted the flap and walked in.

When a room is that dark, it has a different feeling to it. Like the air is thicker, heavier. Like it's not actually empty, but in fact fuller than it ever could be in the light. It's a nice feeling at first, but then it blankets you with cold pinpricks and wraps its pointy fingers around your throat, and suddenly you feel like an intruder who just busted into the wrong home.

I fumbled a matchbook out of my pyjama pocket, plucked a match and struck it—it was a stillborn. I plucked a second one and scraped it across the matchbook's rough strip. It lit.

The burning match cast just enough light to confirm that I had hands and wrists—two of each, in fact—and that I hadn't been absorbed by the shadows the moment I stepped through the flap. I stared at the flame, watching it blacken the head of the match and then blaze its way down the cardboard stem. The flame struggled the closer it got to my fingers, and just as its heat began to hurt, it vanished, as if pinched out between an invisible thumb and forefinger. Observing the lifespan of a flame was a soothing pleasure. It was lulling and it was mesmerizing, and it sometimes felt voyeuristic. I found my pocket and grabbed the matchbook again, ready to light another, but then a distant voice rattled me, causing me to fumble and drop the matchbook into the hungry darkness.

The voice I'd heard was far enough away that I couldn't make out any words, but I recognized that guttural pitch anywhere. I turned around and walked toward the voice, which was coming from somewhere outside the big top, but when I reached the canvas wall, I couldn't find an opening. I pushed at the canvas, trying to uncover the flap that had let me in.

But the dark was so disorienting.

I began working my way along the perimeter, as I'd done earlier on the outside. Navigating was a lot different in darkness, though. More than once, I'd prod at an area that seemed to have more give to it than the last spot I'd touched, so I'd think I was close to the opening, but when I'd reach further to where the flap ought to be, I'd only get a fistful of rough canvas, so I'd go back to pushing and prodding and groping my way along the big top wall. I imagined the tent flap tip-toeing away from me, taking a couple steps further every time I got too close, leading me all the way around the big circular void.

I could still hear the voice in the distance. It would start and stop, start and stop.

Just as my struggle to find the exit was beginning to boil into a frenzy, I felt a faint hint of the night's breath brush across my face. I stretched my arm out and reached with my right hand and found the loose flap, yanked it open, and rushed out of the big top.

Once I got out, everything was quiet. For what must have been a few minutes, I stood there, drinking up my surroundings and trying to establish where the voice had come from. I thought for a second that maybe I'd imagined it all, that the voice I heard over and over was only my mind playing a departing trick on me, and that I'd finally achieved with I'd set out for: exhaustion.

But then I heard it again. It whipped me back to alertness, undoing anything I'd accomplished in my quest for weariness.

The voice was coming from Rowland's trailer, which stood about thirty feet to my left. The window had a faint glow pulsing across it that suggested a light was on some-where inside.

The voice I heard wasn't Rowland's.

The voice belonged to no one but Wally Jakes.

I walked toward it, crouching low. I'm not sure why, but for some reason I felt compelled—no, *obligated*—to investigate.

The dim murmur of Rowland's voice could be heard as I closed in on the trailer, but I couldn't tell what he was saying, either. All I could make out was the tone of the exchange between him and Wally. It didn't sound like a friendly late-night visit.

I halted and knelt down in the grass a few feet from the trailer when the sound of Wally's voice evolved from an indiscernible mucky racket into a string of words I could actually understand.

"Go to hell."

This was followed by Rowland saying something I couldn't quite hear. By nature, his voice was much softer than Wally's, but this time, there was something different about his tone. It sounded...calming. Or maybe nervous, but try-ing to be calming.

I had to get closer.

I got up from the grass, but made sure to stay low. I could have stood up a bit more and still remained below the trailer's window sill, but I wasn't in a tempting mood just then.

I took one step forward, paused, took a second. I went to take a third, which would have got me nice and snug against the wall of the trailer, right below the window, but as I stepped down, the ball of my foot slid over something beneath me, tipping me flat on my back.

The fall felt huge, and I was certain that the resulting thud had been heard from inside. I remained perfectly still. A few seconds crawled by without either voice sounding from the trailer.

The creak of the trailer door opening got my heart mov-ing double time.

From where I sat, I couldn't see who was standing in the doorway, but a moment later, I heard Wally grumble, "Huh."

He sniffed, coughed, and cannoned a gob of spit over the railing, then slammed the door shut and returned to Rowland.

I let a minute pass and then crawled forward to see what I'd slipped on.

An empty wine bottle.

I picked it up, running my hands over its hard, rounded body, which was wet from the grass. Because it was so dark, I couldn't tell for sure if I'd cracked it, but based on feel, the thing was still in one piece.

"You won't just be fucking *me*," I heard Rowland say from inside. His voice was still soft, but it had a desperate, ugly quality to it now, a sludgy green film floating on the surface of a pond. "You'll be fucking everyone. Don't you understand that, you selfish son of a bitch? You're not only punishing me, you're punishing every hard-working soul *here*."

"I understand that just fine," Wally said, and the image of an accompanying shrug came to me with little effort.

On my hands and knees, I crawled over to the bottom of the stairs. The door was ajar. I guess that when Wally had shut it earlier, he'd used enough force to cause the door to bounce open a little before it had a chance to secure itself shut.

I crawled up the first step. When I crawled up the second, I noticed I was carrying the empty wine bottle with me. I was holding it upside down, by the neck, like it were a club. I don't know why, but it felt necessary to have it with me, and if I was going to have it with me, then that felt like the right way to be holding it.

"Only thing you seem mixed up about," Wally went on, "is that it's me doing the fucking. What I'm doing, old pal, is seizing an opportunity and getting out while there's still out to get. The fucking? That's all you. You're the fucker. You're always the fucker."

I stopped at the top step. Through the open crack, I saw part of Wally's back, and Rowland's left hand, which was resting on a table in between him and Wally. Rowland was fidgety. He thumbed his cuticles back. He sped from index to pinky, then repeated. The second run looked painful.

"Now, I don't know why you're making this so hard on yourself. The way you're dragging this out, Rowland—I bet you're the kind of guy who takes a full hour to yank a bandage off. We can stay here talking all night, but it's not gonna change a thing. Now, you reach in that drawer and give me what I know is in there—every damn penny of it—then I'm gone. You'll never set eyes on me again, and you can take me at my word that I'll keep my mouth shut about hiding the retard carnie and all the other shit-filled pots you've got on the burner here."

"And if I tell you to go lay down on the train tr—"

"If you tell me anything other than, 'Here's what you asked for, *Mister* Jakes. Now you take care and go and enjoy the rest of your days in comfort,' then you'll see what a workingman's callused, dirty hands feel like on your face, and you'll wake up to chained wrists and ankles, your own new pair of striped pyjamas, and a pile of questions that you're not gonna want to answer."

Rowland's hand disappeared from my view. A drawer—which must have been somewhere below his desk, because I didn't hear him get up—slid open and thunked to a halt. "This will be the end of us. We won't be able to come back—you realize that?"

"Cut the shit and quit lying to yourself. You did this, Rowland. All I'm doing is removing myself from 'us.'"

Rowland spoke as if he hadn't heard Wally at all. "Everything I've done," he said, his voice beginning to crack. "All of it...was for this circus. To keep us going, to keep us alive. I...I did what I had to, damn it. I did what I had to and now you're taking it away. Just like that. You're taking it away and leaving us with nothing. Sticking a knife in our side and leaving us to bleed out."

"I'm doing this because I have to!" Wally barked. "You've made a big fucking mess and you dragged me—*you dragged all of us!*—into it!" he said. "Don't you cry to me. Don't you *dare* cry to me, try to make me out to be the heel here!" He shoved an accusing finger in Rowland's face and took a deep breath like he was about to start with the *real* lecture, but he didn't get to say anything else. I bashed him in the head with the wine bottle, and Wally Jakes didn't say anything else ever again.

He fell to his knees. He raised a shaking hand to the side of his head, to where I bashed him, and he touched the dripping wound with his fingertips.

He brought his fingers to his face and shuddered out a trembling breath at the sight of his wet, red fingers.

Blood gushed from the side of his head. There were shards of glass on the floor around him, and a few smaller bits lodged in his skull. He turned and looked up at me. I'll never forget those eyes.

He reached for me with open hands. I'll die without ever knowing if they were pleading hands or if they were hands that sought to wrap themselves around my throat and squeeze until my head popped clean off.

I bent my elbow back and angled it upwards, brandishing The Unholy Grail as if I were holding a sword; a hobo cavalier with a knack for improvisation. With a quick jab, I brought what was left of the bottle down, into his throat. Again and again, I brought it up and down until I knew I didn't have to bring it up and down anymore.

THE THIRD LOAD OF DIRT COVERED THE REMAINDER OF
Wally's face. Rowland picked up another load from the pile with his shovel, but before he threw it in, he looked at me over his shoulder.

"Thank you," he said. They were the first words spoken in what must have been at least an hour, since I'd shut Wally up back in the trailer. I didn't say anything in reply. I don't think I was expected to.

Rowland continued filling the impromptu grave. I could smell his sweat from where I stood, a good ten feet back. The soil was hard and he'd done all the digging himself. I figured that was fair.

When the grave dirt was flush with the ground, he tamped the area down, then added some more dirt and tamped that down.

He speared his shovel into the ground, wiped the sweat from his brow—which took the full length of his arm—and then walked to a nearby tree, leaned against it, and puked. Once his stomach was emptied, he wiped his mouth on his remaining dry sleeve, and went about collecting branches and fallen leaves from the ground. When an armful had been amassed, he dumped it onto Wally's grave and spread the mix around with his foot.

If you were looking for it, you could see difference in colour and texture between Rowland's fresh plot and the ground surrounding it. But no one would have any reason that I could think of to venture this far into the woods outside our encampment, and even if they did, Wally Jakes wasn't the type of person anyone would be looking for.

"You saved us, Toby," Rowland said through wheezing breaths. He'd found a spot to sit a couple trees away from where he'd puked. "I know you must feel about as rotten as a person ever could, but I promise you, you did the right thing. Wally was going to bury this circus. Our circus. He was blackmailing me. Said—" a phlegmy cough barged in. Rowland rode the sucker out, spat up some stringy stuff. He found a dry spot on his shoulder, wiped his lips on it and continued. "He said if I didn't give him everything I had, he'd tip the cops off about us letting Ke—about us letting *Eddie* hide out here. He said he'd rat on the mob deals and everything else I did...I had to do...to keep us afloat."

Our eyes met. I'm not sure what mine conveyed, but they did something to stir him up. "Don't you go thinking I was just worried for myself. You hear me? Don't you think that for a goddamn second! If Wally took that money, that would've been the slow, miserable end for all of us."

I nodded, and at least one of the angry wrinkles on his forehead went neutral. Rowland looked to the sky. I joined him. The sun hadn't come up yet, but it wouldn't be long. I walked over to him, offered my hand, and pulled him up. The shift in position triggered another coughing fit from him. When it finished, I was amazed that he didn't have to slurp at least one of his lungs back inside. He caught his breath again, looked me in the eye, and gave my shoulder a squeeze. "Thank you," he whispered.

I swatted his hand away and began my walk back to my trailer, with the sinking realization that my sleep troubles were about to get much worse.

"WHAT DO YOU MEAN WHAT THE HELL DO I MEAN?

You heard me, Toby. I said, do you lie to everyone, or am I just special?"

"I have no idea what you're talking about. I'm not a liar, Gloria. If you're sore about something else, you'd better come out with it, because I don't have much patience when it comes to false accusations."

She throws her arms up in the air. "Oh, *you* don't have much patience? Well, forgive me! I suppose I ought to thank you for using one of your precious little crumbs of patience up on me."

"Christ," I mumble, fishing a cigarette from my holder and sinking back into my chair.

"Yeah, 'Christ,' that's about what I expected for an explanation." Gloria reaches across the table and snatches a cigarette from my case. She lights, crosses her legs, and puffs. She mumbles something to herself that I can't hear.

"Oh, be my guest," I say, pointing to my case. "What's mine is yours."

"Well, I *am* your goddamn guest, aren't I?"

"Sure you are, but there's such a thing as being a good guest. I mean, hell, coming in here and being distant all night, drinking my liquor, smoking my cigarettes, then accusing me of being a liar and refusing to elaborate at all—that kind of guest isn't really the type you're itching to have back in your home any time soon, you get me?"

My blood feels electric. Sitting still makes it worse, so I stand up and pace the room, get things circulating before bolts come shooting out of my eyes and ears.

When I'm on about my third lap of the room, she says, "You want me to elaborate? Fine. I want to know what it is you do."

"What I do?" I shout. "What I do is I'm a fucking clown in a fucking circus. That's what I do."

"That's not what I mean," she says.

I pour myself a drink. I notice Gloria's glass is near empty and set the bottle down without offering her a refill. "Then please, enlighten me." I wave an after-you gesture.

"What do you *do*, Toby? What do you do when we go to the city, and why have you been lying about whatever the hell it is?"

"What are you talking about? I do a lot of things when we go to the city. I go to movies, I go for walks, I go to the track, sometimes I go to a tavern a have a couple drinks. All that all right with you, honey?"

"Don't speak to me like that, Toby. Don't you dare." She stands up so fast her chair shoots back a good foot or so. "Back when we were in Pensacola, Margaret, one of the girls in my group who commutes with us, went down to the track. She said that after she watched a few races, she got up to use the ladies' room. When she came out of the ladies' room, she spotted you standing by the entrance. She said you looked like you were watching for someone and that you were peeking out from behind a newspaper, like you were hiding. She thought you looked odd, but she went to say hello to you all the same. But before she got a chance to, you bolted after some fellow."

"Some fellow? What fellow?"

"Margaret didn't see his face because his back was to her, but she said you were zig-zagging through the crowd, in hot pursuit of this man—whoever he was."

"Oh, for Pete's sake, Gloria," I laugh. "I remember that man. The buffoon dropped his wallet when he walked by me so I rushed after him to return it. Can't do much at the track without a wallet, can you?"

She crosses her arms. "Oh, is *that* it?" she says. "Then thank God that Toby, the patron saint of gamblers, was loitering behind that newspaper, hmm?"

"Sure, thank God all you want. Call the Vatican and see if you can get me on a stained-glass window while you're at it."

Gloria lets out this banshee's howl I never would have guessed she had in her. She picks up her empty glass and whips it right at my head. I duck just in time and the glass shatters against the wall behind me.

"What in almighty hell is your prob—"

"My problem is that you're not only a lying son of a bitch, but that you're making fun of this situation!"

"Making fun of? I'm sorry, whether I'm remembering correctly or not, is there something so scandalous about me walking after a man at the track?"

"No. No there isn't. And if the fishy behaviour ended there, we wouldn't be having this conversation right now. But it doesn't end there, does it, Toby?"

"You tell me. You seem to know more about what I do than I do myself."

"When Margaret told me about what she saw, I thought it was odd, sure, but I didn't think much of it. But then when we went to Atlanta, Margaret decides she wants to go to the track again. She says to me, 'I wonder if I'll see your friend Toby hiding behind a newspaper again.' She didn't intend it in a rude way, she said it like she was kidding around. Anyhow, I told her she definitely wouldn't see you at the track that day, since you were going to the movies that day. I told her I knew so for a fact. So imagine, Toby, imagine my surprise when I see Margaret later that day and she tells me that she saw you at the track again. Well, at first I didn't believe her. I told her there was no way it was you because you didn't go to the track that day. But she kept on insisting, Toby. She swore that it was you. So I said to her, 'Tell me what he was wearing when you saw him at the track, then,' because I was on my way to the Piedmont to meet you, and I figured if she said you were wearing one suit and I got to the hotel and saw you were wearing another, well, then I could get Margaret to give it a rest, and maybe talk her into seeing an eye doctor, too. So, Margaret tells me, 'Oh, he was wearing navy trousers, a white shirt with a gray tie that had red stripes on it.' I told her I'd remember that and then I went to meet you at the Piedmont. Now, when you greeted me at the door, do you know what you were wearing, Toby?"

I don't respond.

"You were wearing navy blue trousers and a white shirt. And wouldn't you know it, when I stepped into your room, what's the first thing I saw? A gray tie with red stripes coiled up on the desk!"

"Aw, Christ, listen, Gloria, I—"

"No!" She stomps her foot for added punctuation. "No! Toby, that night when I saw what you were wearing and the tie on your desk, I gave you the benefit of the doubt. I thought maybe at the last minute, you decided not to go to the movies and instead went to the track. So I asked you what you did that day, and what did you tell me? Hmm?" She slaps my arm. "What did you say?" Slap. "You said that you went to the movies, Toby!"

She grabs the bottle off the table in a quick whipping gesture and takes a long drink right from it. "Now, let me be clear here," she says, wiping her mouth on her arm. "I'm not asking you if you lied. I already know the answer to that. I'm asking you why, Toby. Why did you lie to me? Because there's definitely something going on that you don't want me to know about. Something at the track. And even though I'm worried that later I'm going to be kicking myself for demanding I get an answer from you, I'm going to go ahead and demand all the same."

"You want an answer?" I shout. "I'll give you an answer!" I stomp over to the door, open it fast. The door bangs against the wall and nearly shuts again, so I fling it back open and stick my foot in front of it to make sure it doesn't try anything funny. "I will not dignify these ridiculous accusations—accusations of I don't even know what, mind you—with any sort of defense. You want a detailed report on my every move over the last few months? Too bad! I don't know what's got into you, Gloria, but whatever it is, I suggest you get it fixed. Now get out before I catch your fucking paranoia!"

I notice her lower lip tremble, but she's quick to rein it in. She opens her mouth to speak, but stops herself, shakes her head, and storms past me, out the door. As she walks by, I see the mist of tears to come glazing her eyes.

I keep the door open and watch her walk away. When she disappears from my view, I close the door. I get a grace period of about fifteen seconds before I feel like the King of the Heels.

It takes me a while to sweep up all the glass, but you have to be thorough when it comes to that sort of thing. There are pains worse than a shard of glass in the foot. Plenty of them. But that doesn't make it hurt any less when you step down and feel that stabbing crunch on the bottom of your foot.

SHE WAS ANGRY BECAUSE I COULD HAVE CHOKED ON IT IN my sleep. "I don't want to wake up next to a corpse," she told me.

The trail from the corner of my pillow to the edge of the bed had hardened by morning. Much of what had pooled on the floor was still wet.

I was embarrassed, so I got down on my knees and began cleaning right away. When that was done, I stripped the sheets off the bed and balled them up. I tossed them outside and assured her I'd wash them that day. She wasn't impressed. "This is getting out of hand," she said. "You need to fix it."

I did need to fix it.

I was only getting worse. I'd woken up to a hellish hangover every morning since Wally went missing. Genevieve could usually tell. My smell would give it away, or sometimes it would be my lack of appetite or my swollen face that betrayed me. There were two or three times, though, when I was able to hide it from her. My head would be spinning and the contents of my stomach would be organizing a coup, but there were a small number of times I somehow managed to sneak under her radar.

Waking up and finding I'd vomited in my sleep, though… well, that wasn't one of those under-the-radar instances.

That morning was the first time that I felt she'd had enough. I mean, really had enough. She'd usually say something like, 'Hungover again?' or 'Is life so boring that you need to poison yourself for kicks?' She'd express her disappointment, but never anything beyond that. And I was usually pretty good at dealing with it. I'd say, Sorry, I was trying to keep up with the fellas last night and I guess I got a bit carried away—you know, try and spread out at least some of the blame. And most times that had been enough.

But not that day.

It was her tone—'Fix it.' She sounded so matter-of-fact, so cold. It was a demand. 'Fix it'— it was a threat.

"I'll fix it," I said. "I promise I'll stop."

THE DAYS WERE NEVER A PROBLEM. I WOULDN'T TOUCH

a drop during the day. Risking even one before our set? Not a chance. No, during the day, that's when I would deal with the hangover. I've always been a resilient man, so the right mix of water, salty food, and sweating would usually cleanse my system and get me on my feet. If everything worked out—which it almost always did—I'd be feeling decent in time to run a few practise manoeuvres and enjoy a couple hours of sober downtime before taking the stage with Genevieve. The days were never a problem.

It always started after the show, with dinner.

Most nights, Genevieve and I would eat outside with everyone else. I'd be coming down from the high of performing and, like clockwork, thoughts of Wally would seep up from the grounds of my subconscious like black oil. Wally was always lurking around in my mind somewhere. I could push him back sometimes, but only sometimes. After performances, he'd always come rushing out at me. I don't know why, but Wally's ghost was irrepressible after performances.

Back then, everyone at the circus drank during dinner. If you didn't, people would either get it in their heads that you were pregnant, or they'd say, Oh, you don't want a drink? What, do you think you're better than us? And that kind of pressure, teamed with Wally stomping around in my brain all the time, well, you're damn right I had a drink or two with dinner.

And that slope, that one or two, even an idiot knows it's a slippery bastard.

I was drunk every night for three weeks and four days before that morning when I woke up in a splatter painting of my own creation. When Genevieve told me to fix it, there were just enough icicles hanging from her words that I knew I ought to fix it before she fixed me.

So I did just that. She told me to fix it and, by God, fix it I did.

Temporarily.

I fixed it like tape and bandages over a leaky pipe.

We started eating our dinners in our trailer, away from other people, their boozy breath and their shiny suggestions.

Wally was still a nagging force in my mind—his betrayed eyes, his bloody head, and his pleading hands, that first shovelfull splashing dirt over his dead old face—but I dealt with it, one way or another. I'd fidget with my hands, I'd chew on the inside of my mouth, I'd grind my teeth, and I'd sleep in short spurts and then wake up teary-eyed, gasping for air.

But I dealt with it.

For as long as I could, I dealt with it.

I stopped dealing with it about thirty minutes before I broke Genevieve's nose and her cheekbone and sent her plummeting unconscious into the harsh embrace of a net.

I was two weeks cold turkey in Albuquerque. I was also celebrating two weeks without a good night's sleep and two weeks of being just about the most miserable bastard anyone had ever set eyes on. I was a fucking mess. A pale, jittery mess who mumbled to himself and had puffy, dark bags under his eyes.

I met Genevieve outside the big top ten minutes before our set. Before coming to the big top, I drank a bunch of coffee and chewed a stick of gum to blanket my booze-breath. We did our stretches. At that point, we hadn't slept in the same

trailer for nearly a week. I guess I had been whining and blub-
bering in my sleep every night the second I conked—when I
managed to conk, that is. Genevieve had tried remedying it
by sleeping with wads of cotton jammed in her ears, and that
worked all right for a while, until I started thrashing in my
sleep. One night, I'd booted her while I was out, leaving a big
fat bruise on her left thigh. She told me that when she woke
up, I was kicking and flailing my arms about, and that tears
were pouring from my closed eyes. After a repeat offense two
nights later, we both agreed it would be best if I sought out
different accommodations for a while. Rowland offered me
the circus's one vacant trailer, which had belonged to one
Wally Jakes, and you can bet I had some choice words for
that suggestion. Plan B was that I sleep on Rowland's floor, so
I opted for that—beggars and choosers, right?

"...for Mister and Missus Angel!"

Raised hand in raised hand, we ran into the big top, lighting the stubby wick on a tumultuous panorama of cheers.
The race up the ladder was business as usual: moving in time
to the beat of our music—high-tension horns and heroic
twin base drums.

I felt great. I wasn't drunk, but the alcohol had calmed
me.

The band cut it when we reached the platform, leaving
us with only a rolling snare. Genevieve grabbed her bar and
swung out. I heard a few gasps over the snare—nothing new.
A moment later, I followed. The two of us took a few swings
to get our rhythm, then we clicked: one clock with two mir-
roring pendulums.

Genevieve set up for her first dismount, a frontend strad-
dle planche.

She leapt. The snare halted.

Gasps and squeals rose from the crowd.

I caught her by the wrists. It was textbook. Cheers burst
all around us, heat searing off them.

I returned Genevieve to her bar.

As I released her, it grabbed me. My head felt light, my
arms felt gone. The fatigue that had been stalking me for
weeks had finally made its big move. I blinked hard, trying to

push it back. I opened my eyes to pure distortion. I opened my eyes and a snare drum I didn't even realize was rolling stopped dead.

A somersaulting woman was coming at me. No. A smear was coming at me. Fast.

I flung my weightless arms out. I connected with something.

Gasps and squeals rose from the crowd. They were different gasps and squeals than before.

Screams followed. Lots and lots of screams.

"IF IT'S ONLY AN APOLOGY, YOU CAN FORGET IT." GLORIA is doing her best to look indifferent. She occupies herself by tracing the lines of her palm with her finger. Her lips are pursed. She's trying real hard. "An apology means jack unless it comes with an explana—hey, what are you doing?"

"What the hell does it look like I'm doing?"

"It looks like you're locking the door. And if you're going to talk to me that way, you can go right ahead an unlock it and let me out."

Ignoring her, I move to the window and close the curtains. I tug the two pieces of fabric closed until they're overlapping and not even a sliver of twilight can sneak in.

"Toby, what on earth are you—"

I shush her. "Be quiet, would you?"

She looks me in the eye for the first time since I let her in. "This is ridiculous!" she says, and gets up off the bed.

I move in front of her and push her back onto it.

"It'd be worth your while to stop hassling me for two goddamn seconds."

She doesn't like that. Not one bit. When she walked in here, she thought she'd brought the upper hand in with her. This turning of tables is getting her rattled, but I can see that flicker of intrigue dancing in her eyes. She's mad, but I've got her. I know I've got her.

I strike a match and light a couple extra candles, double check the door, double check the curtain. I motion for Gloria to slide over to one side of the bed and I kneel down and reach underneath.

"Toby, what in the hell are you up to?"

"Shh!"

When I slide my Samsonite across the floor, a miniature galaxy of dust floats out from under the bed. Once the suitcase is out, I take it by the handle and place it on the chair that's facing Gloria. The opening end of the suitcase faces her.

Both latches pop. I force it open. The Vampire Master is on top of the magazine stack, staring me down. Bit by bit, I take everything out—magazines, elastic-fastened postcards, nudie pictures—and place them neatly on the kitchen table. Once the belly of the case is empty, I unzip the top half and pull out an envelope.

Gloria doesn't speak. She looks nervous. Her fingers are resting on her lap, laced together. In one corner of her mouth, she's biting down on her lip. I tear the envelope open and dump its contents into the empty suitcase. I pull another one out and do the same, then another and another. Her eyes are wide and lit now. She's still biting her lip.

I keep at it with the envelopes. Ever the showman, I start adding a little flare to each tear. When I dump the contents into the suitcase, I shake the money out like I'm peppering a dish.

More envelopes.

More envelopes.

Gloria doesn't speak. Her eyes are at capacity, her posture tenses and her shoulders rise. She's still biting. I'm starting to feel sorry for that lip of hers.

I keep pouring.

The bill pile is moving closer and closer to the brim. I need to direct the flow of the last few envelopes to the middle of the pile so they don't start spilling out from the suitcase. When the final envelope has been emptied, I whip it into the air. I cross my arms and take a step back.

"Whose money is that, Toby?"

"It's my money."

"Yours?"

"Every goddamn penny."

"No kidding?"

"No kidding."

"How much is there?"

"Lots. Enough to for me to leave here and get settled somewhere else. Somewhere better."

"So…so you're planning on leaving, then?"

"That's something I'm planning. But I was thinking maybe I don't have to go alone."

That gets me a smile, but as quickly as it appears, it's washed away like shoreline sand. "Where, Toby? Where would we go?"

"Wherever we want to. There's enough here to take us anywhere and get set up some place decent."

She stands up and walks toward me. No, toward the suitcase. She dips her hand in and swishes the money around. A bunch of bills fall onto the floor. She picks them up and returns them to the case, then swirls some more. "What would we do, though?" She looks from the suitcase to me but keeps her hands submerged. "There's plenty here, but the well would run dry eventually."

"Eventually is a long way away. This could get us set up. Away from here. Away from this dead end, Gloria." I reach into the suitcase and grab a fistful of bills. I raise them to her eye level and squeeze. "Just think, we could take this and go to New York. You could dance in Broadway shows."

"What would you do?"

"I could do anything I wanted to out there. A performer of my calibre? There'd be a mile-long list of things I could do in a city like that. And, hell, New York is just one place. We don't have to go there. We could go to Los Angeles and work in pictures—I bet I could find work as a stuntman in a snap. And there'd be no shortage of pictures needing talented, easy-on-the-eyes dancers like yourself. Imagine that, Gloria, going to the movies and seeing yourself up on that screen. Dancing up front, where you belong."

She thinks about it for a minute, her face set in deep concentration, looking around the room, looking at the money. Nodding to herself every now and then.

Finally, she gears those big hazels up at me.

"All right," she says, "I'll go with you. If I stay here, I'll never amount to anything more than a pretty background fixture."

I wrap my arm around her and pull her in.

"When do we leave?" she asks.

"After Baltimore," I say.

"Why wait until Baltimore?"

"Because Baltimore's where I'm going to kill Andrew."

If that rattles her, it doesn't show on her slate-calm surface. Her set face, the firm unwavering line of her mouth, you'd think her expression had been chiselled on.

I'm all double-time breaths and gushing adrenaline. I'm the first one to blink.

"You've got to kill him, then?"

"I've got to."

She nods. "Can I ask why?"

"Yeah."

"Why?"

"Because I hate him. Because it feels like the right thing to do. Too much time's passed since I've put an end to the show, and too long ago it occurred to me that headlining isn't the only way to do that."

She mulls that over for a minute and then gives me an approving nod. "All right," she says. "And we leave after Baltimore?"

"We leave after Baltimore."

She likes that very much.

"WHY NOT HER, TOO?"

At first, I'm not sure if I'm awake or not, so I don't respond. If it's a dream, I can reply however I'd like, but waking life is big on follow-through and consequences, so a more tactful answer would be needed if that were the case.

It's been five days since I told Gloria. She's hardly alluded to it since. She said nothing about it on our second day in Charlotte, or on the first day in Raleigh. Yesterday, on our last in Raleigh, shortly after I'd flicked off the lights and we pulled the covers over our bodies, she gave my side a squeeze and whispered, *I think Los Angeles would be just about perfect*, in the soft, almost slurring voice you only ever hear from people on the cusp of sleep.

But now...

Had she spoken, or was I drifting into a dream?

I wait a minute. Maybe more.

Then: "Hnnh, Toby? Why not—" she's interrupted by a yawn, "why not her, too?"

I pretend I'm out.
Gloria falls asleep without speaking again.

MANY OF BALTIMORE'S TREES HAVE ALREADY BEGUN their autumn blaze. Their bursts blend into one another, creating a gorgeous fiery orgy when the whispering breeze animates their branches. There's a last-rites-thin fog hanging in the air, a shade short of invisible, as if it were caught between here and another dimension. The bench I'm sitting on in Druid Hill Park faces the water, leaving my back turned to the path. Every so often, I'll hear the shuffle of footsteps rising and then falling behind me, but there aren't many people out yet at this hour, and those who are, it seems, aren't the type to stop and chat with a stranger.

That suits me just fine.

I came to town last night, after performing. I'd convinced Julian and Susan to swap act times with me (a change that Rowland wasn't at all pleased about), claiming that I was beginning to come down with a fever and time was of the essence. Once I'd finished my act, I rushed to get my paint off, changed my clothes, and then bummed a ride to Baltimore from a pair of locals I found in the parking lot who were also leaving before the show's close. They told me that they'd heard the headliners were amazing, but the driver, Earl, hated traffic and, besides, his wife, Helena, wasn't one for late nights. I told them I was from the city, too, but I was staying in a hotel because my wife's family was living with us for the next month and I needed some time to myself.

"Nothing like a night at the circus to pull you away from the tedium of reality," Earl told me, the lines of his smile rippling so high I could spot them in the rear-view mirror from where I sat.

"Pal, you're telling me," I said.

Before they dropped me at the Bellingham, Helena threw in her two unsolicited cents, saying that the clown who went on before the knife-thrower and his target-girl was talented, but not very funny. "The bigger circuses, they always get funny clowns. Even the ones who flip around and all that are still funny."

I told her I'd be sure to catch the Ringling, Barnum, and Bailey show next time it rolled through town, and she told me that I absolutely must.

The Bellingham—a towering pale fortress with its name announced in the kind of white, glowing letters you see introducing a fairy tale—is my shot in the dark. It's not entirely necessary for me to be staying at the same hotel as them, but it will make keeping track of Andrew a hell of a lot easier on me. When the Bellingham's glass doors were first opened for me last night, a walk through the lobby to the desk confirmed what its exterior teased: pure swank. Yes, if Genevieve and her soon-to-be late lover are to rest their heads anywhere in this city, I thought as I signed a fake name and took my room key from the clerk, it will be here, at the Bellingham.

Of course, the ideal venue for the deed itself is the race track, Laurel Park. If Andrew shows and conditions are just right, I'll wait until he needs to slip away to the men's room and I'll take care of him right then and there. The track is my safest bet because if there's one thing I know, it's that whenever he goes to the track, he goes there alone. If he pulls any weird shit—if he throws a bunch of money down and splits without watching a race, as he's got a tendency to do—I'll have to improvise.

Shops will be opening in a few hours. First thing I'll do after I get myself breakfast is go get a new suit and hat—maybe in beige or a patterned green…something he won't recognize me in. Then I'll go and get a pair of glasses, the blackest, thickest frames they've got. Andrew, he won't know me from Adam, not even if I walk up and boot him right in his ass.

There's a chill in the air, and as the sun's bleed spreads across the water and moves up my body and onto my face, I feel the softest touch of warmth, telling me to get up, to get moving. Telling me to begin my day.

I walk back through Druid Hill Park the same way I came in. I return nods and hellos when I have to. I drag my feet a little whenever I walk through a patch of fallen leaves because I like the sound it makes.

There's a diner a few blocks from the park. Its OPEN sign has a nervous tic. I push through the door and my presence is announced by the jangle of a bell. The twisty-haired brunette waitress leaning against the counter closes her newspaper, straightens up, and smooths the front of her robin's-egg blue uniform with a quick brush of her hands. "Good morning," she says, and as she does, a cook who's definitely the kind of guy you want to keep out of sight when your business hinges on appetites pokes his head out from the kitchen and shoots me a look. She waves her hand at the roomful of empty tables. "Take your pick. You're our first of the day."

I take a seat at the counter and order scrambled eggs on toast with a side of bacon.

I'm not very hungry—haven't been for a couple days now—but I force myself to eat every bite. Hungry or not, you should never work on an empty stomach.

"You know of a decent place that sells men's clothing?" I ask as the waitress as she places my tented cheque and a couple peppermints in front of me.

She scrunches her face and looks up to the ceiling as if there's a directory pasted on it.

"Men's clothes?" a gruff voice that I can only assume

belongs to the man who made my meal booms from the kitchen.

I cup a hand around my mouth. "Yeah!"

"Go to Hutzler's!" the cook shouts. "Corner of Howard and Clay Street!"

"That where you shop, pal?"

"Surrre, buster! I'm a real suit and tie man! I just crack eggs in a diner because it's my passion!"

"Well, they're lucky to have you here," I say, putting my money on the counter. I take a peppermint and crunch down hard. "Aren't you?" I say to the waitress.

"Aw, sure," she says. "We really won the lottery with Steve there."

The trolley gets me to Howard and Clay in just under half an hour. Hutzler's is a behemoth of a building, the kind of place that ought to have someone put a map in your hands the moment you come through the doors. I manage to find the men's department without needing to stop at base camp, and by the time I've taken my first step into the suit area, this dainty bald man in a sharp checkered number is on me with his measuring tape.

"My good man, my good man," he says, stretching the tape from one of my arms to the other and then wrapping it around my chest. "Just as I suspected: a thirty-eight regular." He folds the tape in half and drapes it over his shoulders like it's a fancy mink. "I always make a point to grab a man's size right away."

"I'll bet."

He almost snickers. "Now, shopping for any particular occasion, or is—"

"No occasion. I just need a new suit."

"Of course, of course. This is certainly the right spot for you."

I brush past him and walk down the aisle, looking left, looking right, running my fingers over textures. He follows so close you'd think he was my conscience.

"You picked a good day for a new suit, sir. Many of these jackets just arrived yesterday evening. I put them out myself before I left for the day. What do you think of this one?" He whips a jacket off the rack, removes the hanger and pushes in front of me, the jacket wide open and ready to be filled.

"I've already got a navy blue suit. I'm looking for something different."

"Ah," he says, and zips further ahead. "I have just the thing." He returns with a light brown jacket. I wave it off.

"Got a brown one, too. I said need something *different*, pal."

"Well, sir, you'll have to be patient, as I don't know what you have or haven't got in your closet."

"What about beige?" I ask. "I've never owned a beige suit. Always wanted one, though."

"Of course!" he beams, as if he were just about to suggest it himself. He walks over a couple aisles and comes back a moment later with a dark beige suit.

I grin. He grins, too.

"Which way are hats?"

BALDY RINGS ME THROUGH AND SENDS ME PACKING WITH my new suit, a matching hat, and a pair of brown shoes. The shoes are a ten, a full size bigger than I normally wear, which ought to steer anyone looking for footprints in the right kind of wrong direction.

Hutzler's sells glasses on the third floor. I find what I'm looking for right away. Rims so dark and thick they could be marketed as a domino mask. When I scope my reflection in the mirror, I think of Gloria's story about meeting Clayton Whatshisface, the Lone Ranger. The salesman directs me to the other end of the floor where they take care of the lenses, and I head in that direction. Once I've gone about halfway, I turn to check he's not watching me, then I head for the escalator.

THERE'S A FAMILY OF SIX APPROACHING THE FRONT DOORS of the Bellingham at the same time as me. I slow down so that they enter ahead of me, then catch up and walk with them toward the elevator. The father tells the elevator boy they're on the seventh floor. I'm on the sixth, but when the father says seventh, I nod at the button-pusher like that's where I'm heading too. I get off with the family, and once they're out of sight, I take the stairs down to my floor. The last thing I need is someone noticing that I came back to the hotel and left shortly after looking like a different person. Well, maybe it's not the absolute last thing I need, but it's one of them.

I change into my new clothes. I do a few laps of the room to get used to walking in shoes that are too big. Once I add the final touch—the glasses—I stand in front of the mirror and stare at myself. Sure, I can spot me, but that's only because I'm looking for me. And even though I'm looking, it still takes me a few seconds before I see that the man staring back at me is the same man who's stared back at me every time I've looked at a reflective surface in my whole life. This disguise, I decide, is damn fine.

I take the stairs down to the lobby and walk out the front door, head down, a few steps behind a group of businessmen. There are two more items I need before I take a cab out to Laurel Park.

It's warmer than it was when I was sitting in Druid Hill earlier, but there's still a faint chill in the air, which I'm glad for, since it means it won't look fishy if I'm wearing a pair of light gloves. The ones I buy are probably the cheapest in the store, but that's fine. They only need to last me one day.

At the hardware store, I buy a flick knife, some screws, and a bottle of glue.

When I'm about a block away, I tuck the flick knife into my breast pocket and chuck the bag in a trash can, with the glue and screws still in it. I wander down West Chase. It's a busy street, so I figure a cab will be by any minute. I check over my shoulder every few seconds and manage to get the attention of a Yellow Cab just as I'm rounding the corner to Maryland Avenue. The driver's got a gold badge that says Safe Driver pinned to his shirt. "Where ya off to, Mac?"

"Laurel Park."

"Laurel Park? You know there's a shuttle goes out there? Save yourself a few bucks, why don't ya?"

"Christ, is your wallet too crowded or something? Take me to Laurel Park. If I want life advice, I'll see a damn shrink."

The driver hunches over the steering wheel and pulls away from the curb. "Miserable son of a bitch," he mumbles.

I tap my chest a couple times in the same spot Buddy's badge is on his shirt. "Don't forget to drive safe, pal," I say.

THE STAKEOUT HAS BECOME ROUTINE TO ME. I BUY A
newspaper, find myself a spot inside the entrance, and wait.

An hour rolls by with no sign of Andrew. I notice the pimply kid tearing tickets shoot me a look a couple times, so I decide to move a little farther down the hall.

A second hour passes. I buy a cup of coffee and bring it back to my post. My legs and my lower back are starting to tire. I lean on the wall to take the pressure off, but I can only do that for so long before my upper back gets sore. The waiting game has become one big fucking juggling act.

Three hours. From what I hear, a horse named Whaler just earned his jockey a ten-thousand-dollar jackpot. Some people scream with joy, others bawl. There's a blister growing on my ankle. Fucking shoes.

I need to piss.

Across the way from me, a father tells his kid to stay put. The kid takes a comic book out of his back pocket and parks his ass on the hard ground. The father and the distillery-scented cloud accompanying him walk past me. He approaches a woman in a blonde wig, palms her something, and the two of them head off together, hand in hand.

Four hours has me feeling like I'm about to start sweating piss. I hobble across to the kid, who's read his comic book cover to cover five times now. I pull a dollar out of my pocket. "Hey, kid. You want to make an easy buck?"

The kid looks at me like...well, like I just asked him if he wanted to make an easy buck. "I don't mean anything weird," I quickly assure him. "I just need help with something. I'm waiting for a friend, see, and I really need to use the men's room. If I gave you a buck, would you watch for this friend of mine and let me know if he comes by or not? I'll only be a minute."

The kid looks up at me. One of his eyes is squinting like Popeye, but I don't know why because I'm blocking the light for him. "What's he look like?" He grabs the dollar from me and I describe Andrew to him. He nods. "Sure, mister. And if this fella comes by, you want me to stop him and let him know you'll be back in a minute?"

"*No*. Absolutely not, you just let me know if he comes by. If I miss him here, he'll head to our other meeting spot and I'll catch up with him there. Got it?"

"Whatever you say," the kid shrugs.

I run to the men's room and take a piss so big you'd think I was Whaler the horse. I leave without washing my hands and I'm still doing my zipper up when I walk out the door. The kid waves at me when he spots me. I rush to meet him. "Anything?" I ask.

He crosses his arms, tilts his head back. I know what's coming. "You got another buck?" Brat probably learned it from his loser father. I peel another bill off my roll and slap it into his hand.

"Out with it, you little fucker!" I don't even mean to call him that, but that's what comes out. The kid actually flinches when I say it.

"He—he didn't come by. I didn't see him. I'm sorry, mister!"

"Don't spend it all in one place," I tell him, then turn and walk to a spot closer to the entrance.

I decide to call it a day around five o' clock. Any of the times I've seen him at the track, he always leaves by five, so I figure there's not much of a chance he'll show at all today.

The cabbie that takes me back to the Bellingham really wants to talk about communists. I play along for a minute or two—"Aw yeah, pal, they're a sneaky bunch, those reds. They could be anyone, anywhere"—but then politely ask him to can it. I need to think.

Why didn't Andrew show? Was it because he isn't in Baltimore at all? Maybe he's in town, but he's off somewhere with Genevieve. Maybe he was in town, but instead of going to the track, buying a ticket and leaving, he's cutting the middleman and going straight from his hotel to wherever it is he sneaks off to.

The possibilities make my head hurt. They make me want to call the whole thing off. He'd made such a habit of showing at the track every other time—where the hell was he today?

Was he onto me? Nah. How could he have known? Gloria? No. No chance. She wouldn't have ratted. What good would that have done her?

I think of my money and reach into my pocket to make sure that the key to my trailer is there, which I know it is, I just need to feel it. It's there, all right. I pull it out and look at it. It's grimier than the spare I gave Gloria. I keep it clenched in my fist for the rest of the cab ride.

"Here's good," I say to the driver.

"Huh? I thought I was takin' you to the Bellingham? It's another few blocks still."

"Yeah, and I'm telling you here is fine."

He pulls over. I pay my fare and slide out. I need fresh air. Since there's none of that available, city air will have to do. Anything to get out of that smelly cab. Christ, how long are their shifts, anyway?

It dawns on me that I've hardly eaten all day. Right as that occurs to me, my body gets hip to it, too, and my hands start to shake a little. I find a drugstore and order a ham sandwich and a glass of milk. I take a seat at the counter, which faces the window looking out to the street. I watch people walk by as I wolf my food down in record time. Once I'm done, I get up and order a slice of blueberry pie ("Yes, I'll take an extra scoop of ice cream, thank you") and a cup of coffee.

The pie is delicious. I take my time with it. What the hell is my rush, anyway? I don't suppose I've got anywhere to be now.

When I'm done my coffee, I order myself another cup. Outside, the theatre crowds are coming and the dinner crowds are going. Lots of people are carrying shopping bags. Fallen leaves are being ushered down the street by a light breeze. It's beginning to get dark. I can see my reflection in the window now; these glasses, this stupid suit—Christ, what a ridiculous getup! There's a crosswalk across the street from the drugstore and the people waiting for the light to give them the go-ahead are far enough away that they look like they're standing inside of my transparent head.

I wonder how Gloria's doing back at the circus. If she was following the plan—and I have no reason to believe she was doing anything but—she'd be bringing meals to my trailer throughout the day today and tomorrow, spreading word that I had a nasty flu and I needed to be left alone. We both agreed that she should spend a good twenty minutes in the trailer each time in order to keep up appearances.

I wonder what she gets up to in those twenty minutes.

I wonder if she's snooped around at all, if she's noticed that my suitcase isn't there.

It's not that I don't want to trust her. It's just that I can't afford to trust her. At least not fully, not as much as I trust myself. But if she does go looking for the suitcase and she sees it's not there…oh, boy. You can bet she'll have a thing or two to say about that. And I'll have a thing or two to say back.

You don't trust me enough to leave the suitcase here?!

Well, what the hell are you doing wanting to root through the suitcase while I'm not there?!

One accusation will follow another, and the next thing you know…

I just really hope she doesn't go looking for the damn suitcase.

It's a funny thing, trust. What a situation like this does to it. You can have two people, with each one pretty much trusting the other with his or her life in almost any scenario, but then you introduce a little bit of money and a couple of secrets, and the next thing you know, those same two people are looking at each other all shifty-eyed, second-guessing each other and thinking toxic thoughts.

Ah, I've got to cut it out. Gloria's fine. She's level. What the hell am I doing thinking any different? It's this situation, that's all. My suspicion is a symptom of this situation just as much as a plugged nose is a symptom of a cold.

I take a couple big sips of my coffee. I need this. Not just the food, but the caffeine. The sweet black elixir of life. It clears my head. Helps me focus. Standing around at the track all day—Christ, what a thing to do to yourself! Staking a place like for that long, it takes a lot out of a guy. By the time I reach the bottom of my second cup, I've flushed the grogginess out of my system. I feel good. I can think clearly.

Andrew.

What to do about Andrew?

Why hadn't he shown today? Had I somehow missed him? I don't see how I could have, but I suppose it's possible. Or maybe he's not in the city at all. Though, I can't see that being the case. The guy comes to the city—any city—every chance he gets. Maybe Genevieve didn't like him sneaking off and she finally said something to him. That could be it. I know better than anyone that when Genevieve tells you it's time to stop doing something, you flat-out stop doing it right the hell away if you know what's good for you. Maybe that's it. I'm not sure, but maybe. The more I think about the whole thing, the less I want to find a way to go through with it. Sure, I think Andrew deserves a nice, long dirt nap more than anyone else I've ever come across, but the way things have gone today...so much planning for nothing, so many unknown variables—so many pesky little what ifs—orbiting me. It's just about enough to turn a guy right off.

I finish off my coffee and take care of any remaining bits of pie left on the plate. My tongue does a couple laps around the inside of my mouth to take care of any specks of food trying to find a low-rent spot for the night.

"Care for another cup? Or maybe one for the road?"

I don't turn to look at the woman behind the counter, but our reflections make eye contact in the window. "I'm all right, thanks. Too much of a good thing, you know?"

"That's fine. You take care."

I tip my hat, still without turning. "You do the same."

Despite Fate's best efforts, I don't believe in Fate. I think whatever happens in a person's life happens either just because, or it happens because someone—usually that person himself—makes it happen. Fate, I believe, is for suckers. But what's that thing people say about the devil's greatest trick? About how the craftiest thing old Lucifer ever did was convince the world he's not real? Sometimes I think maybe Fate's like that. Like its life work is making guys like me think it's all a crock. And most times that works just fine, but every now and then, you see, Fate slips up. It goes and stumbles over its own feet, and then I notice it, and next thing I know, I'm considering its existence for those few seconds it takes to dust itself off and run back into the shadows. Sometimes it takes a little longer than a few seconds. Just as I'm about to get up and leave, Andrew appears in my head. My reflected transparent head. At first he's tiny, so I think my eyes are screwing with me, but then the traffic light changes and he starts crossing the street, moving toward the drugstore, getting bigger and bigger, and by the time he's halfway here, he's so big that he can't fit inside my head and I know for sure it can't be anyone but him that I'm staring at. For a second, I'm worried he'll spot me, but as he steps up onto the curb, I notice he's not looking in my direction. His hands are stuffed into his pants pockets and eyes are on the ground, like he's trying too hard to look inconspicuous or he's avoiding someone. He turns and walks up the street, past me, past the drugstore. I give him five seconds and then walk outside and begin following him from a safe distance.

Every now and then, he turns around and takes a look behind him, but he doesn't spot me. Or if he does, I just look like another someone, so he keeps going. There are plenty of people out and about right now, and I make sure to keep close to the storefront side of the walkway because the streetlights have trouble reaching there. I follow him down West Eager Street, then across Cathedral and up Morton.

A squeal of delight escapes me when I notice he's approaching East Chase Street, but I turn it into a cough when I notice its pitch catching the attention of a man passing me by; last thing I need right now is to draw attention to myself. He rounds the corner onto East Chase and I waste no time thanking my lucky stars.

He's heading toward the Bellingham.

Careful to maintain my distance, while at the same time keeping close enough, I follow Andrew up the street. His pace quickens as he approaches the hotel. He jogs up the steps, passing the doorman without dropping a penny in his upturned palm. I quicken my pace. I've got one hand in my pants pocket, sorting through the few coins I've got jingling around in there in search of a nickel. The game's called incognito. The doorman is sure to remember a man who doesn't tip as well, and he's sure to remember a man who tips exceptionally well. A nickel is a good tip. Standard. Forgettable. Just right.

I walk up the steps, nod without making eye contact, and hand the nickel to the doorman. He thanks me, and I don't respond. Inside, I spot Andrew snaking toward the elevator. I make my way to the front desk.

"Good evening, sir," the man behind the desk says. He's standing with his arms stretched out, his fingers splayed on the desk, reminding me of a blackjack dealer waiting at his table. "Checking in?"

"No," I say, "I'm meeting a friend of mine here, and I can't remember what room he's staying in."

"I see."

"His name is Easton. Andrew Easton."

"I'm afraid, sir," he starts, sounding, actually, a little afraid, "that we can't give out the room numbers of any of our guests. What I can do, though, is call his room on your behalf and let him know you're here."

Before I have time to protest, he's got the directory out and open. He slides his finger down one page, flips, repeats. "You said the name of the fellow was Easton, sir?" he asks, his eyebrows warping into a confused scrunch.

"Yeah, look, pal, that's okay. Forget it. You don't need to disturb him in his room. I'm sure he'll be right down. I can just grab a drink and wait for him in the—"

"There doesn't appear to be a Mister Easton checked in here, sir. Is there perhaps another name he may have checked in under?"

"Nope, he…um, he wouldn't do that. He said he was staying here at the Albion."

A closed, condescending smile steals across the man's face. "Sir," he says, "this is the *Bellingham*. The Albion is on Cathedral Street."

"Ah, hell!" I let out a big laugh. "Well, that explains that. Cathedral Street, you say?"

"Yes, Cathedral. Not far from here. You go down North Charles, right onto West Eager, and then Cathedral will be your second left."

I repeat his directions. "Sounds easy enough," I say.

He smiles at me and I walk away from the desk, but before going far, I stop and turn back to him. "Say, pal, I don't suppose you've got a restroom here I could use?"

"Why yes, it's just down that way."

"Thanks. You have a good night now."

I walk in the direction he's pointed, but then zip over to the elevator. The kid operating is a different kid than before. When he spots me, he straightens up and pulls his finger out of his nose, in that order. He puts his working hand in his pocket and a flush splotches across his cheeks. "Good evening. W-what floor, sir?"

"I'm not actually sure," I tell him, stepping in close. "A friend of mine just came up here a second ago. I forgot his room number, though. Maybe you remember him? He's about my height, wearing a burgundy suit with a matching hat. You must have just taken him up."

The kid clears his throat. Before he gets a word out, I lift up his goofy little pencil-eraser hat and pop a dollar underneath it. "Come on, kid. He's a pal," I say, at the same time giving my glasses a little push up the bridge of my nose to draw attention to them.

The kid looks to his left, then to his right, probably letting both devil and angel plead their cases. He gulps, then reaches past me and pulls the gate shut. "Floor ten."

We ride up in silence and I exit without a parting word. The gate clacks shut behind me, and a moment later, the elevator begins its cacophonous descent. The lingering silence that follows freezes me where I stand. My heart thumps double time. My breaths become fast and shallow.

What am I doing here?

At the end of the hall, a doorknob turns, clicks, and a door squeaks open. A woman steps out from the open door. An electric shudder spreads through me. Genevieve? The hallway is so dim. Is it her? She closes the door and locks it and starts walking toward me. I'm paralyzed. Little puddles of light pour from the lamps mounted outside of each door, giving the darkness in between a grainy texture. She steps through light and dark, light and dark, becoming dimmer and clearer, dimmer and clearer as she nears me. Does she recognize me? Will she? Of course she will. The tap of her heels grows louder. The short void between each step is filled with the frantic thumping of my heart. I can feel it pounding in my ears, pulsing through the vein on my forehead like an angry river. She's two light-puddles away from me.

Tap tap tap.

One puddle. Her hair, not the inky black I'm used to.

Tap tap tap.

Her hair is a deep, dark red. Thank Christ. Not Genevieve.

She—whoever *she* is—passes me without so much as a glance and pushes the elevator call button. My heart slows down half a notch. I start down the hall in the direction she'd just come from, moving slow because it occurs to me that I have no idea which room Andrew is in, and if she doesn't step into the elevator before I reach the end of the hall, well, that sort of thing might look suspicious. A man walking down a hallway, pausing, then turning around and walking back… that's the sort of thing you might mention to whoever's at the front desk while you're on your way out for a night on the town.

I'm three rooms from the end of the hall when I hear the ding of a bell, followed by the metallic slide and clamorous halting of accordion doors. A second later, I hear the same two noises, then the familiar fading ruckus that accompanies a descent. For now, I'm alone.

At the end of the hallway is a window looking out on an alley. Making sure to keep quiet, I try lifting it open. It doesn't budge at first, but a few upward jerks crack it and I'm able to get my fingers between the window and the sill. I pull up, not opening it all the way, but just enough for me to fit through and get out onto the fire escape. Once I'm out, I slide the window back down, leaving only enough space for me to fit my pinky in on my way back.

On my way back from ending a man's life.

It's cool outside. My eyes need a minute to adjust to the darkness. Once everything takes shape, I scan the alley a few times. No one else is here. From where I stand, I can only see one room's window—the room that the redhead came from—and its lights are off. To get access to any of the other rooms on the tenth floor, I'll have to climb over the fire escape railing, onto the stone ledge that stretches around the building, and shimmy around the corner where I hope to find more fire escapes waiting for me. The ledge sticks out about eight inches. The bricks that the outer walls are made of look like they'll allow me a little bit of grip, but what's most important is that I make sure to keep my chest pressed as close to the wall as I'm able to. There's a breeze, but only a light one. Nothing I can't handle.

I step over the fire escape gate and wipe my hands off on my pants, one at a time. Some chalk would be great right about now, but if I was going to stand here and list off everything that would be great right about now, well, I'd be here until the second coming. I reach out with my right hand and find a good spot on the wall to press my fingertips into, keeping my left gripped around the rail of the fire escape's gate. I extend my right foot onto the stone ledge, which is about half a foot lower than the fire escape, and once I've got it safely on there, I let go with my left hand and begin to ease my chest against the wall, carefully moving my other two limbs out to join me.

Looking at a ledge and standing on a ledge are two very different experiences. I don't start moving right away. I need a moment to situate myself, to get used to the ledge. The breeze feels colder out here than it did standing on the fire escape. My hands, stiff and white, are already beginning to feel the chill. I dig the tips of my fingers into the wall and start shuffling along, my toes and the balls of my feet flat on the ledge, my heels standing on air; ladies and gentlemen, Mister Angel!

The cold nipping at my hands rushes me a bit; I make it to the corner of the building pretty fast. Rounding the corner, though, that's a move you don't want to be hasty with. I press my body harder into the wall and, once my right side runs out of wall to lean on, reach one foot and one hand around the corner. My hand finds a spot, no problem, but the tip of my foot scrapes the ledge. Before my brain has time to realize the ramifications of such peril, I shove the foot forward against the wall. I'm hugging the intersection of two different sides of the same building. I then slide my left half around the corner. Not quite a cake walk, but almost.

The window closest to me is dark. It's the redhead's, too. The windows after that go lights on, lights off, lights off, lights on. Andrew's got to be in one of the lit rooms. Each window has a fire escape outside of it. The fire escapes aren't connected, but I won't have any trouble taking the ledge from one to the next.

So that's just what I do.

Shuffle, hoist, climb, shuffle.

I crouch low when I reach the fire escape outside the first lit room. I can hear people talking from inside, but the closed window and the soft whoosh of the breeze muffles the voices so I can't make out what's being said. Keeping low, I move past the window, so that I'm right against the gate of the fire escape. From there, I sit up—just a little—so I can get an angle on the place. In the sliver I'm privy to is the animated torso and arms of a heavyset man in his undershirt. He's moving his arms around like he's trying to make a point, and his gut, which looks host to a couple of bowling balls, is bouncing along with each movement. There's a woman standing in front of him, but the glimpses of her that I see are subject to the whims of the man's moving arms. The next lit window is two rooms down. I hop the gate onto the ledge and make my way to the next fire escape. Just as I'm about to hoist myself up, the window of the dark room comes open a crack.

"Get some fresh air in here." The words are almost carried off by the swirling night air, but the voice...I know that voice! One second later—*just one measly second!*—and Andrew would have opened the window right in time to see me climbing over the gate! My feet are still on the ledge, but both hands are wrapped around the lower part of the fire escape gate. I stay dead still. I don't know if he's still by the window, but if he is—even the slightest movement of my hands could be enough to catch his eye and...

And I won't even think about that.

Dead still. Dead still for a minute. Two. Five. More.

My hands are entirely numb when I finally get the nerve to pull them from the gate and back to the wall of the building. Who was he talking to? Anyone? No one? I didn't hear any response when he spoke—not a peep—but who's to say that meant a damn thing at all?

I wait a minute longer and then place my hands back on the lowest of the gate's three horizontal bars. Slowly, I pull myself up so that my feet are on the floor. On all of the previous fire escapes, I'd gone over the top bar of the gate. This time, I poke my head in the gap between the second and top bar and then snake through, bringing myself inside the gate.

The window is only open a few inches. It's still dark inside, and I've heard nothing since Andrew opened the window however many minutes ago. I don't know where I found the courage to sit up enough to peer in, but wherever inside me that courage came from, I knew it was the sort of thing that a person could use once and once only, the sort of thing that's plucked from soil that turns salty and barren the instant the lone vine feels a tug.

In the half-second glance I take, I see a bed with the lump of a person on it, a nightstand with a half-empty bottle of something on it, and a chair in the corner with a suit draped over it. The bathroom door is closed, but the light has been left on, and the beam it casts touches just enough of the corner chair to show me that the suit resting there is the same one Andrew was wearing when I spotted him outside the drugstore earlier tonight. I sink back down, out of view, and wait.

Minutes pass and not one sound comes from the room. When I sit back up and take a quick look in, I see that nothing has changed. The bathroom light is still on, the door still closed. The shape on the bed is moving up and down with the sort of steady breath that comes from someone in a deep sleep. My eye moves to the bottle on the nightstand. The dumb bastard was probably half drunk when I spotted him earlier. He probably came back to the room, took a few swigs, and passed out like a bag of bricks. It's a wonder he managed to get himself under the covers.

I give the window the slightest push up, moving it only about an inch at first to make sure that it doesn't squeak or anything. A light snore drifts out through the widened gap. I push the window up a bit more. Then a bit more.

I've got to be quick about it. In and out. I've got to be quick so that the bubbling mass of fear—and maybe reason—in my stomach doesn't have time to climb up to my brain.

In and out.

The window is open wide enough for me to crawl in. So that's what I do.

I'd gotten used to outside the building—the October wind's shushing, the clamour of cars from the street around the block, the infinite hum that every city seems to have if you know to listen for it—so the quiet that greets me once I spill into the room is a bit jarring. Steady breathing accompanied by an intermittent snore, the faint whir of a ceiling fan left on in another room. I'm down on all fours. With my right hand, I reach into my jacket and take out my flick knife. Light from somewhere behind me, somewhere outside, catches the tip of the blade when I open it. For a second, I'm mesmerized by the tiny shining star glinting on the steel in my hand. But then...

In and out.

I stand up and move over to the side of the bed, my hand tightening around the knife handle. Andrew is sprawled across the bed, lying on a sort of diagonal slant. His head, covered by the bedsheet, is barely touching the pillow closest to me. His feet poke out from the covers on the bottom corner on the opposite side. Sunnyside down, his back rises and falls with each deep breath. I plant my hand on the back of his head and plunge the knife into the side of his neck. His body jolts. Every limb thrashes. He tries to roll over to face me, so I put more pressure on the back of his head and dish out three more stabs: two in the side, as close to his stomach as I can reach, and one square in the back.

His body tenses, but he's shaking like he's plugged into a generator. Pools of blood expand across the blue bedsheets. A sickening, desperate gurgle that I know I will never forget for as long as I live escapes him. I give him another one in the side. Then another, and another. In and out.

How the hell is he *still* moving? Tremors race through my arms. For one second, I'm lighter than air. My grip on the knife slackens. The pressure I'm putting on him goes down.

Andrew is jerking about like a fucking spastic, tangling himself up in the sheets.

My God, all the blood.

How the hell is he still moving?!

He manages to roll over onto his back. I hammer the blade into his chest twice. I'm on top of him now. When the hell did I get on top of him? His arms have found their way up from under the covers. I feel his hands clasp my shoulders, but they're weak, useless. I swing my arms out, whipping his hands off of me. They fall away, limp.

I push myself up from the bed. The sheets move with me; I've managed to get myself tangled, too. When I twist free, I see his face for the first time. His mouth gaping, blood trickling like water from a broken faucet; his tongue pokes out and his face is frozen in a rigid expression of terror.

And I'm being stared at. The eyes on me are wide and confused. They are misty—wet with tears from a well that will never be pumped again—and they are lifeless. They are also not Andrew's.

The bathroom door clicks open.

FAST AS HELL. THE STAIRS ARE STEEP. THEY'RE HALF-ladder. I'm surprised I don't trip over my feet and tumble down face-first.

I have two flights to go. I'm halfway down the first set when I hear the scream. Andrew's scream. It spears me. I jump down to the last balcony, landing with a metallic rattle. Fuck the stairs. I hop the railing. The drop is longer than it looked pre-jump. When I hit the street, I tumble and roll, shoulder to concrete. I know how to land. Shoulder to concrete: it hurts, but I know how to land.

He'll be looking out the window now. He'll see me getting to my feet. I get up and charge left, toward the street.

"Help! Jesus Christ, somebody help!" His scream is sharp, cutting. It makes the night that much colder. "STOP HIM!" His voice cracks into a sob: "Somebody fucking stop him!"

Together, the Bellingham and the brown-brick office on the other side of the alley frame the street. I force myself to slow down when I get close. Rushing into a crowd isn't the sort of thing you do when there's someone screaming for help in the darkness behind you. The infinite city din greets me when I cross the threshold between street and alley. It's not much noise, but it's enough. I can still hear Andrew scream-ing in the swelling distance, mind you, but I'm listening for it. The street isn't busy, but it isn't empty. An older man standing across the street shoots me a look. I go to pull my hat down.

Fuck.

No hat. It would have either fallen off in the alley or in the hotel room. Either one is bad news. But one is worse news. I try to push the thought out of my head.

I notice my hands shaking.

What the hell is that old man staring at?

I turn my foiled hat adjustment into a forehead scratch. I check to make sure my glasses are still there and then turn left as nonchalantly as I can and start down the block, toward the front of the Bellingham.

The door is opened for me when I hit the first step. The doorman smiles and says, "Good evening, sir." I don't want to appear in a hurry, but I don't know how fast word will reach the lobby. If it hasn't already.

I nod and smile, accept a good evening and wish one back. I'm halfway up the stairs when I notice the wetness on my right hand. I shove the hand into my coat pocket, then use it to open the coat so I can reach into the inside pocket with my shaky left. My hand doesn't go in too far. The knife is taking up most of the pocket space. I forgot to close it, but at least I remembered to take it with me. One less thing to worry about.

There's a small group of five or six men and women chat-ting with a bellhop. I walk around them, using their uniformly plump suit and gown-clad bodies as a curtain so I don't have to walk directly past the front desk. The man behind the desk is on the telephone. He's not talking, he's only listening. His expression is grave.

I slow down a bit when I see that the elevator door is open. Two guests and the same operator who took me up earlier stand in the doorway. A bell dings a moment later. The door closes. I quicken my pace and push through the door that leads to the staircase.

I half expect to run into Andrew on my sprint up to my room on the sixth floor. But I don't. I don't run into anybody. A quick look left, then right, and I rush to my door, fumbling—and nearly dropping—the key twice before I get in and close the door behind me. I twist the deadbolt and slide the chain lock. I push the sick feeling that's been creeping over me back as far as I can and rush to the bathroom.

These goddamn shakes won't let up. When I lift the lid off the toilet tank, I nearly drop it against the sink—Christ, what a thing to do! *Hello? Front desk? I don't know if it has anything to do with the murder a couple floors up, but a loud crashing sound jut came from the room next to me. It sounded like something breaking.* I place the lid on the bathroom floor, then start undressing. My clothes are pasted to my body. I peel my shirt and pants off like half-set wallpaper, then place them along with my glasses and jacket into the toilet tank. The lid doesn't go on all the way, so I take both hands and give everything a hard shove down. That does it.

Instinct takes me to the shower, but common sense gets me out. A shower during a time like this? All that noise? Water rocketing up, from the boiler room to the sixth floor, through a maze of metal pipes, hissing so loud it can be heard from the end of the hall. If the cops haven't arrived at the hotel already, they will any minute now. The sound of a shower might be just the kind of thing that'd tip them off. I turn the bathroom sink tap to a drizzle and give it a minute to warm up, then I wash my hands, my face, and my neck, working up a foamy lather with the cheap hotel soap. Why is it that even nice hotels have the cheapest, shittiest soap? I dry off quickly and put my fresh suit on. I move to the mirror and check myself over. No blood. I'm quite pale, and anyone who knew me might think I look maybe a little tired, but there's no blood. I double and then triple check; definitely no blood.

The elevator doesn't show. I didn't want to take the stairs down—thought it might look shifty, a guy avoiding the elevator after someone had just been…

During a time like this.

I give it another minute and then take the stairs.

That sick feeling's a persistent bastard. Something about the echoing tap of my footsteps bouncing around the concrete stairwell makes it worse. I'm thankful for railings.

The lobby's buzz can be heard two flights up.

Because I have to, I pull myself together before pushing through the door.

Holy hell, what a scene to walk into!

Newspaper men. A horde of gossips bouncing around like molecules. A medic tending to an unconscious woman who looks to have fainted in her husband's arms. I spot two police officers, notepads out, interviewing guests on opposite ends of the lobby. The front desk clerk is pacing back and forth, back and forth, like he's supposed to be tending to something but he's not sure what. I move through the crowd, not rushing, but not slow enough to rouse suspicion, taking in snippets of chatter on my way.

"...and in a classy place like this. My God!"

"...heard it was a suicide."

"...resisting arrest. They'll probably drag him through here any minute."

A bunch of curious men and women are peering in the front window. For the moment, the door to the street is unattended. My first thought is that the doorman is being interviewed by police. You'd think he'd be one of the first ones they talk to. *Who came in? Who came out?* But as I near the door, I see the doorman is out on the street, doing his best to shoo away all the nosy folks congregating outside.

Another black-and-white (there are two that I can see already parked) pulls up in front of the hotel as I step out. I make my way down the steps, doing my best to look like I've no clue what all the fuss is over, like I'm rather annoyed by all this racket. The cop who just pulled up steps out of his cruiser, kicking the door closed with such force that the vehicle gives a little wiggle when door meets jamb. He looks at the gathering crowd. His face is a carved hunk of wood that someone gave up on. His hands are clenched into fists, and his neck is hunched forward in a way that reminds me of a wolf getting ready to pounce. He looks at me. He opens his mouth to say something, but then someone from the crowd shouts, "Hey, officer, you want to tell us what the hell is going on in there?"

The cop doesn't like that one bit; he's the one who asks the questions. He turns in the direction the voice came from. Looking at the bunch, it takes about two seconds to figure out who the smart ass is. He's wearing a checkered suit and a face full of regret. Everyone is looking at him in a better-him-than-me way. That's my out. I weave around a few scattered onlookers and head up the street. I don't look back once.

After walking a couple blocks, I flag a cab. "Where's a decent place to grab a drink?" My voice cracks as I speak. The way the words tumble out, forced, rigid, I sound like a Martian taking his first stab at earth chatter.

"There's a bunch of decent places around here. What kinda—"

"Not around here. I'm sick of this area. You know anything on the other side of the expressway?" This time I sound more natural. The driver scrunches his face. You can tell the gears need some grease.

"There's a nice little place on East Lafayette," he says a moment later.

"Sounds perfect."

He shrugs, turns around, and pulls into traffic.

He's not the chatty kind of cabbie, which suits me fine. No small talk bullshit, just one man taking another from Point A to Point B. No need to exchange life stories, or even pleasantries. No need for any exchange beyond the two dollars I hand him when we reach my destination. The sign outside the place casts a sickly blue neon glow on the sidewalk. I think about baptism as I pass through it and enter the tavern. It's neither busy nor dead. A waitress smiles at me and tells me I can sit wherever I like, so I head to a small corner table. I look the drinks menu over without actually reading it. When a different waitress comes by a moment later, I order a double gin on ice.

By the third drink, my nerves begin to settle. But with the settling of nerves, my mind begins to race.

How long do I wait? Will cops be scouring every inch of the hotel, knocking on every door and interviewing every man, woman, and child registered? Did anyone spot me? Yes. Yes, someone did. There was an old man staring at me from across the street when I came out from the alley. I remember. He was staring at me when I went to pull my hat down, only to find it gone. Where did that damn hat end up, anyway? I was wearing it when I climbed out onto the fire escape, wasn't I? Yes, I'm sure of it. So where did it go? Had it blown off my head? It's possible. There was a breeze, and if the hat blew off, I might have been too preoccupied to notice. Or maybe it fell off when I was in the room. Christ, if that were the case...

Maybe I'm worrying about nothing. A hat in a room. So what? What's so suspicious about a hat in a room? A hat seems pretty inconsequential when you put it next to a dead body. A dead body and a live one, too. A hat is the least suspicious part of that picture. And that's if the hat is even in the room at all. It's got to be in the alley, and in that case, so what? A hat in the alley: it blew off some guy's head—any guy's head! A hat in an alley means jack.

But then there's the matter of my clothes. Crammed into the toilet tank in my room. I need a bag. A sturdy plastic one. But where would I get one at this hour?

"Can I get you another?"

I look up at the waitress. She looks like she's reached that point in her shift where even the faintest smile is too much of a burden. "Another drink?" she says, gesturing with her head at my empty glass.

"Yes, thank you. I'll have another."

Without responding, she turns and heads toward the bar. Something about her walk is funny. She's not quite limping, but the way she moves, you'd think she were walking across hot coals. My eyes move down her backside, down her legs, to her feet: there's the problem. The high heels she's wearing are the source of the torture. A plastic bandage pokes out of the back of each shoe.

The room has thinned out a bit now. Everyone in here looks distinctly middle class. There are a few dates, a few double dates. A few other lone drinkers like myself, men and women who don't look happy to be here, but who also don't want to leave just yet; wherever they're from or wherever they're going, here is better than there for the time being. A few tables down from me, a salesman type is dabbing at his tie with a napkin. There are a couple little puddles on the table in front of him and a larger puddle around his half-empty beer glass. Something occurs to me.

"Miss!" I shout, "Excuse me, Miss!" The waitress whips around and shoots me an irritated look. She comes over and stops at the edge of my table in a way that reminds me of the way a hockey player comes to a stop. "Yes, what is it?" Her tone is the accompanying spray of ice.

"I'm sorry, but could I please change my order?"

"I've already *placed* the order," she says. "Eddie's probably already poured the gin. The *double* gin. If you can't make up your mind about—"

"That's fine, I'll still take the gin. I'd just also like to order a beer."

She regards me for a moment, then: "Sure. I'll bring you a beer. What kinda beer you want?"

"Something good," I tell her.

"Sure. One of those, coming right up. With your double gin."

She brings both drinks over a minute later. I tell her thank you and she gives no indication that she hears me. I down the gin in quick mouthfuls. Once I'm down to ice, I slide the glass out of the way and take a sip of the beer. Whatever the hell it is, it isn't the something good I'd asked for. I take a few more sips, then take a quick look around the room to make sure no one's paying attention to me. No one is. Everyone sharing a table is chatting away and everyone sitting solo is staring down, either into their glass or at the empty chair across from them. The waitress is standing at the bar, leaning on the counter with her back to me. I take my glass—still at least two-thirds full—and pour it on my coat.

"Aw, goddamn it!" I groan. "Isn't that just great?" I look up at the waitress. She's already on her way over, cloth in hand. She's got this expression like she knew I was going to spill that drink five minutes before I even walked in here.

"Geez, I'm sorry, Miss."

"You forget where your mouth is?" She tosses me the cloth.

"I guess I must have." I take the cloth from her and start dabbing at my coat, where I'd tried to get all the beer. Some got on my lap, and, naturally, the table, and a bit got on my shirt, but my coat got most of it.

While I dab away, the waitress walks back to the bar. She returns a minute later with another cloth—this one wet—and starts wiping down the table. "You know," I say to her, raising the now sopping cloth she'd given me, "I appreciate this, but I'm not sure the cloth is going to do much good here. Do you think I could bring me a plastic trash bag to put my coat in?"

"I suppose so," she sighs. "And I think I'll bring you your cheque as well."

I check my watch. "Are you closing up soon?"

"I wish."

I pay my cheque and leave her a dime for her trouble.

I've got this queasy feeling in my gut the whole cab ride back. Relief washes over me when we round East Chase and I see that there are no black and whites parked in front of the Bellingham. The man at the front desk assures me that they will have my jacket cleaned for tomorrow morning when I leave. I ball the plastic bag up in my hand while he finds a hanger for the jacket. He makes no mention of what happened here earlier tonight. And, really, can you blame him?

When I get back to my room, I remove the lid from the tank, take out my dirty clothes, and place them in the plastic bag. I tie two tight knots and place the bag next to my suitcase. After a few hours and a few handfuls of rocks, it'll be sitting at the bottom of Druid Lake, out of my hands and out of my mind.

IT'S EARLY, AND STILL DARK WHEN I RETURN TO
Rowland's World Class Circus. I notice the unfamiliar car
as my lift pulls into the lot. It's parked on a sharp diagonal,
the way people park when they're in a rush and simply can't
be bothered. I step out of the clunky old pickup that brought
me back and go to take a closer look at the car, but Julian's
voice pulls my eyes away from the car. I look up and see him
charging toward me, a man possessed.

"Toby," he shouts, waving his arms at me. "Holy hell,
Toby!"

I quicken my pace to something just shy of a jog. When
I meet Julian, he is hunched forward, hands planted on bent
knees, supporting his upper half. "Toby...my God, you...you
wouldn't believe..."

"Easy, pal," I say, giving him a light pat on the shoulder,
"it's a lot easier to speak when you can breathe."

Julian nods and then takes a few seconds to catch his
breath. "The police are here, Toby," he says a moment later.
"There...there's been a murder!"

"Jesus Christ!" I say. "You better not be pulling my—"

"I'm not, Toby!" Julian insists, straightening up and looking me in the eye. "Two plainclothes officers got here about an hour ago. That's their car right there," he points out the mystery car, the black Chevrolet behind me. "They've been going around questioning people. I know they've spoken to Genevieve, and—"

"Julian," my voice comes out louder than I intend it, "are you saying someone from here *was* murdered, or someone from here *is* a murderer?"

"Both!" he shouts, grabbing my shoulders and giving me a light shake for emphasis. "Both!" he repeats.

"Who?" I ask.

"That Syc," he tells me. "What's his name...Reuben. No. Raymond?"

"Rupert?"

A spark of recognition flashes in Julian's eyes. "Rupert!" he says. "That's him!"

"Rupert was—"

"Killed, Toby! Rupert was stabbed to death last night in Baltimore, and they think your pal Andrew did it!"

I can feel the colour leave my face, as though a plug hidden beneath my chin has been tugged free and all but the sickliest white comes spilling out onto the dirty ground. "Did you say they were questioning Genevieve?" I manage after a moment.

"Yes. Genevieve, Rowland. The other Sycs. They're making their rounds, Toby."

"And they *know* Andrew did it?"

"How the hell would I know? You think they let me sit in on each session? Take notes?"

"Christ, Julian, you don't need to be that way. I meant... it's just hearing this...this whole thing threw me for a real loop."

"Not just you, Toby."

"All right, all right," I say, giving him a pat. I need to get out of sight before he clues in that I'm not cooped up in my trailer like I'm supposed to be. "Look, I think I need to take some time here. Go back to my trailer for a bit and make some coffee. Christ, to think—I mean, if it is what you say it is—to think we could have been working with a murderer all this time. Holy hell."

"Holy hell," Julian agrees.

SHIFTY-EYED MEN AND WOMEN CONGREGATE IN CLUSTERS,
talking in whispers to one another, hands obscuring mouths. Trailer windows are manned by snooping sentinels. Many gazes are geared toward Rowland's trailer. Nearing my trailer, I fumble my key out of my pocket. I'm almost at the steps when Gloria approaches, her hair a frazzled mess, her eyes bordered by dark, puffy circles. "Toby," she whispers and grabs for my arm. I flinch away. She gets the message. This time, she speaks even softer. "Toby, what happened in Baltimore?"

I don't answer her. It takes all the restraint I have not to grab her by the shoulders and give her a good shake. What the hell is wrong with her? Sneaking up on me like that. Approaching me out in the open at a time like this, suspicious eyes everywhere and two cops sniffing around the place. I walk up the stairs and open my door, motioning with my head for her to follow me inside. When she enters, I reach around her and tug the door shut. "Waiting outside my goddamn trailer—what's the matter with you? Do you have any idea how shifty that looks?"

"I-I'm sorry, Toby," Gloria snivels, "but I needed to know! I hardly slept a wink since you left for Baltimore. And since the police showed up this morning..." She can hardly keep herself together. "People—people are saying all kinds of things, Toby, th—"

"About *me*?"

"Well, no, no, not about you. About what happened with Andrew and that...*boy*. Oh, God, he was just a boy! And now...now..."

I grab hold of her face. "Damn it, Gloria, don't break down on me. Not here, damn it, not now. You can't do this right now, you understand?"

She nods yes, her hazel eyes wide, unblinking. She's afraid of me. "Y-yes. Yes, I understand, Toby," she says in a tremor of a whisper.

"Now, about Rup—about that Syc biting it. He wasn't supposed to. He wasn't supposed to be there at all. As far as I knew, it was just me and Andrew in that room. I thought it was only the two of us, you understand that? It was dark, and I thought it was only me and him, and what happened, well, what happened wasn't supposed to happen, but things can still work out for us, all right?"

Gloria nods.

"As far as I can tell, the cops have pinned the murder on Andrew. I mean, hell, how could they not? It happened in his hotel room, to a fella in his bed. Hell, the poor bastard probably even ended up with some of that Syc's blood on him. All we have to do now, me and you, is play it safe. You got that? Play it safe. We'll have to stop hanging around each other for a while. The last thing we want to do is rouse any suspicion. Right now, as far as I can tell, Andrew is taking the blame for this. Sure, I bumped the wrong guy, but shit happens, right? We make the best of the situation—he's taking the fall? He's ruined? Good enough for me. But the last thing we want is to fuck that up. Last thing we need is someone noticing how close that one pretty spec girl is with the clown. The clown who has a few damn good reasons to hate Andrew and who might be sore enough to set him up for a fall. Someone notices that and then notices that the two of us jump ship at the same time? It wouldn't take a genius to connect the dots."

Gloria nods. "All right, Toby," she whispers. "I can do that."

"I know you can." I open the door a crack and peep outside. No one around. Gloria comes up next to me and shoves the door shut.

"You won't leave without me, will you, Toby? You won't just take the money and split?"

I pull her close and give her a long kiss. "Never," I say once we've both come up for air. "Now get out."

THAT EVENING, ROWLAND CALLS A MEETING. EVERYONE—

and I mean everyone—has gathered in the area that was used as a parking lot for the audience during our stay here. Everyone, of course, except for Rupert, who is keeping cool on a slab somewhere in the city, and Andrew, who, I have since learned, is locked up in jail, presumably awaiting trial. Rowland is standing on top of the circus-owned 1945 Ford truck, eyeing the restless crowd before him, shushing with hand gestures and probably wondering if there's a single fish and a loaf of bread he can try anything fancy with under these odd circumstances. Gloria is standing close to the front with the other spec girls. I find a spot to stand off to the side, which I notice, too late, is right next to Genevieve.

"Hello, Toby." Her expression is sullen, but because she is who she is, she makes sullen look like an attractive face to be wearing. She's wrapped up tight—crossed arms, hands hugging her sides—in a forest-green cardigan, one leg straight, the other bent, creating a form that says, Get on with it.

"Hi, Genevieve." I'm unable to look directly at her while I speak. I shove my hands into my pockets. "Look, I. Whatever happened in Baltimore with Andrew, I know he and I had our differences, but I hope that you're—"

"Whatever happened?" she says, a snide thread running through her tone. "You're referring to the fact that *my* Andrew, who was going to the city under the pretense of hitting the track but was, in actuality, shacking up with—and subsequently murdering—a young man? Is that the 'whatever' you're referring to, Toby?"

I shrug. There are still a few people trickling in, joining the crowd. Rowland, looking more and more impatient, is waving for them to hurry it up. "Anyhow, I wanted to say that despite all of the bullshit that's happened between us the last little while, I hope you're doing all right."

Her body tenses and her mouth twists into a sickened line, as if a screw somewhere inside her had just been turned to its tightest. "I am *not* all right, Toby." I turn to face her, and for a second, I think I notice her eyes misting over. But whether they actually do or whether I'm merely imagining it, one forceful blink returns them to their status quo. She continues, "I'm not all right at all. My...partner, who is currently sitting in a jail cell, has been sneaking around on me for God knows how long. Bringing God knows *what* home with him." She looks down at her own body, moving her hands down to her hips and then looking away with a shudder before bringing them back up to her sides. "That son of a bitch has embarrassed me, he has left me without a performing partner, and for all I know, he has contaminated," she almost chokes on the word, "me."

Acting purely on instinct, I reach my arm around her. She lets it rest there for a second and then pulls away from me. I turn and look across the crowd, at Gloria, who is looking back at me, but the moment our eyes lock, she averts her gaze, turning and saying something to the spec girl next to her—Carol. I think that's her name.

"All right, now! Okay, let's quiet down here!" Rowland shouts. The chatter evaporates quicker than it normally would for Rowland. It's been a long day full of gossip and hearsay. I know Rowland well enough to know that despite the grim conditions, he's enjoying feeling like a leader right now. "I'm sure we all know what we've gathered here to discuss. Tragedy has befallen our little family." He takes off his hat and bows his head. I wonder how many times he practised that bit. A few of the men in the crowd remove their hats as well, but most don't. "Last night," Rowland continues, "our dear Robert was taken from us—"

"*Rupert*, you son of a bitch!" someone shouts up at him.

"Rupert. Yes, I'm sorry. Excuse the mix up. I'm under a lot of stress right now."

"Well, Rupert's under a lot of ground!" another voice hollers back, getting a couple laughs and twice as many gasps. The crowd starts to shift around a bit. I notice that one of the remaining Sycs is pushing his way toward the centre, to where the voice came from. A moment later, there are more gasps, a couple cheers. The crowd continues to stir. Someone yells, "Yeah, hit the smart-ass again!" but a few seconds later, the kafuffle comes to an end. The Syc makes his way to the periphery of the group. People are patting him on the back and saying, '*atta boy*, and *well done*.

"That's enough!" Rowland yells, stamping one foot on the roof of the truck. "By no means is this a time to joke around. Please, keep it together. We don't need any fights. Not today. Now, for those of you who haven't already heard, *Rupert* was killed last night in Baltimore. Many of circumstances are still unknown at this time, but—and it pains me to say this—but we do know that at the time, Rupert was in the company of Andrew."

More gasps from the crowd. Christ, what a misinformed bunch. Rowland raises his hands to shush. The crowd complies quickly. "At this time, Andrew is in police custody." Gasps. "I know little more about any specifics beyond that, but earlier today, the Baltimore Police asked that until they have sorted out some more details, that we stay put here." Groans. "Now, now! Come on, folks! Come on! I know it's an inconvenience, but the police still have some unanswered questions, and I believe there are some of you that they would like to interview—not that anyone here is a suspect, but because they need help piecing a few things together and some of you may have information that could assist them. So, for at least the next few days, we will remain where we are. We have been given permission to set the big top up again and put on a show. Even though that will make for a rather lengthy stay in one location, I'm hoping that the amount of attention the case has received so far will bring big crowds out and that we'll still be able to take in a fair share."

Rowland says thank you and dismisses us with a wave of his hands and the group crumbles, spreading their gossiping and grumbling in all different directions. Genevieve is no longer next to me. She's gone, and the hell if I know when she left. A hand grips my arm just as I'm about to head back to my trailer. Rowland.

"We need to talk," he says in a hushed voice.

"Do we?" I ask.

"Yes, Toby. We do. Can you come by my office in two hours?" His expression is severe.

"All right," I agree. "Two hours."

IT'S FULL DARK WHEN I LEAVE MY TRAILER TO MEET

Rowland. I spent the last couple hours—actually, more than a couple hours…Chet Rowland is a man who I don't mind making wait—counting out the money in my trailer.

I give three swift knocks on his door. As I wait for an answer, I hear the faint mummer of indiscernible voices from inside. A few seconds later, Rowland opens the door a crack and shoves his face out through the nearly too-slender gap. "Toby, my boy. Come in, come in." He peers over my shoulder, then left, right, before opening the door further and stepping aside so I can come in, come in. Once I'm inside, the door is hurriedly closed behind me, the deadbolt twisted. Genevieve is sitting with her back to me. Her arms are crossed, her head tilted forward.

"Hello," she says without turning.

Before I have time to say hello back, Rowland places a hand on my back and ushers me to the vacant chair next to Genevieve. I take a seat and he shuffles around to his desk and sits down opposite Genevieve and myself. "We have—" he begins, but then stops himself. He opens his desk drawer and brings out a bottle of scotch and three glasses. "Drink?"

Genevieve shakes her head no while I nod mine yes. I notice that two of the glasses don't look to have been cleaned properly. Each of them has lip marks around the brim. I reach across the desk and grab the clean—or I should say cleanest—looking glass for myself.

"Allow me." Rowland splashes some scotch into my glass, then does the same for himself. I continue to hold my glass out, and a second later he gets the idea and pours me some more. Stingy bastard.

Rowland and I both take a drink. Genevieve sighs and reaches for the bottle and the third glass. She's just about to pour herself a drink when she notices the lip marks on her glass. "Yuck," she mutters and places the empty glass on the desk, slides it across to Rowland, and then takes a drink right from the bottle. "Let's get on with it," she says.

"Right," Rowland agrees, then takes a big gulp of his drink, pauses, and nods, more at his desk than anyone in the room. "Toby," he begins, "Andrew is in some hot water. I know you know that, but what you don't know—what no one at this circus except for Genevieve and myself know—is that even though he's currently locked up in a jail cell in Baltimore, the two detectives I spoke with earlier today don't expect him to be convicted of murder. Now, that's not to say that he won't be charged with something—there's a mile-long list of things they could pin on him, given the…messiness of the whole situation—but what Genevieve and I learned earlier today was that the primary reason for keeping Andrew in custody at this time is for further questioning and maybe even more so for his own safety. See, although Andrew—and this information isn't to be shared—" he leans forward and cups a hand around his mouth as if he were whispering, "although Andrew was found alone in the room with the body of Rob… er, Ra…of the deceased, the police don't consider Andrew a suspect in the murder."

"They don't?" I reach for my drink and notice that my hands went and turned into a set of balled fists. I unclench them. My fingers have a slight shake to them as I take the glass. I drink a quick mouthful and then place my hands on my lap, out of view.

"No," Rowland continues. "From what I understand, they think that someone had broken into the room with the intent of killing Andrew as well as, um—"

"Rupert," Genevieve jumps in.

"Yes, with the intention to kill the both of them."

I nod. I nod because I don't think I can speak.

"Now, all in all, the detectives were pretty tight-lipped on the matter. I guess they have to be, don't they? But they did tell me that they have a suspect—or maybe they'd said person of interest—they're searching for. Apparently, a number of people had spotted Andrew and his companion at some nearby dive that was a known hangout for men with…er, those kinds of tastes. A few other patrons of this place had told the detectives that there was a man harassing Andrew and company outside the bar as they left for the night. Insults were hurled, threats were made, and the three of them got into a tussle. Anyway," Rowland waves his hands, "the question is, where does this leave us? For starters, as you know, we are stuck here until the police have finished their investigation. They didn't make clear to me whether that was because they still wanted to interview some of the folks here, or what, but whatever the reason, we are stuck here for a bit. The other matter that I need to address is the fact that while we are here, we need to be working. Right now, we should be on route to Philadelphia. After Philly, we're scheduled for three nights in New York. None of that is happening now. We're creeping toward the end of our touring year, and, I'll be frank, if we don't take in some serious money, we are collectively fucked. So, we need to be drawing crowds here for what I hope and pray is only a few more days, and we need to do this while one half of our headliners is imprisoned. Do you see where I'm going with this, Toby?"

The onslaught of information is too much for me right now. I feel like there's a traffic jam in my head. A few seconds walk by. Rowland gives me a funny look. "Toby, what I'm getting at is we're in a real tight spot. I've always been able to count on you to do what's best for the show, and, well, I guess that's what I'm asking of you right now. I need the two of you to headline the show. For at least a few nights. Now," Rowland holds up his hands in a defensive gesture, "I know you two are not on the best of terms, but I'm asking you, I'm begging you to find it in your hearts to either sort things out, or at the very least set it aside for a little while and do what we—*what everybody here*—needs you to do."

No one speaks for a minute. Genevieve has knotted herself up further. Hunched forward, her arms crossed tighter, her legs overlapping. She is looking away from me, at the wall. Rowland has found something fascinating to look at on his desk. I'm still at a loss for words, so I take another drink. Genevieve recoils at the noise my now-empty glass makes when I place it down in front of me. Because we haven't heard enough from him tonight, Rowland starts up again. "I forgot to mention that you will both be very well compensated for all this." Look at him, talking like the bunch of us have all just agreed on something. He eyes my empty glass and continues, "Genevieve, I should mention, has already agreed to participate, Toby. She does have a condition, mind you. Genevieve requires—"

"I can speak for myself, damn it."

Rowland holds up his defensive hands again and Genevieve unknots herself and sits up straight in her chair.

It's a funny thing to think of at the moment, but it dawns on me that anytime I've seen anyone else straighten up from a sitting slouch, they always do it in a sort of wiggling shuffle. When Genevieve does it, though, it's in one grace- ful movement. For the first time since this secret little ren- dezvous started, Genevieve turns and looks me in the eye. "Toby, I don't know what to make of this whole situation. I don't know where I'll be two months from now, but Rowland has…persuaded me to stick it out here for the remainder of the touring year. And to be fair, I owe this circus that much."

Rowland nods appreciatively.

"If that means performing with you," she continues, "well, then that's that. I'm not willing to forgive and forget, but I'm willing to set our troubles aside temporarily if it means keep- ing the show on its feet. I have one condition, though. I need you to be stone-cold sober the entire time. That mouthful of scotch you took a minute ago? That's your last drop until we're done. If you can't accommodate that, then forget it."

A few seconds pass before I answer. But in that few sec- onds, the traffic jam in my head decongests a little, leaving me with only one question to consider. Do I want to be a headliner again? For a few nights, do I want to climb back up that platform and do what I was born to do?

"Of course."

"Good." Genevieve slides her chair back and stands up, making to effort no hide the fact that she's been dying to make that move for probably this entire meeting. "We'll spend the day tomorrow working out a routine. Rowland has assured me that the big top will be back up by dawn and that we'll have the place to ourselves for the day. We won't per- form tomorrow—"

"Yes," Rowland cuts in, "we'll push the next show to two days from now. I know you'll still be rushing a bit, but you're both top-notch professionals. Even at your worst, you're bet- ter than most."

"You can quit with the ass-kissing, Rowland," Genevieve says. "We've both already agreed to go ahead with it." She turns to me. "Toby, if it's all right with you, I'd like to start early tomorrow morning."

"It's tomorrow morning now," I tell her.

She consults her wristwatch, nods once. "Right. Seven *this* morning, then. Rest up. We've got a lot to do."

THE CRISP OCTOBER BREEZE MOVES THROUGH THE makeshift streets and avenues of our trailer maze with a soft, ghostly whisper. Very few windows have lamps burning behind them at this hour. In the distance, I hear the cacophony of the big top going up. The barking of orders, the disgruntled chatter that accompanies late-night toil, the creaking of pulleys, the rustle of wind tonguing across limp canvas. I know I'm being followed back to my trailer. But tonight the marvellous clamour of the tent coming to life is enough to make me not care right away. When her fragile dancer's steps finally grow close enough that the hushed brushing of feet over dead and dying grass no longer blends in with the rest of the night, I turn around to greet Gloria. She freezes when she's spotted.

"What all did you hear?"

"Hear? I-I didn't, Toby. I'm sorry. I followed you to Rowland's trailer, but I didn't do any snooping beyond that."

I take a few steps and close the gap between us. "You remember what I said? About us playing it safe?"

"*I am* playing it safe. I'm looking out for myself."

"Goddamn it." I grab hold of her arm and hurry her to my trailer. "Shut the door. And lock it," I say as I feel around the table for the box of matches that I know is there somewhere. Once I get the lamp going, we both take a seat at the table. "Now, what the hell's got you so worried that you're sneaking around and following me like this?"

"Damn it, Toby, I'm scared! I mean, our whole plan—you come back here yesterday morning all flustered and telling me how things went south in Baltimore, saying we can't leave like we're supposed to and that you killed the wrong guy—"

"*Don't say that.* You *cannot* say those words, Gloria."

"I'm sorry!"

"And keep your damn voice down, would you?"

"I'm sorry!" she says only slightly quieter this time. "Can…can we have a drink before we talk about this?"

I get up and fetch the half-full bottle of gin and plunk it in front of her. "You have a drink. I don't need one right now."

Gloria gets up and finds her own glass. "I don't need one either," she says as she pours. "I want one. To calm me down. Christ." She takes a long drink, then another. Then she needs a refill. She takes a sip of the refill and sits back down, content to nurse it for the time being. "Like I was saying," her tone is more cautious now, "things went south in Baltimore and now we have to deal with the change in plans. That's fine. I understand that, Toby. But I can't help but be at least a little worried—and can you blame me? First you tell me we can't be seen together for a while, and next thing I know, I catch you sneaking off to some secret meeting with Rowland and *Genevieve* of all people?"

"There's nothing to worry about," I assure her. "Everything's going to be fine. Rowland just told me that even though Andrew's locked up, the cops don't think he did it. Earlier that night, some chump got something started with him and Rupert, the Syc. I guess the bunch of them got in a fight and this fellow—whoever he is—made some threats, and boom! He's suspect number one."

"So there's no reason to think that they suspect you had anything to do with it?"

"That's right."

"But what about Andrew? I mean, the reason we went to all this trouble in the first place was so we could bump him off before we skipped out of here."

"Yeah. Yeah, that part isn't ideal, but it's not so bad. As far as I can tell, he's through here. Ruined. Genevieve seems like she loathes him now. You should see it. The way she cringes at the mention of his name. I figure, at most, she'll finish the touring season with him if she can stand it, but after that, he's done." Gloria smiles at that and takes another sip of her drink. Her smile is quick to fade, though.

"Why was she with you tonight in Rowland's office?"

"Rowland needs the two of us to headline the show for a couple nights until Andrew gets back."

"*What?* The two of you, headlining—well, you can say no, can't you?"

"Sure, I could say no, but I don't see why I would do that."

"Why the hell not?"

"Will you tone it down a notch here? Holy hell. For one thing, I don't want to do anything that'd throw any suspicion on us. Rowland knows I'm the kind of guy who'd do whatever needs to get done if it's best for the show. He and I aren't pals or anything—far from it, and you know that—but I think it'd look fishy if I just up and left after all that's happened. Besides, I don't even think we can leave here until the police have given the go-ahead to do so. So if I've got to stay here and if Rowland wants me to headline, then that's what I ought to do."

Gloria nudges her chair back, crosses her legs, and looks away, her drink cradled safely in her hands. "I'm sure that's the only reason you want to headline," she says with a roll of her eyes.

"Well, I'd be lying if I said the idea of headlining a couple nights wasn't part of the appeal. But that's just icing, Gloria. The main reason I'm going ahead with it is because it'll make sure we don't have any heat on us when we ditch this place."

"Right." There's that eye roll again.

"Yeah. That *is* right." Out of instinct, I grab the bottle. I raise it about an inch off the table before I realize what I'm doing and set it back down.

"You don't want a drink?"

"It's not that I don't want one. I don't think I should have one. Need to be tip-top first thing tomorrow morning."

"Yeah," Gloria mumbles, "better make sure you're tip-top for that bitch."

"Aw, Christ, would you give it a rest? The reason I'm doing this—the *main* reason—is because it's the smartest move for us. Do you not understand that? I don't like the idea of working with Genevieve any more than you do, but if I just stick it out for two or three shows, we can still walk out of here in a few days with the money. And actually, it'll be more money than we've already got. Rowland is paying me a pretty penny to go through with this. Really, you're benefiting from this just as much as I am—maybe even more, considering that you don't need to do the work—so I'd appreciate it if you'd lay off with the goddamn attitude."

After mulling it over for a few seconds and a few sips, she says, "Fine."

I grab her hand and give it a squeeze. "Thank you."

"You don't have to thank me," she says with a hint of reluctance. "It's late and you've got an early start tomorrow. I should go."

"All right."

I walk her to the door. She gives me a kiss and then leaves without saying another word.

IGET UP A FEW HOURS LATER AFTER A NIGHT OF TOSSING
and turning and not really getting much sleep. Or maybe
I didn't get any sleep at all. I'm not sure. For all I know, I
closed my eyes and slept a quick, dreamless sleep, only to
return to consciousness minutes later and commence my fidgeting. Or maybe I slept all night, but I dreamed that I was
lying awake in bed. Who the hell knows? The mind is funny
like that. Something could have only just happened to you
and your recollection can be mint, or it can be spottier than a
litter of Dalmatians. When you've spent a night teetering on
the cusp of sleep, you can go through your entire day—sometimes even longer—thinking that whatever you dreamed
about really happened until something triggers a thought
and makes you believe otherwise. Once I got up this morning, as I cleaned myself up and got dressed, left my trailer and
got some breakfast, I found myself bouncing back and forth
as to why I was up that early in the first place. One second I'd
be thinking, Sure is something that I'm getting ready to go
work with Genevieve after all this time, and the next second

I'd think, Odd that I'd have a dream where Genevieve and I agreed to work together again.

At any rate, despite my lack of rest, by the time I've eaten a small breakfast, I feel as fresh as ever. The sun is still inching up as I make my way to the big top a few minutes before seven.

The flap has been pinned open; she must already be here. Must be eager to get started. I step inside and see Genevieve sitting on the ground, leaning forward, stretching with her legs spread out in a wide V. Her hair is tied up with a kerchief that matches her navy blue shorts. She is wearing a black swimsuit top covered with white polka dots. The audience's door, which is much wider than the performers', is pinned open too, so the whole place is lit with a cozy, ethereal glow. With the exception of Rowland, who's standing a few feet from Genevieve puffing away on a cigar, the place looks perfect.

"Top of the morning to ya," Rowland says. I don't know if he's trying to be cute or funny or chummy or what.

"I didn't realize that you wanted this to be a three-piece act."

Rowland barks a laugh. "I don't think you'd be able to keep up with me." He lets that remark hang for a moment, then says, "I'll be out of your hair in a second, but I just wanted to pop by and see that things get off to a good start."

"They won't get off to any start until you march out of here."

"Yes, yes. Thank you, Toby. I always appreciate your subtlety." He pauses for a beat, then tugs on the lapel of his jacket. "Is seven hundred each reasonable? I can tell you right now that I think it is, but I'm not the one putting on the performance."

"That's fine with me," Genevieve says, her tone carrying a hint of indifference.

"Me too." I try to mask my surprise. Seven hundred? I hadn't given the money much thought really, but I sure wouldn't have figured it'd be that much.

"Good, then. I'll leave you two to it. Just remember not to overexert yourselves—I know neither of you is rusty, but given how long it's been since you worked together, I want you to make sure you're doing a straightforward, *safe* routine." He starts to make his exit, but as he's leaving, he tags another point onto his goodbye. "Especially since we're not using the safety net."

"Hold it, Rowland," Genevieve commands. Rowland obliges, freezing in his tracks, his back to us. "You've somehow got it in your thick head that we're going to do this without a net?"

"You and Andrew perform without a net. And Toby, if I may say so, is a far superior acrobat," Rowland says to us over his shoulder.

Genevieve walks around Rowland so that she's in front of him. She pokes her index finger into his gut with such force, I'm surprised some of his breakfast doesn't come shooting up. "You son of a bitch. This has nothing to do with Toby's skill. Andrew and I do a simple act and we know each other's moves inside and out—*that's* why we're able to perform without a net."

"But I would expect that you and Toby would come up with a new routine that is equally simplistic and no less dazzling."

"*In a day?*"

"You're both professionals."

"You're even more full of shit than I thought," I tell him.

"Am I?" Rowland shouts. "We've already done a run of shows here. Do you realize how difficult it will be to fill this place for another two, three—hell, maybe more—nights? If we can't give them more than we have the previous shows, we've got to at least match the standard that we set. You and Andrew," he points his finger at Genevieve, "did your act without a net. How are we supposed to entice people to come? 'You've seen acrobats without a net, now, Rowland's World Class Circus is proud to present: two acrobats performing *with* the safety of a fucking net!'"

"Well, I wouldn't make that your pitch," I say.

"And I'm giving you seven hundred dollars each!" he says, stomping his feet.

"You think the money matters that much? Rowland, you could give me ten thousand dollars a show—if it's me and

Toby up there, I will not perform without a net! Now, you can pay us less and still get a good performance with a net, or you can just not pay us at all and we won't have to worry about performing. Your choice, buster. At this point, I'm fine either way."

Rowland's face goes through a couple different shades, all of which remind me of different root vegetables. "Five hundred each," he growls after some consideration, "and you can keep your precious net." With that, he straightens his lapels yet again and then marches—*actually fucking marches*—out the audience's entrance, grumbling all the way.

It takes close to an hour to get the net set up. Genevieve sticks around for the length of one cigarette, then takes off somewhere. I stick around and oversee the whole operation, puffing my way through almost half a pack before the damn thing is ready to go. When the five crewmen leave through the audience's door, Genevieve enters through the performers' flap. "A bit of a later start than I was planning for." She sticks her arms out and arches her back, then winds her torso from side to side like a kid playing airplane.

"You and me both."

"Let's waste no more time, then. For obvious reasons, we'll need to keep this simple. We'll have to stick to a limited repertoire of manoeuvres. I was thinking we could do a back-end planche, a layout half—those ones always worked well in the past. The double angel return is one I think we could pull off, but let's see how the easier ones are for us and decide from there."

I nod along. "If we do a double angel—which I think we'll be fine with—we should make that as complicated as it gets."

"Of course."

"What about a whip?"

She thinks on that for a second. "A whip will be fine. Full twist?"

"That's what I was thinking."

The way we talk to each other is so different from the way it used to be—all rigid and business-like, as if we're two acrobats meeting for the first time, feeling each other out, which, in a sense, I guess we are. The way we talk feels different,

but standing under this roof with Genevieve, hashing out a
routine...

That part feels nice. That part feels right.

We come up with an order of manoeuvres, starting with
the elementary and working our way up the more complex,
which really aren't a fraction as complex as what we used
to do. Once we've got it all worked out, the two of us walk
toward the ladder.

I pause and motion for her to walk up first. She gives me
a nod that you could almost call cordial if you looked at it in
the right light. I start climbing once she's about halfway up.
Goosebumps sprout up all over me, moving in a wave further
and further across my body with each step climbed. When I
reach the top, I move the centre of the platform and look out,
my eyes moving from the rigging, then across to the other platform, then slowly down to the ground. Maybe I did fall asleep
after all. And what a beautiful dream to splash around in.

I look to Genevieve. She's clapping chalk onto her palms.
I walk over and do the same. She unhooks the bars from
where they are fastened against the frame and hands me one.
I start laughing. Real hard. At first, Genevieve just stares at
me, her face blank. But after a while, blank becomes confused, then confused becomes curious, and then next thing I
know, she's laughing along with me. Not as hard, mind you.
I'm practically doubling over by the time she gets going,
tears leaking from the corners of my eyes. But she is laughing. Laughing her darling laugh. It's a sound I haven't heard
in years, a sound I'd forgotten about altogether. And I didn't
know just how much I've been missing it until this moment,
when I was reminded that it even existed at all.

She recites the plan we came up with when we were on
the ground. "You got that?" she asks. I nod yes. "Then say it
back to me."

"We do a knee hang and then a backend planche. We
return to the platform and repeat that three more times."

"All right," she says, then she takes a second to brace herself and swings out.

I follow. The only nervousness I feel comes just as I step
off the platform, past the point of no return, but the feeling

washes away an instant later and the thrill of soaring replaces it.

During the first couple times, I can feel the tension in our limbs as we meet midair, but by the third run-through of the knee hang and backend planche, we move with the fluidity we moved with years ago. In the following set, we work on a layout half twist and a full twist whip. Both manoeuvres evolve to perfection in the same way the earlier two did—the first couple attempts going fine but being a bit rigid, and the following two being bang-on.

From there, we move to the double angel return. It's not a particularly difficult move to pull off, but as Genevieve and I stand on the platform talking through it before attempting, I notice a note of hesitation in her voice. A double angel requires me to flip her upside down by an arm and a leg and then return her to her bar. It takes some convincing, but eventually she caves. Her eyes are bright and eager as we discuss the timing of the manoeuvre. Our success up until this point seems to have instilled faith in her.

Again, I follow Genevieve off the platform. The manoeuvre goes off without a hitch on the first try. And as Genevieve leaves my arms and returns to her bar, an exclamation of glee escapes her. Like all the others, we practise the double angel three more times, and, after that, run every move a few more times, adding a couple new parts to the routine as we go.

It's sometime after noon when we decide to call it a day. I don't even realize how much my body aches until we've gone down the ladder and returned to the ground. And anyhow, it's a good ache. "That went well." I'm still catching my breath as we make our way to the performers' door.

"It did," she agrees, dabbing her towel on her chest, her forehead, the back of her neck as we cross the vast floor of the big top.

When we're just shy of the exit, I stop. When she notices, Genevieve stops as well. She turns to me. "What is it?"

"I, uh. I just wanted to say I'm sorry. About all you're going through with Andrew and all. I know that he and—"

"Don't, Toby." Ice dangles from each of her words.

"Look, I don't mean to—"

"Toby. Please, don't," she says, then turns and continues walking. "We'll run through it a couple more times tomorrow morning and that should do it. If things go half as smooth as they did today, we'll be in great shape for the show in the evening."

THE TWO OF US WERE GUZZLING BEERS, SITTING ON A fence that marked the border between private land and the field the circus set up in. It was dusk. The sun had fallen just behind the big top, back-lighting it in a way that made its boldest colours—the yellow on the flag at its peak and the swooping thick red and blue stripes that lined it—look stronger, more defiant, than ever. I felt like I was looking at a backdrop from a Hollywood movie.

Together, me and Wally watched the crowd funnel in. It was the first night in many that I wasn't performing.

"Because it's my home," Wally said. It was an answer to a question that I forgot I had even asked—*Why do you care so much about a place like this?* Maybe it was the couple beers that I'd already downed loosening my tongue, widening the gaps in my internal filter, but I hadn't meant it to sound so rude when I said it.

It was something that I'd wondered about for a long time. *Why?* I could understand if Wally had been a performer. If you're a performer, the answer is simple—you care because it takes care of you. It brings you the glory and the validation that, admit it or not, you are so desperately addicted to. But when you're not a performer, when you're stuffing suppositories into elephants' asses, or you're out on a cold, early morning hammering stakes into the ground until the skin on your chapped hands cracks open, or you're down on all fours in a vacant lot picking up litter—empty bottles, popcorn containers, dead balloons, shitty diapers ditched before the car ride back to the city—how do you do it?

Because it's home. That's how. Because it's home and you take care of your home.

"Yup," Wally said, but I got the sense he wasn't really speaking to me, "it's home right up until it's not."

I nodded. Wally popped the lids off two more beers and handed one to me. I hadn't finished the bottle I was working on, but when he handed the fresh one to me, I pounded what was left of it back as quick as I could. "Shame about your friend there," Wally said as I was catching my breath.

"Yeah, it is a shame." Clay had been goofing around on a horse late last night. For the life of me, I don't know what would have enticed Clay to go anywhere near a horse—he was very allergic to horses, and anytime I'd seen him get within ten feet of one, little red bumps would erupt all over his skin and he'd sneeze so hard and so often you'd think his head was going to explode. Anyhow, while I don't know what got him on the horse, I sure know what got him off. He'd been bucked and landed flat on his head, leaving him with a broken neck and leaving me down one performing partner. The doctor said that Clay likely wasn't paralyzed, but that a full recovery—if there was such a thing—would take a long time. If it hadn't been for Wally, though, Clay could have been much worse. Wally was the one who found him shortly after it happened, and the doctor said if Clay had ended up spending the night like he had landed—lying in the cold, damp grass in only his tights and an undershirt—he could have gotten hypothermia and died.

Wally and I stayed out there for the duration of the show, the cheers, the applause, the music all softened by the distance and carried over to us by the rambling night air. The two of us were flat-out drunk by the time the Fly De Lis, now boasting a third member—their daughter, Genevieve—closed the night. An unmistakable crashing of cymbals marked the end of their routine, and the audience trickled out into full dark shortly after, followed by Thunder and Blazes.

Noticing that that was our cue to hurry back in time for the barbecue and bonfire, Wally pulled two final beers from the leprous brown paper bag he had brought out with him, then balled the bag up and tossed it over the fence. He popped the caps off both, handed one to me, and we began to make our way. We didn't say much on the walk back. I was having trouble walking straight, but Wally seemed fine in that department. His only tell was the volume of his voice. Whenever he drank, his voice would rise and fall, rise and fall. One minute he'd be barking about everything wrong with the goddamn place (which was a list that covered topics ranging from the logistics of moving from one city to the next, to the existence of a secret hierarchy that decided the names of new animals coming to the circus), and the next he'd be mumbling in a manner that was so soft and guarded that the words he spoke couldn't have been for anyone but himself.

The fire was alive and raging when we arrived. Flames shot high from the tipi of burning wood, licking at everything around them like tongues sprouting up from hell, eager to get a taste of things to come. I don't know when Wally left my side, but by the time I felt the warmth of the fire on my face, he was gone. I stood there for a moment, enjoying the sobering heat, mesmerized by the movement of the flames. Then someone came along and gave me a slap on the arm.

Rowland's wrinkly face was scrunched into a drunken grin. His eyelids had jammed up at their halfway mark, and his mouth was trying to decide between three or four different makes of smile. I smelt the booze wafting from him and took a few steps back from the fire, realizing that at that moment, he and I had more corrosive potential than a human ought to have.

"C'mere," Rowland said to me.

"Where?"

He waved his hand, pointing nowhere specific. "Over there. With me. We have a meeting."

I followed him through the crowd of hungry performers and crew, taking a few pats on the back and a few more *Tough break about your partner, kid,* comments on the way. Rowland stopped near the edge of the fire's throbbing glow. He looked confused for a second, but then, scanning the crowd, saw who he was after and called out. "Hey...*hey!* Over here!"

Genevieve was at his side a moment later. He went to put his arm around her, but she deflected it, doing so with such subtle grace that even a drunken pig like Rowland couldn't be put off by the refusal. "You two have met, I presume?"

"No," she said, "I don't believe we've had a proper introduction in all this time."

"Tragedy," Rowland said.

She extended her hand. I reached out and shook it. "Toby. Very pleased to meet you."

"I'm Genevieve. And likewise, naturally."

Rowland clapped a hand on both of our backs. "You two are top-notch. You're top...top-notch, and I want..." he turned and belched over his shoulder and then paused, belched again, then stood completely still for another few seconds, looking rather worried. He relaxed again once it became clear that nothing more substantial was coming up. "I want you two to start training together once we hit Ottawa in a couple days," he said.

Genevieve flashed her smile at me for the first time. It was the kind of smile that didn't let go of you until it was good and done. The kind that pierced you with its pointy morphine tip and lulled you and carried you off. And you let it. No matter who you were, you let it. Because it belonged to a queen and because it made you feel so damn good.

THE MORNING IS A CAKE WALK. PROFESSIONALS—*true professionals*—are creatures of instinct. From the time we both step onto the platform, neither of us says a word. We don't have to. We run it, then we run it again. After the second time, Genevieve turns to me. "Let's not wear ourselves down. We've got it, Toby. We'll be fine tonight."

We climb down the ladder, first Genevieve, then me, and walk out of the big top together. Outside, we part ways without a word.

I stop by Rowland's and tell him we're good to go for tonight. I know he wouldn't have any doubts that we would be, but hearing the news from me gets him all giddy and chummy and over-the-top-thankful to the point that it seems phony. I get out of there as quick as I can and head to my trailer.

On the way over, I spot Gloria. She's sitting on a fold-out chair, flipping through a magazine—*Life*, I think—with her hair rolled up in curlers. She takes quick, modest puffs from a skinny little cigarette that pokes out from between her fingers. I walk over to her.

I pop a cigarette in my mouth. I can't find my lighter anywhere. Gloria sparks hers. She holds it up for me, but she doesn't
get up from her chair, so I have to bend down to light up.

"How are you doing?" I ask her once I've taken a few
puffs.

"I'm fine."

"Yeah?"

"All right, I'm anxious. But I'm fine."

"What's got you anxious?"

"What hasn't?" she almost laughs, but only almost. "A few
days ago, I figured you and I would be zooming down the
highway together by this time."

"So did I, but things change."

"Boy, do they ever." She hooks a loose strand of hair
behind her ear, then fidgets around in her chair and leans
forward. Before looking up to me, her eyes shift from side
to side a couple times. "I understand why we have to stick
around a little longer. It'd look shifty if we split right after
Andrew got caught up in that mess."

"Gloria, it's not just that we *should* stick around—*we have
to*. Police orders. Everyone in the circus stays here until they
give us the go-ahead."

"Right. Right. I get that, and it's fine. I just…it bothers me
that you're performing with her."

"Aw, come on, would ya? What am I supposed to do? I
don't like it any more than you do, but if we need to keep on
like everything's tickety-boo, then I don't really have much
choice, do I? It'd look suspicious if I were to say no to headlining for a few nights. Rowland knows how much it hurt
having that gig taken away from me in the first place. And
not only that, but the money he's throwing in—I'd be an idiot
not to take it, Gloria. An idiot."

In the moment she takes to mull it all over, I flick my cigarette stub away and get started on another, this time reaching down and snatching the lighter up off her lap.

"All right," she says. "All right. I'm sorry, Toby. It's just
nerves."

"It's all right," I tell her. I take a quick look around to
make sure no one's watching, then I lean in and plant a quick

one on her cheek. Her cheeks flush red right away. I've never done that before, kissed her out in the open like that. She smiles up at me and I smile back.

"What's a couple extra days, anyway?"

"Exactly," I say.

THE PARKING LOT IS NEARLY FULL AN HOUR BEFORE

the show starts. I don't know how they did it—whether it was rock-bottom admissions, two-for-one-entries, or whether I'll be performing to a tent full of hostages held at discreet gunpoint—but Rowland, and whatever razorbacks went back to Baltimore today, found a way to wrangle up enough of a crowd that it looks like we'll have a close to a sold-out show tonight. From the top step of my trailer, I watch them scurrying about like ants, hitting the concessions in mobs and stocking up on popcorn and drinks. I look at the big top. My eyes move to its highest point—the flag that stands on top of it, flapping in the wind like a pervert's tongue—and without warning, I puke all over the steps of my trailer.

It's a good puke, though. A healthy puke. Cathartic.

A few packs of stragglers quicken their pace when the first notes of the night are played. Children with balloons on sticks rush ahead of the crowd, their squeals cutting through the music and drifting over to me. I can't help but laugh.

Back inside, I put my tights on, then drop to the floor and do fifteen push-ups. I sit on the bed and sip some water and run my hand over my bristly head. It feels strange having this much hair before a performance. And no makeup. If this were any other night, I'd be dragging a razor across my scalp and getting ready to put the paint on. I'm leaving the clowning to the clowns tonight; Biff and Boppo and Mucko and Fucko. Have at it, boys.

I light a cigarette and do my stretches. I'm antsy. The trailer feels small. I throw on an undershirt and start making my way to the big top.

Julian and Eva, his substitute target, greet me. I think Eva usually dances with Gloria and the girls, but someone new was needed to fill in for Susan, who's been looking mighty pregnant lately. Thank God we had someone else with a

230

talent for getting knives thrown at them. "How does it feel, pal?" Julian says, cigarette smoke blowing from his nose as if he were a cartoon bull.

"Right," I say. "That's how it feels." He throws his head back and laughs.

"You're damn right it feels right!" he says. "I can't wait to see ya up there again, Toby!"

We stand there shooting the shit for a while. Eva stays with us. She laughs politely whenever we laugh, but her eyes keep drifting to Julian's knife belt, which lies on the ground a few feet away. Other performers pop by intermittently and tell me to break a leg and that they're excited for my act and all that.

As if on cue, Genevieve shows up right as Julian and Eva are announced by Rowland. The way she arrives, it's as if she materialized out of nowhere. She steps into the shard of light that's being cast from the opening in the big top, and my breath is snatched from me. "I thought it would be appropriate," she says, noticing my eyes moving up and down her. "I mean, if we're going to do this, we might as well match, don't you think?" Her old costume: a one-piece scarlet number covered in twinkling sequins, black boots with silver lightning bolts blasting down the sides. She's even done herself up the way she used to—a swooping black tidal wave of hair at the front, clouds billowing down each side, cat's eye makeup.

"If the shoe fits," I reply, realizing how stupid I sound about a second after the words leave my lips.

She ignores my response and goes to take a peek inside. "You feel ready?" she asks over her shoulder.

"Of course," I assure her.

She comes back over and takes my hand.

Neither of us hears Gloria sneak up.

I figure this is the sort of situation where the sooner someone speaks and gets things rolling, the better. "Hey, kiddo. Great set tonight," I say.

Gloria ignores me. She takes a couple steps toward Genevieve and I, stops, eyes us both. "I came by to wish you luck," she says.

I'm right about to thank her when Genevieve chimes in. "Honey," she says in a tone that is anything but honey, "luck has no place here. Luck is for the hopeless. When you're a performer of our class, you don't wish for luck. You don't wish for anything. You decide what you're going to do, and then you do it."

"Come on now," I say, "she just wants us to have a great show."

"And we're going to," Genevieve says, addressing me but looking—glaring—at Gloria. "With or without the aid of wishes."

Rowland's voice booms from the big top before I can get another word out. Without thinking, I turn and look in. I turn back a second later, just in time to see Gloria storm off.

"Toby, I wanted to thank you," Genevieve says, pulling my focus back to her.

From inside, Rowland shouts, "...but, ladies and gentlemen, never before have two angels pulled such devilish stunts!"

"You don't have to thank me," I tell her. "Truth be told, I'm just thrilled to be headlining again. Brief stint or not."

"...a man and a woman who laugh in the face of danger!"

"No, Toby, not for that. For what you tried to do for me."

"I don't understand."

"...gives me great pleasure to present to you..."

"For exposing that rotten son of a bitch Andrew for what he is."

"Mister and Missus Angel!"

The big top explodes. Shrapnel applause—Jesus Christ. I can't speak. Genevieve smiles. A warm, knowing smile. She leans in and plants a kiss on my cheek. I can't speak. She takes my hand and guides me toward the entrance. I take the lead once we enter the big top.

Right—that's how it feels.

We kill.

THERE'S A CLUSTER OF TREES A SHORT WALK FROM
the big top. They're the only trees in the field. They look
diseased. The stump I'm sitting on in the midst of them
might have once been the only decent one of the bunch.
Maybe after whoever was tasked with clearing the place cut
it down, he took one look at the rest of the trees—their soft,
scabby bark, their limp limbs—and decided they weren't
worth the effort. They'd be gone soon anyway. Rotted out
from the inside.

I can see the parking lot from here. Only a few cars remain.
I don't know how long I've been sitting up here. The rush that
comes with performing a set like that, it's like being drunk.

My cigarette case is empty now. The breeze is cool, and
while my body registers its chill, I still feel warm all over.
What a night. I'm just about to get up and head back to my
trailer—where I know I won't get a wink of sleep—when I
hear someone coming.

His clumsy steps are punctuated by the sound of liquid
sloshing about in a bottle.

He—no. *She*. She is crying.

When I spot her, I can tell she doesn't see me. She yanks the cork out of the bottle she's carrying and takes a long drink. When she's done, she snivels and wipes her eyes with one side of her arm, her mouth with the other.

"Eva, what's the matter?"

She screams and jumps, causing booze to splash out from the bottle. "Toby—what the hell is the matter with you? You scared me half to death!" She shakes her head all disgusted, like I'd been waiting up here all night for the sole purpose of making her leap out of her skin, and then takes another drink. "You want a sip?" She points the bottle at me.

"Nah. Thanks for the offer, though. Next time, ask me a week ago."

"Huh?"

"Forget it. What the hell are you doing wandering around here for?"

"Aw, I don't know." She shrugs and crosses her arms, slouching a little. "I needed some space, that's all."

With both arms, I gesture in all directions. "I can't fault you for that."

She comes over and stands next to me, offers me the bottle one more time. "You sure?" I shake my head and she takes my drink for me. "It's your buddy," she says, "Julian."

"Oh?"

"That baby can't pop out soon enough."

"Not enjoying the knife gig?"

"Not one bit."

"Well, I guess it takes a certain type. I can certainly see having knives thrown at you every night being the sort of thing that takes a toll on a person."

"You know what? The knives I don't even mind all that much. It's him that's taking a toll on me. My God, what a piece of work that man is. Every day, accusing and nagging, nagging, nagging. I swear, Toby, I can do no right in that man's eyes. He gets on my case for the most trivial things. I don't walk right when I go to the target. The way I wave to the crowd is all wrong. I look like shit in the costume. I show up too early for our set. I show up right on time for our set. And now, tonight, the jackass accuses me of losing one of his precious knives!" The whole spiel looks to have exhausted her. She takes an appropriately long drink and mutters, "Stupid man," as soon as she's got the air to.

"Yikes. Well, if you lost one of his knives—"

"I didn't lose one of his fucking knives!"

"All right, all right. All I was going to say was that even though Julian's awfully picky about those things, they're not irreplaceable. If one got lost, the world will likely keep on turning. He's probably just stressed about the baby coming and all that."

"Well, if you know any way to speed a pregnancy up, would you let me know? The sooner that thing pops outta Susan, the better." She takes another drink.

Before tonight, I'd never really said much to Eva. Nothing beyond the occasional nod or good day. Still, something tells me that Eva did lose Julian's knife. She strikes me as the kind of girl who loses a lot of things. "Yep, the sooner the better," she echoes. "Time to push the little demon out and get your behind back to the bull's eye, Susan."

She pulls out a cigarette. I ask her if she's got an extra one and she produces another, pops them both in her mouth and lights them, then hands one over to me. We sit there together in silence, puffing away, not quite rushing. When I'm done, I stand up, stretch, and snuff my stub out on the bottom of my shoe. "You know, if you hate it so much, you could just pack up your shit and leave."

"Pardon me?" she says in the irritated way people say it when they've heard every word you just said.

I shrug. "I said you can pack up your shit and you can leave. No one's holding you hostage here, are they? If you don't like it and you can't be a professional, you can hitch a ride to the city, head to the bus terminal, and go to Los Angeles and star in a stag film."

"Son of a bitch," she mumbles, then reaches for her bottle. I kick it away before she gets to it.

"You don't like L.A.?. Go to Des Moines and become a waitress. Go to Minnesota and become a school teacher. Go to the fucking North Pole and raise reindeer. But whatever you do, get the hell out of here, because if you don't want to do it, I guarantee there are a dozen other girls who'd jump at the chance to stand in the spotlight and have knives whipped at them."

She doesn't say anything else, at least not while I'm still in earshot.

WHEN I NEAR MY TRAILER, I NOTICE THAT ONE OF THE drapes in my window is twisted up near the bottom. The window, as always, is closed, so unless a windstorm had happened inside the trailer while I was out, it's safe to assume that someone had snuck inside.

I open the door to a deeper darkness than the starlit night sky has to offer.

"No one saw me." Her voice comes from the corner where the bed is. My eyes are still adjusting; I can barely make her shape out.

"How do you know that?"

"I just know."

"I guess I must be pretty oblivious if I've managed to go all this time without noticing the eyes you've got on the back of your head. And eyes that can see in the dark, no less. Cat's eyes."

"Aren't you a riot." She stands up and moves to the nightstand. Something slides, something clinks. A match head scrapes, then hisses.

"Why are you here, Gloria?"

She picks up the lamp and walks over to me. The flame's light dances across her face spastically. "Don't you want to see me?"

"Oh, cut the shit, will you? You know what I mean." It all comes out in one quick breath and she gives a little start. I walk over to the drapes on the window and straighten them out. When I turn back around, Gloria is right in front of me.

"What are you planning?" she asks, a slight tremor rocking her voice.

"What the hell are you talking about?"

"What are you two planning?"

"What do you mean *two?*"

"You and her! You and Genevieve!"

"Keep your voice down, would you?" I place my hands on her shoulders. They're shaking. "I don't know what you've got in your head, but whatever it is, I'll tell you right now that you're being paranoid. There's nothing going on with Genevieve and I. Our relationship is strictly professional, get it?"

Gloria considers that for a moment and then swats my hands off her shoulders. "Strictly professional—like hell! I've been watching you two. The way you look at her, Toby, the hand-holding, everything," she shudders, "it makes my skin crawl."

"Can you hear yourself?" Now I'm the one who needs to keep his voice down, but damn it, I can't help it. "The way I look at her—Christ! I don't know what the hell's gotten into you, but you need to cut it out! We're in a tight spot here. No one suspects we had anything to do with what happened in Baltimore. We've got some serious money stashed away—and we're going to get more as soon as I'm done this stint—and we've got a *plan*. The cops are probably this close to wrapping the whole Andrew thing up. I bet he'll be back here in a day or two. *A day or two*—that's all it is! By this time a few days from now, we'll be cruising down the highway together, away from this damn place, on to better things! All that can muck it all up right now is you acting crazy, seeing things that aren't really there, making up stories in your head and sneaking around like this. You know one of the detectives was here earlier today, don't you? They're still interviewing people. I don't know why—by the sounds of it, they know who did it—but they're still sniffing around here. All it takes, Gloria, is one person noticing that something funny is up with us. That's all it takes. They don't need to know what. They don't need to figure it out, that's the detective's job. All anyone here needs to do is say, 'You know, Detective, I noticed Gloria sneaking into Toby's trailer last night. It sounded like they were arguing about something.' And that'll be it. That's all the excuse they'll need to come over here and start sniffing around. We're so close here." I put my hands back on her shoulders. This time, she lets them rest there. "So please, stop looking for problems that don't exist. A few more days—tops. That's all."

She nods. "Yes. A few more days. I can do that, Toby. I'm…I'm sorry. I'm acting crazy."

"As long as it's only an act."

She smirks and takes my hands, gives them a squeeze. She kisses me. "Maybe I'm just practising for Hollywood." What a loon.

I'm escorted to the edge of the bed. When I sit down, Gloria steps away and starts rummaging around my cupboard. She takes out two glasses, places them on the table, and goes to fetch the bottle of gin from the cabinet. "Oh no," I say. "I can't have anything to drink tonight."

"Why not?" she asks innocently, not looking up from pouring.

"I don't want to drink when I've got to perform tomorrow."

"Is there an early morning matinée show no one told me about?"

Gin sloshes into the second glass. I open my mouth to protest again, but then I figure, what the hell? What's one drink? Well, one drink is one goddamn drink—and that's all it is.

Gloria walks over to the bed, hands me my drink, and takes a seat next to me. I wrap my arm around her and the two of us sip away in silence.

Gloria notices that my glass is empty before I do myself. She brings the bottle over and pours me some more. "That's good," I tell her when the gin passes the halfway point. Two drinks is two goddamn drinks, and not a thing more than that.

A few sips has me buzzed. My mind finally has the courage to go to that place it's been avoiding all night. I don't know how to bring it up, but that's one of the best things about booze—it takes care of that for you. "Genevieve knows." With the words out of my system, I feel a throbbing void in my guts. I pound back my drink, getting about half of it down before I erupt into a sputtering coughing fit.

Gloria shoots up from the bed and stands in front of me. "She knows what, Toby?" I can't stop coughing. She bends over and gives me a few hard whacks on the back. "Come on, Toby, what is it? What does she know?"

She goes to give me another whack, but I push her hand away and bury my mouth in the crook of my elbow and ride the remainder of the cough out. Gloria doesn't ask me again. I look up at her, and, well, I guess my expression says a lot, because after about two seconds, she gets this petrified look on her face. She wants to speak—I can tell that much—but wanting to and being able to are two very different things. I get up from the bed and hold her in my arms. "Don't worry," I tell her, "don't worry." I heard somewhere that when people are in a panic, it's best to repeat yourself because it takes a few times for words to sink in. I rub her arms. "Don't worry. Don't worry, okay, Gloria?"

"O-okay," she finally manages, her voice barely even a whisper.

"Now, I told you she knows, but you went and had a series of heart attacks before I even got around to telling you how much she knows." I guide Gloria back to the edge of the bed. "Are you with me here?"

"Yes."

"All right. So, she knows that I was the one who did it, but don't go all crazy just yet, okay? See, the thing is, even though she knows I did it—and you're gonna love this—she's *glad* I did it. You hear me, Gloria? Genevieve is happy about the situation. She even thanked me. I don't quite know why, but she did. She thanked me."

Gloria, crossed arms, shoulders perked like she's got a chill crawling up her back, sits on the bed in silence for what seems like a very long time. She stares down at her feet, looks up to my concerned eyes, then decides she prefers the first view. "We don't have a choice," she says in her hushed ghost's voice. "We have to kill her, too."

"Jesus Christ. Come on, now."

"We have to, Toby," she says without looking up at me, as if a swirling pool of possible futures were playing out on the floor in front of her. "It doesn't matter how she feels about the whole thing—whether she's glad about it or not, it doesn't matter. She knows, and she can't know. She's a..." she straightens up, her eyes searching the room for the right word. "Liability," she says after a moment. "That's it, she's a liability."

My body tenses. Veins throb. I walk over to the table and slam my fist down on it. Hard. It takes three blows for me to loosen up a bit. Three blows before my throat unwinds enough that I can speak. "You're way off, Gloria. Way off. She's not a liability. Not at all. If she knows about it and she hasn't gone to the police, that would make her involved, too. If we were figured out, she'd be in just as much hot water as you and me."

"But Toby, we don't have any proof that she knows. If we were found out, we could tell the police she knew about it until we were blue in the face, but it wouldn't matter. Not without any proof."

"Yeah, but who says she has any proof on her end?"

"Who says she doesn't?"

"I do, because I was the one who did it, damn it! She couldn't have any proof." I've got this nagging voice in the back of my mind telling me that's not true, though. I did a good job of covering my tracks, but there are always unknowns. Unknowns, I realize, like Genevieve's whereabouts the night of the murder. As far as I knew, she was back here at the circus the whole time, but that's not a certainty. She could have been in Baltimore. It's not inconceivable. But I can't think like that. I can't let myself go down that road. The Road of Unknowns—of What Ifs—is an easy road to get stranded on. Best to avoid it altogether.

I boot the nagging voice back down the well it crawled up from. "Gloria, Genevieve can't have proof because *nobody* has proof, you got that? For all I know, she just has a hunch. And it's not as if I confirmed that I had anything to do with it when she thanked me. I didn't go, 'The pleasure was all mine—anyone else you need bumped off?' She just thanked me, and two seconds later, we were called in to perform. Nothing more to it."

After a moment of consideration, Gloria says, "All right," but her eyes tell me the opposite.

I get down on my knees, reach under the bed, and pull out my Samsonite. I place it on the bed and pop the latches, then I grab the lamp, angle it toward the suitcase, and open it up. I look over to Gloria just in time to see her pupils shrinking from the light. "We're gonna be fine," I assure her. "Just a couple more days, and that's it."

She nods.

"I can't blame you for being worried, but we can't be stupid about this. Killing someone else is the last thing we should be considering right now. It'd only serve to complicate things, make an even bigger mess for us to sweep under the rug."

"You're right," Gloria says. Her eyes move from me back to the money in the suitcase. "Just a couple more days," she whispers.

She finishes her drink. I don't opt for a refill myself. When she's done, we say our goodnights and we kiss our goodnights, and I walk with her to the door. As I turn the knob, I say, "The window's out of service, so I hope this will do."

She forces a snicker. "It's fine for now, I suppose."

I watch her walk away until the dark absorbs her and she vanishes from view, then I close my door, lock it, and return my suitcase to its home under the bed. I fish out a copy of *Fantastic Novels*. That shitty old nagging voice is causing a ruckus down at the bottom of the well, and sometimes reading something really out of this world—something with lunar conquests or gladiators on Mars—is the best way to slide a cover over the well's opening and shut the voice up for good.

I can't focus. I have to read the same paragraph over and over again, retaining nothing each time. After two glazed pages and zero plot digested, I close the magazine. I'm not tired yet, but I need to be. It's late, and a headliner needs his rest. There's an ad for Prestone Anti-Freeze on the back of the magazine. Five or six reads of that (No rust, no foam, no freeze, no failure!) and the sheep are lining up beside my bed, ready for a quick inventory.

SOMETHING'S GOING ON.

I feel it the second my eyelids flip open. I don't know how, but by God, I swear I feel it.

I feel it as I pull my clothes on, and I feel it as I splash cold water on my face and neck and as I brush my teeth.

Too much chatter. That's the first thing I notice when I step out of my trailer: too much chatter from too many people. It's too early in the day for that sort of thing. Except apparently it isn't. When I step out of my trailer, the place is buzzing with men and women who, up until now, I could have sworn were the type who didn't even know there *was* a seven a.m. Some of them are still in their trailers, conspiratorial faces peering out with eyes shifting back and forth like a Kit-Cat clock; they peer and then they mutter over their shoulders and then they get right back to peering.

Others are out and about, congregating on steps in twos and threes, craning necks, concerned faces, whispering behind cupped hands.

Something's going on.

I begin making my way to breakfast, but something catches my eye and pulls me off-course. Three men are standing outside of the big top at the performer's entrance. One of them is Eddie. He's holding two syrup-slathered pancakes in his hand. As I draw closer, I see that the side pockets of his overalls are covered in sticky globs of syrup. They're loose overalls, and I figure he's got at least one more pancake rolled up in each pocket—whatever's happening is interesting, but it isn't forget-about-breakfast-altogether interesting. The other two men I recognize, but I can't recall their names for the life of me.

"Morning, boys," I call.

They all look at each other like I'd just tossed a live grenade between the bunch of them, then look at me, and smile the three phoniest smiles I've ever seen together in the same place. Eddie speaks for the bunch of them: "Morning, Toby. How's things?"

"I'm not sure. Maybe I'll know once I get a look inside there."

Eddie steps aside, but he's not really one for effort, so I still have to brush past him to get into the big top. I hear Eddie mutter something behind me, but I'm not really interested in whatever he's got to say. What interests me is the five men inside the big top: Rowland—standing near the edge of the ring with his arms crossed and one foot sticking out like he's waiting to trip someone—and four crewmen taking down the trapeze safety net.

When Rowland spots me walking toward him, he gets this sheepish look on his face and gives me a half-assed wave without uncrossing his arms. "Good morning, Toby." The crewmen stop what they're doing when they hear his greeting, but Rowland's quick to motion at them to get back to it.

"What the hell's going on here? We're not doing the act without the net. Even if I wanted to, there's no way Genevieve would go for it. You know that."

"Yes. Yes, I know that," Rowland says to me. His crossed arms inch up his chest a little, and I could be mistaken, but it looks as if he tightens his grip on himself slightly. "Toby, Andrew is back. He arrived late last night—too late for us to pack up and be ready to leave this morning—so I've decided we'll do one last night here as we'd originally planned and then leave first thing tomorrow morning. Let me tell you, though, I am more grateful than you'll ever know for you stepping up and filling in in Andrew's absence. I know it was asking a lot of you to not only help develop a routine on such short notice, but also to work with Genevieve again after so many years."

"Are you telling me—" I start, but my voice peters off. My head feels light. My knees weak; I shift my stance to correct the feeling and try again: "Are you telling me that I'm not performing with Genevieve tonight?"

"I'm sorry, Toby." Rowland's sympathetic eyes sicken me. I want to rip them out and feed them to him. "I won't need you to perform with Genevieve anymore. But you'll still be performing your regular act tonight." He unknots himself, opens his arms to me, and smiles like a salesman trying to distract you from the pointy tail poking out of his pant leg. "The best part of the show, as far as I'm concerned."

I leave without speaking another word, realizing once I've exited the big top that that was probably the best-case scenario response as far as Rowland was concerned.

"SO THAT'S IT, THEN. WE'RE LEAVING TONIGHT." SAYING IT

out loud does something to her. Her chest rises and falls, rises and falls, she starts nodding and doesn't stop, she's biting down on the corner of her bottom lip. "Tonight," she echoes.

I nod. "You got it. We'll catch a lift to Baltimore, spend the night, and then buy a car first thing in the morning. You have a suitcase, right?"

"Yes. But I don't want to pack while any of the other girls are around." She thinks for a moment, then: "We always leave our trailers at least half an hour before the show starts. I can tell them I'm not feeling well and that I want to lie down while I've got a bit of time. That's when I'll pack. It'll only take me a few minutes."

"Perfect. Now, I'm not organized at all," I say, gesturing around the trailer, which, now that I'm actually paying attention to the state of the place, is pretty damn messy. "You'd better be on your way."

Gloria nods in agreement, gives me a kiss on the cheek, and heads for the door. She opens it a crack, pauses, and closes it. "Toby," she says, turning back to face me, "we're really doing this, aren't we?"

"You're damn right we are," I assure her.

Once she leaves, I start rooting around for my old green duffel bag. It baffles me how it could take ten minutes to find anything in a place this small, but I spend that much time rummaging before I find the bag in the back corner of the top shelf of the closet.

The duffel is spacious, and, being a duffel, it's got some give to it, but I know I'll still have to leave a lot behind. I stuff it with clothes and toiletries, which I keep in a little buffalo-hide bag that I've had for years. The contents of the Samsonite will go untouched. The money—I just like it there. And there's no way my old magazines are going to be rolled up and forced into a jam-packed duffel bag. I lay my favourite brown suit out on my bed with a fresh cream dress shirt and powder-blue necktie—might as well look half decent for the road—and then give the place a quick once-over.

The show doesn't start for another few hours.

I do some push-ups. I juggle. I smoke and I pace around a whole lot. I'll need to go and see Rowland soon so I can collect my money for the work I did with Genevieve. Knowing him, he probably hasn't even budgeted for the money he'd promised us, so he'll likely try and get me to hold off on collecting until after tonight's show. I decide to break ritual and shave my head early. How do I get Rowland to pay up before the show? It'll be damn near impossible to pin him down after—especially if Gloria and I are in a rush to split.

The idea hits me as I'm rubbing shaving cream across my poky scalp. A gambling debt. I'll tell Rowland that back when we were in Richmond, I went and made a stupid move by stiffing the wrong guy after a card game. I'll tell him that I got word that this guy—a real tough customer—has made the trip all the way to Baltimore to settle up, and that if I don't get paid right away, I'll be looking at some serious trouble.

That'll work. Rowland will go for it. Not because he's worried about me, but because he knows if some thug smashes my head in, I won't be able to perform, and if he's down one top-notcher, it'll hurt his wallet.

I give Rowland's door three swift raps, which are immediately followed by the sound of shuffling feet from inside. Rowland opens the door seconds later, but he doesn't open it all the way. He greets me with a grave face. "Toby?" he says as if he were expecting the Pope.

"Yeah, Toby," I confirm his suspicion.

His eyes widen and he presses a finger to his lips and shushes me. He opens his mouth to speak, but before he gets a word out, another voice drifts out from inside, somewhere behind him.

"Is that fucking Toby?" The words are so slurred, like they came from a puddle. Somehow, though, I can still recognize the voice.

Rowland steps back from the door, closing it almost all the way, and hisses a response, "Goddamn it! It's not Toby! Now will you just shut up and sleep?"

The door opens again—this time wider—and Rowland squeezes out. "Walk with me," he says, securing his trailer.

We walk around the back of his place, in the direction of the big top. Once he's determined that enough distance has passed, he glances over his shoulder to make sure no Russian spies are trailing us, and then turns to me. "That fucking idiot. He's done, Toby."

"He sure sounded done," I say.

"I don't know if I've ever seen someone so drunk. It will be a miracle if he doesn't need to get his stomach pumped."

"What the hell happened?"

Rowland shrugs. "Well, you know most of it. He went to Baltimore, fucked a young man who ended up dead in his hotel bed, and spent a few days in police custody. Thanks to me greasing the right palms, though, he's not even going to get a slap on the wrist for the fairy stuff."

"So why's he in such a state?"

Rowland looks at me like I'm king of the dunces. "Why the hell do you think? Genevieve, Toby. My God, you've never seen a woman so cross."

"Well, can you blame her?"

"Of course not! But, hell, her and I, we had a talk about this. Her and I had an *agreement*." Rowland slams one fist into his open palm for emphasis. "She said she'd stick it out and work with him until the end of this season. And, boy," Rowland huffs, "you better believe I promised her a pretty penny for it." He shakes his head and drags his palm down his face, forcing his wrinkles to rearrange themselves. "But when he came back, Toby…holy hell."

"What do you mean? Stop beating around the bush."

"I was there when he first came back. I figured I ought to be, you know. When he came back, he had this look, reminded me of a dog who'd shit on a fancy Persian rug and knew a beating was coming. You could see it in his eyes, Toby—pure guilt, pure shame. So I watched the two of them greet each other, and you know, despite the tension—and make no mistake, you could feel the tension—but despite it, I thought they'd actually be okay. I had no illusions about them patching things up, but I honestly thought that they'd be able to work together for as long as I needed them to. But once I left them alone, well, you can imagine that was another story altogether.

It was shortly after I'd spoken to you earlier today. We'd just finished putting the safety net away when Sal comes in and tells me he'd spotted Andrew wandering off in the field, stumbling around like a zombie or something. I left the big top right away, went with Sal to go see what was up. It took the two of us a while to track him down, but when we did… Jesus Christ. We found him lying on the ground, in the shade beneath some trees. The smell…you wouldn't have believed it. Now that I think of it, we might have smelt him before we saw him, Toby. It was just rotten! You'd think we'd stumbled across a hidden distillery. He was lying there at the base of a tree—we couldn't even tell if he was breathing—as drunk as a man could ever be, blood all over his face and shirt. Naturally, we assumed at least some of it was Genevieve's blood. We panicked. I sent Sal to her trailer to check on her. Once Sal was gone, I leaned in and got a closer look at

Andrew. I noticed some of the blood on his face was coming from scratches—looked like the work of a sharp set of fingernails by my best guess. Then I noticed that the blood on his shirt wasn't on the outside, but that it looked to have seeped through from inside. I undid the buttons on his shirt and took a look. Toby, it was…" Rowland just shakes his head.

"Come on," I say, "it was what?"

"Awful. That's what it was. It looked like he'd been jabbed repeatedly with something. Not stabbed—I don't think she took a knife to him—but jabbed with something that wasn't too sharp but could still break skin. Maybe it was the pointy end of a high heel shoe. I don't know. Whatever it was, it had sure tenderized him. He was covered in purple bruises and bloody holes—five or six of them—messy things. Every breath he took sent a trickle of blood oozing from him. I waited until Sal came back and the two of us carried him to my trailer. I had Harriet Lane come over and patch him up, but she's still awfully worried about him. Worried about infection and about alcohol poisoning."

"Well, wouldn't that be a shame."

"Oh, come on now, Toby. I know you two hate each other, but if you could see him right now—"

"I wouldn't bat an eyelash."

His gaze fastens to mine, and for a moment, neither of us speaks.

"I need something from you," Rowland says, breaking the silence, but not the stare. He digs into his breast pocket and pulls out a stuffed billfold, empties it into my hand. It's more than he owes me. So much more.

I guess I can save that fake gambling debt for another time.

PRIMEVAL DRUMS POUND. MY HEARTRATE ADJUSTS
to their pace. Someone once told me this rhythm was
called Ferry Through Acheron, but I can't remember who.

Rowland bellows through his megaphone: "Ladies and
gentlemen! It is with great pleasure that I present to you our
final act of the night!"

Genevieve gives my hand a squeeze. Together, we step
toward the curtain. I haven't spoken to Gloria since this
morning. I looked for her after I saw Rowland, but I couldn't
find her anywhere. I wanted to tell her about what happened
with Andrew, about how I'd be headlining the show one
more time. I wanted to tell her about the money Rowland
had given me—more than I ever would have even considered
requesting for headlining another string of performances—
and I wanted to tell her to take her suitcase and head for my
trailer right after the show and wait for me. She probably
knows to do that, but I get anxious.

It's been a while since I've watched her perform, but I
did tonight. She seemed a little off. It wasn't overt, but it was

there. Every step seemed to come the tiniest bit late. It's not the sort of thing most people would notice—probably not even other dancers—but I sure noticed.

And it wasn't just her movements that were off. Her smile looked so phony you'd think it was pinned on. You can't get nervous like that. I know we're pulling a real stunt here, but you can't let nerves get to you. Not if you want to call yourself a professional. If you're top-notch, you go out there with steel nerves and you make people gasp, no matter the circumstances.

Hell, look at me and Genevieve. Most performers would probably have a fit if they were in our shoes. Getting to the big top and seeing that the show had started and the damn safety net hadn't been set back up. But we're professionals. Sure, Genevieve took some convincing, but I got her to come to her senses eventually. I reminded her how smooth our act was. How it was all elementary stunts with a bit of spice thrown on to make them look more daring than they actually were—the kind of stunts even a novice could pull off.

"Knock 'em dead, you two!"

"Break a leg out there!"

I smile and nod. Genevieve doesn't react.

"A man and a woman who gravity *fears*!" Rowland paces about like a demented preacher, the roving spotlight following him around the ring, his shadow a menacing silhouette.

Father-to-be Julian catches my eye. He raises his cigarette in a toast, and gives me nod and a wink. I notice that his knife belt is fully stocked and that one of the handles is a fresher shade of red than the others. I wonder if he'll let Eva live it down before Susan returns to the target.

"Please join me in welcoming Mister and Missus Angel!"

Through the curtain, into a tent full of cheering, whistling, applause so deep you could drown in it. The rest of the band joins the drums as Genevieve and I run to the ladder and climb, up, up the writhing ladder, one hundred fifty feet.

We step to the middle of the platform, hand in hand, and strike a pose, bringing the music to a clean halt.

One, two beats of silence, then the drum roll starts. Genevieve's dismount is punctuated with gasps. I follow her out a moment later. More gasps.

Tick-tock, tick-tock, we pendulum, syncing our rhythm. Tick-tock.

Redemption.

After so many years. After all I've done, redemption. Tonight I leave this tent an acrobat.

Tick-tock.

Two rhythms meld into one. The rolling snare drum below grows in intensity. Genevieve lets go of her bar, drifting through the air toward me, and...

"NO! TOBY, NO!" The scream is shrill and desperate. The scream is familiar. It tears through the air from somewhere below. It doesn't affect my timing. I'm a professional. I catch Genevieve, my hands locking us together at the forearm. That's when I feel it.

"NO, TOBY!"

The wire breaks with a crisp ting. We slide off the bar. The gasping crowd sucks every mouthful of air from the big top.

"NO!" That fucking scream, it cuts through everything.

Genevieve screams, too. Her body is rigid, but her arms and legs flail with such intensity that for half a second, I think they might actually save her.

The ground is rushing to us. I won't scream.

I have just enough time to correct my form.

ACKNOWLEDGEMENTS

Bottomless gratitude to all the wonderful folks at NeWest Press, a publisher that I am proud and privileged to work with. Thank you to the remarkable Jenna Butler for lending her editorial talents to this book and for providing vital guidance and insight throughout the process. Many thanks to Marketing and Production Coordinator (and noir enthusiast) Claire Kelly, for her tireless work and unwavering dedication. And thank you to NeWest General Manager Matt Bowes, who, in addition to believing in this story, taught me the importance of answering phone calls every now and then, even when you get one from an unfamiliar number. You never know, it might be good news.

Thank you to the talented and telepathic Kate Hargreaves for her brilliant book design.

Special thanks to Micheline Maylor and Richard Harrison for their mentorship and inspiration, and also to Beth Everest for her guidance and encouragement when I was first scrambling to find my footing as a writer. I'm still scrambling, but much less frantically thanks to the three of you.

My good friend and fellow writer Jason Wall was kind enough to offer much-needed feedback on an early draft—Jason, many thanks for that. You are definitely not a squid. Huge thanks are also due to the (now) Victoria-based poet Alex Williamson, who shared his insight on early sections of the book.

To my parents, Jim and Ann Howell, I am grateful for your support of my creative endeavours over the years. Thank you for that, and for creating a home where stories of all sorts were appreciated. Thank you as well to my top-notch sisters, Mariann and Claire, the Pawlak family, my Grandmother Marty Hollox, and to all of my fantastic in-laws.

I must also extend my gratitude to my friends. There are too many to mention here (which I realize makes me very fortunate), but you know who you are, and I thank you for inspiring, supporting, and indulging me while I rambled on about crime novels and film noir over beers.

Lastly, thank you so much to Alicja, my amazing wife. Without your endless patience, love, and encouragement I never would have finished this book. This is for you.

NIALL HOWELL was born and raised in Calgary, where he still resides. His short fiction has been published in *The Feathertale Review* and *FreeFall* and he holds a Bachelor of Arts in English from Mount Royal University, and a Bachelor of Education from the University of Calgary. He enjoys playing bass, and obsessively collects records and comics.